CLASS DISMISSED

CLASS DISMISSED

REDONDO AND ROSE NEIGHBORS IN CRIME
BOOK 4

BONNIE HARDY

ON THE OTHER HAND BOOKS

"Aging is not lost youth,
but a new stage of opportunity and strength."

Betty Friedan
(1921 - 2006)

1

VIVIENNE ROSE

Rex tugged the spiral notebook from Viv's hand. "So you're going old-school, taking pen and paper notes for the class?" His voice, filled with amusement, made her feel prickly.

"I remember details better if I write them down. So in answer to your impertinence, yes, I'm going old-school." She took the notebook back with a sniff.

Eyeballing his laptop, she retorted, "I see that you've bought a brand-new computer. It probably cost three times more than the community college tuition, and I bet Sutton had to teach you how to turn it on."

He grinned. "True. But I'll be the envy of all the rest of the students." When they reached the stairway, he gestured for her to go first. "Shall we get aerobic and take the steps to the second floor?"

She sighed. "Of course. Good start to my day."

"Ladies first." He gestured again.

Viv stepped lightly, but she felt uncomfortable. Every time he offered for her to go ahead, it meant one thing. He liked observing her fanny from behind.

"Who do you think will be in this class with us?" she asked over her shoulder. He didn't answer right away.

"I was distracted," he admitted. "But look, there's room 236 right there." He pointed. "We're five minutes early. Why don't we linger in the hall? I don't want to be the first ones to arrive."

Viv stopped to look at a board with announcements. She read aloud, "Mojave Mesa invites you to our fall back-to-school night. September 29." Her eyes drifted to a second notice. "Plus there's a student rally. Reminds me of the old days." She turned to him. "Students still protest."

Rex came closer to have a look for himself. "Why would we attend back-to-school night? Not like my parents want to meet the teacher."

"Community colleges aren't just for second-career people," she reminded him. "Younger students attend, who may live at home. They often have limited finances. After two years they may transfer to four-year colleges. Community colleges provide a first step."

"Did you go to college?" Rex asked.

"I went to community college for an AA degree. I studied to be a nurse practitioner." She felt proud of her brief time in higher education. "Of course, that was ages ago. Afterward I heard about doula work and took classes. Most of my education was online. What about you?"

He dipped his chin with a characteristic *aw shucks* grin. *Is he a Harvard man?*

"Parents sent me to a state school," he said. "I wasn't that great of a student. Got the degree but didn't show up for the graduation ceremony." Viv watched his face with approval. *No wonder women call him a silver fox.*

"Hey, is this the Introduction to Private Investigation 101 class?" a young man asked. They both turned at once.

Possibly in his late twenties, he had blonde hair, one strand falling over his eye. "I'm Brad May," he said, extending his hand to Rex.

"I'm Rex Redondo, and this is Vivienne Rose." He shook Brad's hand vigorously before letting go.

"Are you here for the eight o'clock class? Do you want to be a private detective too?" He seemed eager, which Viv appreciated. *Young men have such energy...*

She liked him immediately, detecting a shyness underneath his introduction. *Handsome but not overly confident.*

"We're considering a second career as private detectives," she explained. "I thought this class would help me make a decision one way or the other. Rex has more experience. He was an intel officer in the military years ago. Plus," she teased, "he likes to think he's Humphrey Bogart."

Brad squinted. "I've heard of him. An actor in old movies..."

"Only the greatest movie star to play a detective in the history of Hollywood." Rex sounded indignant. He ran his hand through his hair.

"Sure, sorry." Brad's eyes grew wide. "I guess I don't watch much TV or movies."

"It's nearly five after eight. Shouldn't the door be open by now so that we can head inside?" Viv glanced at her phone.

Brad stepped closer and looked inside. "Electronic entrance," he said. "Maybe administration changed the classroom. I didn't check my messages."

"I did get a notice early this morning." Viv read aloud, "Mr. Wallace Walker's class has been moved to the main building, first floor, number 236." She glanced above the door. "This is it."

Rex looked through the glass panel. "Lights are on.

Someone's inside." He stared harder. "Looks like he's doing some work at his desk. I bet that's Professor Walker." He firmly rapped his knuckles against the door. "Maybe he lost track of time."

"I think he's taking a nap." Viv felt a niggle of irritation. It had taken a great deal of persuasion on Rex's part to even get her to this class. She'd rescheduled three of her doula clients to free the early morning time. And now the instructor was asleep at his desk. *So disrespectful.*

"Try knocking again," she said.

Brad used the palm of his hand to pound against the door.

"He's still not moving." She could hear the tone of concern in Rex's voice.

"Is there a problem?"

A man wearing a custodian's jumpsuit joined them. The name Eddie had been embroidered over his left pocket. "Wally's not opening the door..." he said, answering his own question.

Viv, Rex, and Brad moved aside.

"If you're the custodian, you gotta have the key," Brad said.

The custodian raised his fist to hammer on the door. "Wally. Wake up. Your students are here."

The back of Viv's neck prickled.

Brad glared at the custodian. "You're the guy with the keys, remember?"

"I have the access code. But I normally don't intrude on professors." Eddie pressed numbers into the keypad. "Funny. The code's not working." He tried again. After three unsuccessful attempts, Eddie turned to Rex. "Did you see any sign of life?"

"No."

"Professor Walker hasn't moved. I think something's wrong. I'm going to call 911." Eddie searched his pocket but Rex had already lifted his phone to his ear.

Viv's knees felt weak. *What are the chances of this? Taking a class in private detecting where the instructor is slumped over his desk. This scene's right out of an Agatha Christie playbook.*

2

______

REX REDONDO

The paramedics pounded against the locked door as a woman used her toolkit to monkey with the panel. "There must be a way to bypass the lock," she stated.

Another first responder peered through the glass. "He's not moving," he said urgently.

"That's it. We're breaking in." She lifted a tool to apply pressure to the closed sliding door.

Rex held his breath, exhaling when he heard a distinctive click. As the door slid open, the paramedics rushed past.

Rex and Viv stood next to the custodian's cart to watch. Lights overhead cast a harsh glow on the scene. "Looks like he's unresponsive," Rex observed. "Time for life-saving measures."

Brad leaned against the wall, his chin set. "I've seen this before," he told them. "In Lily Rock."

Viv wanted to ease the tension. What better way than to engage him in conversation? It didn't take much prompting. "You're from Lily Rock?"

Brad nodded. "I've been on several murder investigations. We have volunteer first responders since Lily Rock is such a small town. We're really good at assessing situations."

"So you're a cop?" Rex asked.

Brad shrugged. "Not exactly."

"You're a fire guy," Rex prodded.

He shook his head. "Not exactly."

"Then you're a first responder," Viv concluded. "Otherwise why would you be so familiar with scenes like this." She gestured with her head.

Before Brad could explain further, the custodian interrupted. "I told Wally over and over not to lock the door. But he wouldn't listen. This isn't the first time, you know."

"First time for what?" Rex asked. "Leaving students standing in the hall, or taking a nap at his desk?"

"Something might be really wrong," Viv chided him. "The man may be having a health emergency."

"That's what I'm sayin'," the custodian insisted. "Wally's always having, what did you call it, health emergencies. This isn't the first time. You watch, they'll take him to the ER. Everything will be fine."

By now a handful of other students gathered to see what was going on. Some held laptops. Others shouldered backpacks. One filmed with her cell.

"Stand back," Eddie warned. "Move on. If this is your class, Mojave will be in touch." He turned to Viv. "You might want to leave," he commented dryly. "One thing seems clear—dead or alive, Wally won't be working today. I'm sure the administration will update everyone with a text."

Rex could read what she was thinking. The way she glanced back and forth from the custodian, to the room, and back to him. *She's going to give up on our Neighbors in Crime business. One obstacle too many.*

It had taken him several months to enroll in the class. She'd been reluctant at first but finally gave in. But now he was afraid she'd changed her mind. *I need to do something fast.* He improvised.

"We'll find another Introduction to Private Investigation 101. Pretty sure this isn't the only college where it's offered." Then his voice faltered. "Walker was an old fart. Maybe we can find another professor. Younger. A woman. You'd like that." He turned to Viv.

She frowned. "The instructor isn't that much older than we are."

"Don't give up." He didn't want to plead, not in front of the others. So he looked at her with his puppy-dog eyes. But he could tell by her narrowed glance that she wasn't having any of it.

Rex tried another angle. He spoke to Eddie. "You seem to know Walker pretty well. How old is he? He kept on teaching. What an example."

"He's retired from the police force and been teaching here for decades," Eddie explained. "He's mid-seventies. Like I said, lots of health issues." Eddie glanced toward the classroom. "We can't stand here forever. It's my job to move people on." He took another look at the classroom. "Maybe they'll let me in. I'll get an update that I can share." With one shove, he pushed the custodian cart out of the way to walk inside the classroom.

Rex called after him. "Can we come with you?"

When he didn't answer, Rex took Viv's hand. "Come on. I know you think this is terrible. But you gotta admit—what an opportunity. We have a mystery to solve right in front of us. Think of the headlines: 'Amateur Sleuthing Duo Solve The Case.'"

"I'm not so sure." Viv's voice faltered. "Most likely this is a situation where an aging professor with medical issues died in difficult circumstances. Not exactly newsworthy."

Brad made no attempt to hide that he was listening to Rex and Viv's conversation. He added his opinion. "Until we find out the specifics, the forensics, we can investigate. Step closer and observe. Listening to what they're saying."

"We?" Rex's jaw clenched. *How did the kid get in on my great idea...*

Viv shrugged. "I don't suppose we'll be welcome. But there's no harm in trying. Let's get closer and have a look."

3

VIVIENNE ROSE

Viv lingered by the doorway, surprised that Eddie didn't acknowledge their presence. She watched Rex and Brad size up the situation. Brad was well-built, strong shoulders underneath a t-shirt that read Lily Rock Woofstock Festival on the back.

Edging toward six feet, he was Rex's height. Brad had a certain energy, an optimism, that Viv suspected was born from overcoming difficult circumstances, not from a privileged upbringing. That would account for the way he wanted to be included.

I wish Rex was more receptive. But his refusal to look at Brad while he talked indicated a certain disdain.

I bet it's his youth that annoys Rex. Once again she realized a distinct difference between men and women. *Dominance for men is often about height and age. For women it's about beauty; who's the youngest, the thinnest, and who has the best hair.* She felt keenly aware of crossing over a recent decade birthday.

When Rex refused to converse, Brad's fingers fidgeted

against his sides. She suspected this nervous gesture was an attempt to avoid feeling hurt.

Her own nerves tingled. *What about the unconscious man, Viv? Pay attention.*

The paramedics worked over the body. One checked for a pulse, the other turned the professor's head to the side to look inside his mouth.

Rex detached from Brad to inch toward the desk. His body language shifted as he came closer. Adopting a look of curiosity, he didn't interrupt, but he appeared to be taking advantage of the paramedics' focus on the body to gather some clues. She saw his dark eyes dart back and forth, focusing mainly on the desktop.

It was nearly impossible to see the instructor's face. Underneath his right folded elbow was a scattering of papers. His ergonomic chair had been tilted slightly toward the right. Viv's glance dropped to papers on the floor.

A laptop had been shoved to the right corner. Next to it was a takeout bag with the Just Desserts logo. A lid had been removed from a large travel cup. One eye squint revealed a plastic pill container.

One of those day-of-the-week kind, Viv thought. *I often recommend them to pregnant clients who forget to take their prenatal vitamins.* "Set up for a week at a time. You'll be less likely to forget."

Her nostrils flared. *I'd expect to see a wallet or his cell. He most likely drove himself here. The key to the vehicle may be stored on the phone. What about the room key? Was that also accessed by an app?*

She cast an eye back to the door.

From the looks of the classroom, Mojave Mesa had spared no expense. Neatly arranged rows of long student tables, each with a built-in computer hookup. A ceiling-mounted projector loomed overhead. Even the familiar hum of the air conditioner purred with quiet efficiency. Viv smirked. She felt her age, remembering when she went to college. Notebooks, pencils, no cells and no computers, let alone the World Wide Web for research.

Viv looked over when she heard a commotion from the hallway. A uniformed officer stood outside with a grim expression on his face. He had a strong chin, and his narrow eyes took in the scene. "I'm Lieutenant Darius James. I'll be in charge of this scene."

Rex stood to his full height. "I didn't touch the body," he stated before the cop even asked.

The officer didn't acknowledge what he said because two Palm Desert first responders pushed past. They made their way toward the victim as Rex stepped back to give them room. Viv knew standing away from the crowd would make her less in the way, so she moved closer to the bank of windows.

"Should I open the blinds for more light?" she asked.

"No," the police officer snapped. "We need to take photos and prints. I'd appreciate it if you'd get out of here, right out this door, and take your friends with you.

"It looks like natural causes," the cop added. "The guy's pretty old. Maybe his heart. But until we get more evidence, I won't know for sure. So..." He glared at Viv, then Rex. "Class is dismissed. Say goodbye."

"What about me?" Brad called. "I work with the Lily Rock Constabulary. I'm Janis Jets's assistant. She'd expect me to offer a professional courtesy, to stay and help out." When the lieutenant only stared, he added, "I'm a professional..." Brad's voice dropped at the end. Viv knew that was a mistake.

When the cop's eyes narrowed, Brad hurriedly

corrected himself. "Okay, I'm almost a professional. The constabulary paid for my tuition. That's as good as..."

"Is there something about class dismissed that you don't get, young man?" The cop's frown deepened.

"Okay then. I'm going. But you should interview me first. I have a keen eye for details. Like that travel cup, for example." He pointed to the teacher's desk. "It didn't contain coffee."

"I'll be the one to determine the contents," the cop stated matter-of-factly. "But you do have a point. Step outside the room. All of you. Including the janitor. I see you over there, trying to look invisible. We'll take contact information before you leave campus."

Viv felt defensive. She was the first to leave the room. "Let's stand over there," Rex insisted. "The cop is a pompous pain. With that full head of hair, I'd call him Lennie Briscoe. Like on *Law and Order*."

Viv fumed. "It's not like we're taking a class in watercolors or stage design. There's a learning opportunity right in front of us."

Brad May sounded equally unhappy. "I'm gonna ask my boss about this guy. She'll do a police background check. It will only take a few minutes to discover everything about him including his past, his favorite color, and the name of his dog. Then we'll know if we can trust him or not."

Brad rattled on. "This is our investigation. Plus I have a hunch. The lieutenant will refuse to prioritize an old dead guy. He'll write him off, 'cause of his age." He glanced at Rex. "Sorry. I know you're old too."

Viv held back a smirk. Rex's jaw had tightened when he heard "old dead guy." Brad's engaging smile would not soften the blow of comparing him to the instructor.

She intervened. "I suppose I'm not welcome in your

investigation. Because I'm a female. We're so delicate and fragile and all." She flipped her hair off the back of her neck with her index finger and winked at Rex.

Brad looked startled, a blush creeping up his neck. "Oh no. I didn't mean to imply... Being female is an advantage. My boss is female. To her core. And believe me, she's no one you want to mess with."

Rex spoke in a dry voice. "Most people tell me I don't look a day over forty."

Viv and Brad locked eyes. She raised an eyebrow. He acknowledged with a slight nod. "Barely thirty-nine," he mumbled.

Rex continued. "Obviously you haven't acquired the wide berth of experience to assess people's ages with any accuracy."

4

REX REDONDO

Viv waited for Rex to unlock the SUV. "What did you think of Lieutenant Darius James?" she asked.

"Pompous ass," he mumbled. He opened her door right as his phone pinged.

"I have a text from the Mojave Mesa principal. Did you get one too?"

Viv checked. "Nope. Have you met her before?"

He took a moment to read the message again.

"What does she have to say?" Viv asked.

"She invited me to come to her office, if possible before I leave campus. Oh, and she's apologizing for the inconvenience of canceling class," he explained.

"An inconvenience," Viv sounded annoyed. "That's what we call a dead instructor on the first day of class..." She shook her head.

His gaze took in the set of her chin and her lips forming a straight line. He loved seeing her indignant expression. Something about Viv expressing her feelings made him happy. Even when she was irritated, she looked beautiful.

"Do we say yes to the summons, or ignore her and go out to breakfast? I'd like a bagel with lox and cream cheese." He rubbed his stomach to coax a smile.

Viv sighed. "I'd like to eat, don't get me wrong. The eight o'clock class disrupted my carefully constructed morning schedule, including my appetite. My entire body expects regular meals at certain intervals. Seems to be an aging thing. A breakfast burrito will be just the thing." She looked down at her trim figure.

Rex put his key fob back in his pocket. "We'll make this quick. Meet Dr. Morales and find out what she wants. Then push off with some excuse so we can go eat."

Inside the administration building they stopped at stairway. "Fourth floor," Rex told her. "Sure you don't want to take the elevator?"

"I wore these just to go back to school." She glanced at her new trainers. "It would be nice to climb these stairs to get in some more steps. Should I meet you in front of the elevator?"

Rex knew she intended to appeal to his better instincts. Delay the next meal and use the stairs. "I'll meet you in front of the principal's office," he answered. Not because he wasn't up for the climb, but because he'd already set his sights on a vending machine chocolate bar. He waved goodbye.

Rex stepped inside the elevator, a chocolate bar in his pocket. He pushed the button for the fourth floor. Two younger students had braced their backs against the wall. Both looked at their phones.

Are they twins? was his first thought. They had similar

bodies, lean and angular. Both had long dark brown hair pulled back into low ponytails with rubber bands. Even their faces had a similar shape. The main difference was that one had a mustache.

Both wore orange tees that read "Meet me at the quad." He suspected they had something to do with the planned protest. Before he could ask one of the students, the elevator door slid open. They pushed past.

"I'm over here," came Viv's voice.

"Nice climb?" he asked.

"I stopped to catch my breath one time," she admitted. "The office is at the end of the corridor right over there."

An administrative assistant ushered them into the principal's office. She pointed toward two mid-century leather chairs. Rex paused to take a read of the room. *Efficient, modern like the occupant,* he concluded.

The back of his neck made him look more closely. *Something's a little off here.* He waited for Viv, then sat next to her. The large sleek wooden desk gave him an opportunity to look at the wall behind it.

A floor-to-ceiling bookshelf had been filled with rows of academic texts. The titles about leadership, psychology, and community engagement felt impressive. There was also a collection of books on hiking and nature conservation.

On a shelf in front of the books, a line of award plaques and medals had been strategically arranged. More certificates in black frames stood on the shelf above. He could see the State of California printed in embossed letters. Underneath was a photo of a tall thin woman. One included the recognizable face of the current Palm Desert mayor. To the sides were photos of students dressed in graduation apparel. They smiled into the camera, seeming pleased to be in the company of the Mojave Mesa principal, Dr. Seraphina Morales. *I wonder how many of those she's posed for over the years...*

Satisfied that he'd seen enough, he glanced toward a bank of windows. A shimmering view of the San Gregorio Mountains provided the background, with jagged peaks softened by a haze of heat. *Nice office. I wouldn't mind working here.*

One towering saguaro in the foreground caught his attention. It stood alone in the vast landscape, resilient and unrelenting.

The door from behind opened. Rex and Viv turned around to look as Dr. Seraphina Morales entered. "I'm so happy that I could meet with you before you left campus," she began.

Rex inhaled right as his temple throbbed. *She's like that saguaro. Alone and singular. Prickly but stately. A strong woman. No nonsense. Maybe ambitious, definitely intuitive. She'd been told she was too bold growing up. So she adjusted, wore a mask, to avoid putting people off. Hiding behind her stand offish exterior. I feel a vast reservoir of concern.*

Dr. Morales made herself comfortable in the chair behind her desk. Her welcoming smile revealed a row of even white teeth. "I so hope the events of this morning haven't discouraged your return to higher education." She paused, then continued. "I'd never want to put you off. That would be most unfortunate."

"At first I thought that the murder might be staged. You know, as part of an immersive back-to-school experience. Like one of the murder dinners," Rex offered. "I thought we'd be handed a magnifying glass and a detective's hat and told to solve the crime with other students. That kind of thing.

"But I could see as soon as we got inside the classroom that it was a real emergency. That the man behind the desk wasn't acting."

"Wallace Walker passed away, Mr. Redondo. That's what the police just informed me, right before I came through that door. Though I do appreciate your initial perspective. Not a bad idea actually, staging a pretend investigation for the first day of class. But Professor Walker had his own ideas about his curriculum and believe me, he wasn't that interactive or innovative."

"I think I read on his bio that he was a retired cop," Viv offered.

"Wally was so much more. He was a beloved part-time faculty member at Mojave Mesa. He'll be missed by staff and students alike." Seraphina Morales sounded sincere. Her eyes filled with tears.

"I'm sorry for your loss," Rex said. "You were obviously close."

He averted her distress by taking note of more details, like her ceramic coffee mug with the college logo. Next to the cup was a stack of neatly aligned papers, along with an electronic tablet and small framed photo of her family. *She's obviously organized.*

"May I get you a tissue?" he offered. "Or I can ask your assistant." He sat on the edge of his chair. This detour into female tears made him uncomfortable.

"Here you go." Viv slid a small pack of tissues past the photo toward Dr. Morales.

"Oh thank you." The principal dabbed at her eyes.

Rex heaved a sigh of relief. *Crisis averted. Good ol' Viv.*

"I have a question," Viv gently began. "We paid full tuition. Will someone else take over our class? Since we're planning to qualify for a private detective's licensing exam by next year, we'd like to keep to our schedule."

Dr. Morales's eyebrows rose. Rex suspected she hadn't expected such a direct question, especially in light of the tragic death. "We have to notify the next of kin and make arrangements, of course. But that won't take more than a week." She looked toward the window. "Poor Wally. The death isn't unexpected. Men over seventy often neglect their health."

Rex felt the return of annoyance. *Even she thinks seventies are old.*

"But back to your question," Morales continued. "I have a list of people waiting to be offered the job. Part-time instructors for adult education are not hard to find. Everyone with experience loves to share their expertise with an apt group of learners"—she cleared her throat—"even to older students."

Viv was apparently done with the conversation. She rose from the chair. "Okay then, thanks for giving us a chance to talk. Do send us the details of the resumed class schedule."

Rex remained seated. "When you texted, I thought you might have a specific question for us."

"I wanted to touch base," she admitted. "As is often the case with Wally's students, you two and that other young man were the only ones to show up. The enrollment for his classes has dwindled over the years. At first he had a large crowd who appreciated his lenient policy about attendance. He often let students slide when it came to tests and papers. Since it was just you three, I thought I'd text."

Viv spoke from the doorway. "You could get a substitute. We could return to class tomorrow."

"I suppose I could do that," she said slowly. "Maybe hire

someone on a probationary status. I'd like to do one hire if possible though. More efficient."

"Of course, I'm not in charge." Viv opened the door right as Rex stood. "How about that breakfast?" she reminded him without a hint of indecision.

5

VIVIENNE ROSE

Viv appreciated the quiet hum of people talking. They sat under an umbrella on the outdoor patio at Just Desserts. Having already ordered, she sipped iced tea, welcoming the cool breeze of an outdoor fan against her arms. "I'm glad we got a table outside," she commented.

"We won't be able to linger, with people waiting for tables," Rex reminded.

"We can take our breakfast to go and eat it at home," she offered. Her outdoor table by the pool was also a welcome retreat.

"Always a good backup," Rex agreed. "But after the morning we had... Plus being summoned by the principal. What did you think of her?"

She took another sip. "She's terribly efficient. I thought her feelings for Wally Walker may have included more relief than she was willing to admit. A loss for her personally but maybe not professionally."

Rex's eyes widened with appreciation. "My take exactly."

"She's obviously ambitious. Did you see all those photos

of her shaking hands with politicians? Oh, and the carefully placed objects on her desk. I notice things like that," Viv admitted.

"You're picking up some of my habit," he said. "Taking in the room with all the details. Did you feel anything, you know, with your other senses?"

"I wanted to leave as soon as we sat down. I felt like I was intruding in her schedule," Viv admitted.

"Is that why you asked about the tuition fees right away?"

"I wanted to catch her off guard. Just to see how she'd react. If I understood correctly, she was impatient to set up a new instructor. Almost as if she'd planned..."

"I bet we'll have a substitute day after tomorrow." Rex lifted a napkin to place on his lap. "One look out her office window and I got a glimpse of a saguaro. I felt my head throb but no images. My focus isn't back, at least not in full force."

She nodded for him to go on.

"When Dr. Morales walked in, I realized she's like the saguaro. She stores information to use later and is prickly on the outside. But the tears... She seemed genuinely upset about Wally's death."

Rex had not referred to his recovery since his return. "Are you okay?" she asked.

"Absolutely. Ready to go," he hastily added. "Like I was saying, only some of my images aren't quite back. That's all."

She felt a certain relief. When he'd returned after his month-long retreat, she wasn't sure how to proceed with their relationship. He'd not been as physically close, for one. She didn't want to push. This conversation was the first sign that he felt comfortable talking about his time away.

A server placed the plates on the table and refilled the iced tea glass. "Anything else?" he asked.

Rex picked up his first half of bagel. "I'm good," he said.

Viv carefully divided her breakfast burrito in half. "I'll take this home for later," she explained after the server left. "Want to share a cookie?"

"Sure," he mumbled. He swallowed. "I'll pick one up at the bakery counter on my way to the restroom and bring it back. Excuse me."

Viv now had a chance to review the details of the morning. When she realized the class would not be starting, her initial reaction was to leave and not look back. But the longer she waited, she realized her genuine curiosity got the better of her.

Rex returned with an oversized chocolate chip cookie. "Here or home?" He held up the bag.

"Here," she said. "I don't see anyone waiting for our table. Are you ready to talk about this morning? I have some questions."

He split the cookie and offered her half. "I never expected to be thrown into another case so quickly."

"So you already think this will be an investigation, not a natural death."

"Of course. What an opportunity. A sure sign we're meant to be in business. I don't believe in coincidences. Our first day of class and ta-da! The professor turns up dead. Now we can show off our considerable knowledge. Maybe get credit for an independent study. They still have those, right?"

Viv savored the dark chocolate chip cookie on her tongue. "I don't know about independent study," she admitted. "But one thing's for certain. Wherever you are, excitement follows."

His eyes sparkled, making his face look less weary and more like his old self. "Is that your way of saying I'm a magnet for murder? But let's get down to how we'd handle this, assuming it's a real case. It would take some poking around to find out more about Wallace Walker, that's for sure. In the course of our investigation we might reveal an enemy or two. Then we'd have people of interest."

"According to Dr. Morales he was beloved by all," Viv reminded.

"That's what they say about all the murdered people in all the detective shows," Rex insisted. "Not an enemy in the world." He pitched to a higher register, which made her chuckle.

"But if we go snooping without including the cops, we might get into real trouble. I mean, he may have died of natural causes."

"Nah," Rex said. "I think he was murdered for sure."

Cart before horse, Viv concluded. *I know I'm a novice, but assuming a murder without convincing evidence couldn't be the best practice under the circumstances.* "What makes you so sure that Walker was murdered?"

Rex grinned. "I have a nose for the truth. And Wally Walker was killed. My gut tells me so."

6

REX REDONDO

Rex hummed as he sauntered his way across the cafe toward the restroom. He'd made a polite excuse, but in fact he intended to pick up some intel.

When the images didn't arrive after the throb in his temple, he'd grown concerned. The last time that happened it led to a downward spiral, affecting his health, bringing back memories from his military deployments. As much as he appreciated the recent wellness retreat in Hawaii, he had no desire to return.

He'd explained to his therapist—they called him Chaps—how he'd get a throb in his temple and then images scrolled behind his eyes.

"When I was a kid I thought that happened to every-one," he admitted.

"When did you find out you are unique?" Chaplain Lightyear asked.

"Years later. I got drunk and was talking to another mentalist. He told me he envied my gift. Up until then I considered it a curse."

"Why's that?"

"Because I get the images but I don't always interpret their meaning correctly."

"Got you into trouble?"

"You can say that again."

As he sauntered toward the men's room he wanted to practice, thinking he was just rusty. *Listen. Observe. Pause,* he told himself. *Let your attention flow.* His eyes immediately rested on a young woman in tears. A man in a suit put his arm around her shoulders.

Rex ducked behind a server station to listen.

"I'm so sorry, Mia. For your loss." Business-suit guy sounded genuinely sorry. But the young woman's tears didn't stop. She wore a perky apron tied around her neck and behind her waist. Her body heaved with sobs.

That's no act, Rex reasoned.

When people pretended emotions, he instantly sussed them out. These two felt genuine. The damsel in distress and the knight in shining armor.

The woman dabbed at her eyes with the hem of her apron. "He was such a nice man, coming in every morning for breakfast. I'd see him come through the door and I'd start his order. The same thing every day. Even on weekends." Her face clouded, giving rise to a fresh batch of tears.

"I know, honey. We all liked Wally. It's easy to get attached to the regulars." The man pulled her closer. *Easy, buddy,* Rex thought. *Not too close. This could get creepy.* He'd comforted many a young woman in his time. He should know.

She sniffed. "I'm sorry about the tears." She pulled away. "I'll fix myself up in the women's and get back on my shift. Gosh, this is turning out to be the worst day." She forced a smile.

Rex made his way to the restroom so as not to be observed listening in.

After washing his hands, he stopped by the bakery counter. He noticed the young woman, now composed, helping another customer. He made his way back to the table with Viv.

As soon as he sat down, he could tell she was distracted. She had that look she got when something was on her mind. "So let's talk logistics. What's next for the Wally Walker case?"

Despite the heat and the dead body, Viv could get preoccupied but still appear calm. One tendril of wavy platinum hair fell over her left eye, softening her appearance. She pushed the hair away to share a smile. *Unflappable,* he thought. *Love that woman.*

Her direct gaze made him feel slightly giddy. He felt his attraction strongly. *Not now, Rex.* He broke his gaze. When he looked back the moment had passed.

A thoughtful expression came over her face. He liked to watch the thoughts cross her mind, the way her brow wrinkled and then smoothed and then wrinkled again.

She came at problems with logic. He found that most enthralling. He'd never expected to meet someone like her at his age. He figured all the excitement was probably over. But she'd proved him wrong from day one.

By the time they paid and left the cafe, Rex had a plan. "I think we should get Wally Walker's address," he said as they got into his SUV. "We can do a stakeout in front of his place—see who comes and goes. That kind of thing."

"I have a few loose ends to attend to first," Viv reminded him. "I postponed a call to a new mom. But after that I'm free."

"That will give me time to talk to Sutton. She'll be able

to get the address." He felt more confident now. With Viv at his side and a problem to solve, he knew his images would return.

A short while later, Viv let herself out of the SUV. "See you soon," she called over her shoulder.

He parked in the garage. Just as he stepped into the house, he called, "Sutton!" Time for her to earn her salary. He found her staring intently at her computer. Kevin shot out from behind the desk, barking and nearly knocking Rex off his feet.

"Hey, boss," Sutton said.

"Get down," Rex ordered the dog.

Kevin sat back on his hind legs. The dog raised both paws to balance on Rex's chest. This was followed by a series of dog licks to his chin.

"I mean it, Kevin." Rex pushed him back.

"Instead of repeating yourself, why don't you mean it the first time," Sutton suggested, eyes still focused on her screen.

On all fours, Kevin wagged his tail. Rex reached down to give his ear a scratch. "You're the trainer," he reminded Sutton. "How come you two are cooped up in the office?"

"When I got up this morning Kevin was hiding in the kitchen. He looked guilty so I figured you forgot to tell me you weren't going on your morning walk with Viv. So there was a cleanup before my coffee. Now I'm keeping him close. In case he makes another mistake."

Sutton wore a white baseball cap pulled over her strawberry-blonde hair. She'd lowered her reading glasses to give Rex a stern stare.

"Is this where I apologize for being an abysmal dog dad?" he asked dryly. "Don't forget, the puppy was your idea."

Sutton slid the glasses in place. "So how was your first day of school? Make any friends? Do you like your teacher? Any homework?"

He ignored her implication. "Not the usual," he confided. "We found a dead body. You should have been there."

She dropped her glasses on the desk. "The first day?" Her face, filled with incredulity, made him smile. *I love getting her attention like that.*

"Class was dismissed before it even started. Kind of disappointing. But Viv and I consoled ourselves over breakfast and a chocolate chip cookie. We now have a plan of action."

"What kind of action? You don't for one moment think this is your case! The cops will take care of things."

He pursed his lips to whistle nonchalantly. He did that a lot to indicate he didn't like her advice.

"Tell me the guy died of natural causes!" Sutton insisted. "I don't believe this happened to you two again. Why can't you be an average middle-aged couple? You two don't need any more dead bodies."

"Do you want to hear what happened?" he asked.

"Oh all right," she sighed.

When he was done describing the situation, Sutton clicked the computer off. "Like I said, probably natural causes. Old people die. I'm sorry to hear your class was canceled but really happy there's nothing that requires you butting your nose in. Think about it. Most likely a heart attack."

If I want to investigate, then that's what we're gonna do, her opinion notwithstanding, Rex thought. "I need to shower." Sutton rose to her feet. "The dog is all yours." She pointed to Kevin.

"Okay, I guess it's you and me, boy." Rex patted the dog's head. He'd planned on assigning Sutton the task of researching information about Wallace Walker. But now that she'd been so dismissive... He sat behind the computer to do his own investigating.

A quick search revealed Wallace "Wally" Walker's name. He had a noteworthy reputation in the community. A large image of the dead man's face stared back from a Facebook page. The skin prickled on Rex's arms.

The photo, taken a good fifteen years ago, showed Wally in a cop uniform. He looked alert and friendly. Weathered skin made him a desert standout. Only the keen stare of his blue eyes made Rex blink. *I wouldn't want to run into him if I were a criminal. Those eyes don't miss much.*

Rex read more of Wally's bio. He'd started as a cop in Palm Springs. After a few years he moved and transferred to Palm Desert. "To help the community," he told the interviewer.

Rex suspected that wasn't the entire story. *Most likely a messy divorce*, he reasoned. In fact, Palm Springs and Palm Desert were rivals. Most people with property in Palm Springs wouldn't move to Palm Desert. Property values aside, if Wally worked in Palm Springs, he most likely had to take a serious pay cut with the transfer.

Even though the towns were only a twenty-minute drive apart, Palm Springs, with its reputation as the playground for Hollywood stars, had always been a haven for the rich and famous. Right when Wally transferred, the late '6os, commerce exploded. Trendy restaurants and hip cosmopolitan tourists added to its allure. People flocked to see and be seen.

They stayed in overpriced spa hotels with a view of the

San Jacinto Mountains. Spotting celebrities was a tourist attraction. And then there was golf. Expensive courses with exclusive country clubs. Lots of celebrity tournaments.

While Palm Desert, the more laid-back younger sibling, attracted full-time residents and had a family-friendly vibe. Of course there was still upscale shopping and plenty of places for foodies from Los Angeles to drop in. You could see all of their Facebook photos as evidence. The golf courses were less traditional. Often designed around housing communities, featuring more modern amenities. But Palm Desert was definitely considered the stepchild to Palm Springs.

The fact that Walker was raised in Palm Springs, got a job on the force, and then moved to Palm Desert felt important to Rex's way of thinking. *Why the move?* He pulled out a paper to make a note and was immediately interrupted by a bark from the living room.

"I'm coming," he grumbled, his annoyance with Sutton renewed.

7

VIVIENNE ROSE

"Meow." Miss Kitty circled Viv's legs. She dropped her purse on the counter as the cat pawed at her foot. She gave Miss Kitty a treat and then braced her hands on each side of her kitchen sink.

Viv glanced longingly toward the pool. *I missed my morning swim. The class disrupted my schedule. Maybe this private investigation thing isn't such a good idea...*

Aging had changed how Viv viewed her life, especially how she took care of herself. Unlike earlier days when she could eat what she wanted and even occasionally drink alcohol to excess, she realized staying healthy would require a different set of habits. Stodgy or not, a consistent moderate consumption of food and drink and exercise made her feel better.

Skip one day of exercise and she'd be drowsy and out of sorts. Skip two and her muscles would ache more than usual. Skip three, well she might as well flop on the sofa and give up. She'd nearly said no to the early morning class, knowing her routine would be off-kilter.

But I can swim this evening, she reasoned. Be flexible,

Viv. Maybe this interruption will give you a chance to reconsider. She turned from the sink.

Sitting at her kitchen table, she opened her laptop. After returning a call to a client and sending two emails, she heard her phone buzz.

I got Walker's address. Want to do a drive-by?

Sure.

See you in ten.

They drove with the air conditioning on full blast. "So what's the address?" she asked.

"It's 43752 Ocotillo Drive," he answered promptly. "I put it in my GPS. We should be there shortly."

"I know that neighborhood." Viv nodded. "I helped deliver a baby there a year ago. Lots of '50s-style bungalows. Some have been remodeled and are quite expensive. Flipping houses in that neighborhood must be lucrative."

Rex took a left turn and another quick right onto Ocotillo Drive. "Right here." He pulled up to the curb. The mid-century home had been dwarfed by two-story dwellings on both sides.

"Wally's lived here for years and had nothing done to the place, but the neighbors renovated and doubled their square footage." Viv knew the challenge. She'd negotiated selling her home a few years ago, before buying into the Desert Tortoise Estates.

"Kinda plain," Rex observed.

"No curb appeal," Viv agreed. "Maybe smaller than my

place or yours." The front yard held one minimalist palm tree surrounded by white rocks. Weeds grew in the midst of the stones.

A series of three windows expanded across the front of the house. "Do you suppose Wally lived alone?"

"No idea," Rex said. "How about we look in one of those windows?" He whistled. "Check out those curtains."

"They look ancient. I'd think he'd at least have blinds," Viv added.

Right then a sleek BMW convertible pulled into Wally's driveway. The engine gunned as it came to an abrupt stop. The driver reached into the backseat. When he stepped into view he carried a real estate sign. Shoving aside the white rock in the front yard with his foot, he began pounding the stake into the dirt.

Viv read aloud. "J.W. Realty. For Sale."

"Now that's fast. The owner's barely dead and a real estate guy pounced. Selling Wally's house before the body is cold," Rex said.

Viv felt her face fall. "Lots of older people have fears about just this type of thing. That someone will sell their worldly assets and hurry them to their grave."

"Not your son," Rex reasoned. "Lucas seems like a good kid."

"He is a thoughtful and considerate son. But don't forget his father's in the mix." She sighed. Divorce was complicated even with adult children.

Rex put his hand on her shoulder. "Don't forget you have me. I've got your back."

The realtor turned toward the front door, then walked quickly to his car. Rex opened the SUV window and called out, "Is this house on the market?" He pointed to the sign.

The man changed his mind. Instead of getting into the

BMW, he slammed his door to come closer. Dressed in stylish slim-fit chinos and a crisp button-up shirt in bold red and blue stripes, he looked every part the realtor. Viv got a patriotic vibe. "Are you looking for a home in this neighborhood? This one's a dandy," the man said.

"I'm Rex Redondo." He extended his hand. "And your name..."

"I'm Jax Walker." The realtor returned a hearty shake. "And the beautiful lady is..." He nodded toward Viv, who remained in the passenger seat.

She shuddered. *I hate it when random men do that. I'm not looking for compliments. It feels like he's tossing an old lady a bone.*

She unclasped her seat belt and opened the door. Once outside she spoke in a brusque no-nonsense tone. "I'm Vivienne Rose. Why don't you show us the house."

His eyebrows arched. "Not wasting any time then. Probably wise. I hope you're prepared to bid right away because a bungalow in this neighborhood is going to go for over asking price."

Rex and Viv followed him inside.

Once her eyes adjusted to the darkness, she saw a well-worn beige sofa with a matching recliner. The recliner faced the flat screen TV, and a maple coffee table with a yellowed surface stood in front of the sofa. Old *National Geographic* magazines covered the top.

She sniffed. *Musty,* she concluded. A shelf with photographs and a shadow box caught her attention. She found mementos behind the glass of the shadow box which included a badge and a few ribbons, along with a photo with Wally in uniform. "Palm Desert cop," Viv said aloud.

Rex pointed to the side table next to the chair. "Looks like the owner is also a diabetic." Supplies had been neatly organized, including a days-of-the-week plastic pill container.

Jax didn't affirm or deny their observations. "Let's take a look at the kitchen," he said. "Now's the time to make an offer. By the end of the week I'll have this place staged and listed. You might be able to get in a bid and save the owner some money and trouble. Something to definitely consider."

Maybe he doesn't know that the owner is dead. Or maybe he doesn't want us to know. Either way this is awkward. Viv shot a glance at Rex before saying, "I'll check out the kitchen. Honey, why don't you get a look at the bedrooms?"

"Good idea," Rex agreed.

Two birds, one stone, Viv thought. *We can get a good look at this place and get out of here before revealing why we've come.*

One glance at Jax's face told her he didn't like them splitting up. "Why don't you come with me." She smiled engagingly, knowing the realtor could hardly refuse.

Her first look into the kitchen made Viv feel as if she taken a step back in time. The avocado-patterned linoleum floor, along with avocado-green counter tops reminded her of her grandmother's house.

One ceramic jar of utensils had been placed next to the stove top. They appeared sticky. *Probably haven't been washed for some time,* she thought. Viv opened the refriger-ator door and then closed it immediately. A waft of stale air and decaying food made her eyes water.

"Did the owner live in this house or rent it out?" she asked.

"He lived here," Jax responded. "He bought it from the original owner in the late '6os. He considered remodeling but it was too much trouble. So the place is ready for the next buyer to put their personal stamp on everything from the landscaping to interior design.

"Invest a quarter of a mil and the price would more than double. I've sold houses on this street that have tripled in value overnight. I've got the comps. We just have to stop by the office. I can recommend a builder who knows the area and he'll cut you a good deal." He handed Viv his business card.

She read his name aloud. "Jackson 'Jax' Walker. Any relation to Wally Walker? I've heard so many good things about him." She hoped her connection would push Jax to admit the man was dead.

His jaw tightened as he crossed his arms over his chest. "Sure. He's well known in this area. A Palm Desert cop. He teaches at Mojave Mesa as an adjunct professor."

Viv scrutinized his face. Before she could ask again if Jax was related to Wally, a loud crash came from the other side of the house.

"What the..." Jax pushed past her, his back disappearing around the corner. "What are you doing?" came his loud voice. "Trying to destroy my listing!"

"I'm in here," Rex said. "I'm just looking around. The drawer fell," he explained.

A quick trip down the hall revealed Rex with hands held feigning innocence. Unfortunately the mess, with the drawer broken at his feet, along with papers spread over the carpet, made it obvious. He'd had been snooping.

"I forgot to remind him not to look in the drawers."

Rex grinned. "She can't take me anywhere."

To Viv's relief, Jax didn't seem too concerned.

"I suppose you didn't mean any harm. Just don't do that again. I'm supposed to protect the seller's valuables. If anything's gone, he'll prosecute."

Rex rolled his eyes. When he caught her looking, she glanced away to hide a sheepish grin.

She'd seen this before. The eye roll when he was up to something but he was afraid he'd get caught. He patted his pants pocket. Not a random gesture.

She'd realized when they first met that Rex liked to learn things about people, and the best way was to hold an item in his hand and see what came up. An intuition. Maybe one of his images. Or just an overall gut feeling. She'd decided from past experience that he meant no harm.

He reached into his pocket. When he opened his hand there was a gold pocket watch attached to a chain. "You mean something like this?"

Jax drew an angry breath.

"When the drawer fell to the floor I picked it up. I didn't want to inadvertently step on something that might be a valuable antique. But now that I've been caught in this embarrassing situation, I'll just leave it right over here where I found it. No harm, no foul."

"What kind of man are you, stealing from a dead guy," Jax sputtered. Phone to ear, he glared at Rex.

Viv wasn't sure if Jax was bluffing. But she didn't want to stick around to find out.

"Just let me clean up," Rex offered. "No need to call the cops." He bent to pick up the strewn papers. Then he shuffled the envelopes and put everything back. His hand hovered over the back of the drawer as he dropped the watch. He slid the drawer closed with a thud.

"Hello, police?" Jax said into the phone.

"We'll be going now. Good luck with your sale." Viv took Rex's hand to make a quick exit.

8

REX REDONDO

"Did you hear what he said?" Viv asked as Rex started moving the SUV away from the curb. "He admitted the owner was dead." She checked the side mirror to see if Jax followed. He ran toward the curb just as they pulled away.

To her amusement, he got halfway across the white rocks when his arms flailed. He lost his balance and fell over, executing a face-plant into the decorative stones.

"Step on it," she said. "Jax tripped."

Despite his quick acceleration, Viv saw Jax stand and brush off his sleeves, looking none the worse for the mishap.

Tires squealed. Rex took the corner and sped toward the main boulevard, merging into traffic. "That was a close call."

"I'm happy you returned the watch," she said. "If he did call the cops you'd be in big trouble."

He slid the SUV behind a truck and lowered his speed. "Jax admitted the owner died. He wasn't saying so at first."

She turned toward him. "Did you happen to get a read on the pocket watch?"

"I didn't have time. But it felt warm in my palm. I don't know what that means, but it's something."

Rex felt his neck flush. Viv believed he left the pocket watch in the drawer. She'd fallen for his sleight of hand. Now he was in a quandary. *She hates when I lie. Do I tell her I still have the watch?*

Viv seemed unaware of his conflict. She asked the next question. "Did you see the photos on that shelf? Looks like our victim was kind of a big deal, shaking hands with the mayor and the governor. In the late '6os."

"Ronald Reagan. There was a photo of Wally standing next to the actor-turned-president," Rex said.

When she didn't ask any more questions, he felt pretty certain that he'd gotten away with keeping the watch. "Wally's desk was stuffed with old papers. I wanted to take a closer look." He pulled the SUV into his driveway.

"If there's an open house this weekend, we can go back and gather more clues about Wally. I could take photos for evidence."

Rex felt a surge of energy. "Good idea. I'll alert Sutton. She can gather some intel about an open house. Maybe there's an electronic gadget that we can wear to help us eavesdrop. Or an infrared camera that would pick up DNA. Wally may have been murdered in his house and transported to the classroom."

"I don't think we need to worry about the body being transported just yet. I think we have to eliminate what's more obvious, which is Wally's health condition and if he died of natural causes."

Rex shrugged. "I suppose. Not as interesting though. Once Sutton gets some info on the open house, I'll ask her to set us up with disguises. And possibly a fake identity. Now that Jax knows us as Rex and Viv, we'll need to go undercover.

Viv opened the passenger door. "Let me know what Sutton says. I have to get back to work."

"Okay, boss." Sutton stood in front of the full-length mirror. Rex sat on the end of the bed. She'd brought two armfuls of assorted clothing.

"Do I have to wear a wig? My hair is my signature feature. It makes me stand out over all the other guys my age."

Sutton sighed. "You can think that. But the truth is you stand out because your

over-the-top energy draws people's attention. Stop being annoying. You called me to consult. I'm just doing my job." He heard her impatience loud and clear.

"Remind me again. I pay you to do work for me." He smiled fondly at his roommate, aka personal assistant, aka former military colleague.

"Put this on." She handed him a blonde wig. "Use the glue and stick this mustache over your lip. Then come back and wow me. I know you have more personas in that bag of mentalist tricks. Just pick one to go with the disguise."

When he returned, he did feel different. He patted his head. "Hair makes the man. I admit I feel protected, hiding the real me." He used his thumb and index finger to twirl the end of the mustache. "Just like Hercule Poirot. But I need wax for the stash."

Sutton looked him up and down. "No you don't. Now for the clothing." She handed him a pair of cargo shorts. He frowned. "I don't wear those. Too many pockets. I'm a slim and trim kinda guy." He waited for her to chuckle.

"Drop your pants and put these on." She turned away.

Rex felt disgruntled. *Not even a smile from Ms. Crabby Pants.*

He took a look at himself in the mirror. "The shorts make me look fat. Too bulky," he complained.

"I've got this graphic tee from Coachella. Put it on and slip the jacket over the front," she insisted.

"Come on. You know jackets don't look good with shorts. Plus it's over a hundred degrees. Who wears these in this kind of weather?"

"A guy whose ego is bigger than his fashion sense, that's who." Sutton refused to back down.

Rex shook his head in disgust. "You just want to make me look bad," he muttered.

"I'm not done yet." Sutton handed him a large pair of sunglasses. "These will cover the upper part of your face. Don't forget eyebrow pencil for the brows to match the stash. And now here's the best part." She smirked and handed him a black fanny pack.

"No! I draw the line. I'm not wearing one of those. It's just...wrong." Rex's protest got lost in her laughter.

"You need a signature accessory to comment on and remember instead of your face." She clipped it around his waist.

"So what do you have for Viv?" he finally asked. "Is she going as an upscale socialite in a tight dress? Low-cut in the front." He ran his finger over his tee to emphasize how low. "And maybe short, to the middle of her thigh."

"She has the body to make that work," Sutton ruminated aloud. "But no. I'm not playing into your fantasies. I've got a great plan for Viv, which I will reveal right before you get ready to go."

"What about backstories?" he prodded.

"You'll be playing the part of business partners from Los Angeles who want to invest in properties that can be flipped and used as vacation rentals. Your name is Rick and she is Vera Steele."

"Nice. The names remind me of Dashiell Hammett's favorite sleuth duo. Nick and Nora. So tell me more."

"Since you'll be mingling with other people, prospective buyers and realtors, you have to sell your backstory. I'll give you lots of fake business cards. Kinda like a spy's passport. Keep them handy to hand out when people start to get nosey."

Rex quirked an eyebrow. "I like that. Plays into my"—he turned toward the mirror to put on his sunglasses—"persona."

"And don't use that word." Sutton handed him a stack of cards. "Practice saying what's on the cards. Sprinkle the phrases into your conversations with people. I'm giving Viv some ideas of her own. Go ahead, try the top one."

Rex squinted. "I've been trying to balance my chakras lately." He rolled his eyes and read the next card. "This house has good flow..." Then he sent her a glare. "What does that even mean?"

"Doesn't matter," Sutton chided. "Just practice saying each one with conviction and keep dropping the phrases as if they mean something. Pretend. You're good at that, right?"

Rex sat down on the edge of the bed to look at the rest while Sutton made her way to the door. "See you later, boss. Tell Viv I'll be over soon."

9

VIVIENNE ROSE

Viv braced her back against the headboard to open a book. Her reading glasses perched on the end of her nose, she planned on falling asleep. Then her phone jingled.

"Hello," she said. "I'm attending to my sleep hygiene by reading before bed." She hoped "hygiene" would put him off and that he'd say goodnight and hang up.

Unfortunately Rex didn't take the hint. He kept talking. "Old Jax must have had the open house prepped and ready. The ad's already on social media. Makes me wonder if he anticipated his grandfather's death."

"Makes him a person of interest for sure." Viv yawned.

"You mean a suspect," Rex corrected.

"Not according to *Law and Order,* my TV reference for all things legal," she responded tartly. "You can't call someone a suspect until they've been arrested and read their rights."

"You must have that wrong." Rex sounded doubtful. "I know Brenda Lee in *The Closer* calls people suspects all the time. And what about Columbo. I'm pretty sure he calls them suspects."

Viv chuckled. "I'd have to fact check you on that one. Maybe some other time." She yawned again. "I'm feeling tired and want to get up early tomorrow for our first undercover operation."

"Okay then. See you tomorrow." The phone clicked, ending the call.

She'd expected him to invite himself over, which would not have been entirely unwelcome. But when he seemed more interested in the investigation than getting close to her, she felt disappointed.

They'd had a moment on the cruise ship where they'd actually shared the same bed. Viv had fond memories of that time. In fact, she'd anticipated a repeat performance once they got back to shore.

But since they'd returned home, one thing led to another and he'd not made a move. Despite living next door and seeing each other every day, the intimacy had not taken up where it left off. He'd not even referred to their time together. She tried to imagine if she'd done something wrong. *Maybe it was a one-off, or maybe he's gone back to dating younger women.*

Viv reached over to turn off her bedside lamp. Snuggling down into her covers, she remembered that sleeping alone had its rewards. *I get the whole bed to myself and all the covers.*

Then she heard a soft, "Meow." Miss Kitty landed on the bed to snuggle into her side. Viv closed her eyes to the sound of a rumbling purr.

Sutton sat on the edge of her bed as Viv looked at herself in the mirror. "Repeat after me," she instructed. "I just love how *Instagrammable* the whole vibe here is."

Viv repeated back the phrase.

"That's really good. I didn't know you were a mimic," Sutton complimented.

"I did some community theater years ago," Viv admitted.

"Try this one." Sutton pulled out another card. "Do you guys have any plant-based restaurants around here? LA has us spoiled."

This time Viv sounded exactly like the teacher, bringing a shared giggle from both women.

"Are you good with the disguise?" Sutton came closer to adjust the hem of the Boho-style maxi dress. The bold gray and black design suited Viv's coloring but was the complete opposite of her usual coastal grandma look.

Viv adjusted her wig. "I remember my mom having a dyed brown bob with bangs when I was growing up. She was always brushing hair out of her eyes." Viv did the same, using her forefinger.

"Here, put these on. They will help with the bangs." Sutton handed her an oversized pair of sunglasses. "Very Liz Taylor," she added. "Are you okay with the platforms? They can take getting used to."

Viv lifted a sandaled foot. "As long as I don't have to run."

Sutton pulled out large gold hoop earrings from her tote. "These will be really distracting. Try them on. And I have a huge black leather bag for you to carry. Try this sun hat. Pull the brim over your eyes for a better disguise. I'll get the identity ready too, along with a burner phone. It's important to keep your surveillance cell separate."

Viv moved her head back and forth to watch the hoops bounce against her cheek. She kept staring at herself in the mirror. "What's the backstory again?"

Sutton explained as Viv only partially listened. She

wondered about her appearance and if Rex would like the new look.

Sutton watched Viv's reflection in the mirror. "Did you hear anything I just said?"

"Most of it," Viv mumbled. "Something about real estate developers..."

"That's right." Sutton nodded.

"I'll let Rex handle that part. Give me another phrase to practice."

Sutton took up another card. "Try this. 'I'm all about manifesting the right space. This one definitely feels aligned.'"

"Manifesting." Viv looked surprised. "Really..."

Both women burst into another round of giggles.

Viv folded her garments and put them on the dresser before walking Sutton to her front door. "You could be a Hollywood wardrobe person," she said.

"More of a hobby. Just so you know, I rented a car—to keep up the appearance that you're big-deal real estate investors from Los Angeles. I suspect Jax would be showing the house and that Rex's SUV would be recognizable."

"So many details in undercover work." Viv suppressed a giggle. "Rex must really be enjoying all of this."

Sutton shrugged. "He doesn't mind playing a role if it's his idea. Having one foisted on him is an entirely different matter. There was some pushback when his signature silver-fox hair got hidden by a wig."

Viv heard Sutton's impatient tone. She didn't like to intrude upon her relationship with Rex. They were a complicated pair. Employees. Roommates. Friends but not a couple.

"Has Rex seemed different to you...since he got back?" Viv asked in a hesitant voice. If anyone would know, it would be Sutton.

She blinked as if surprised by the question. "Not really. Maybe his energy is a bit more subdued. He's definitely as irritating. I wish he'd pick up after himself and take responsibility for Kevin more seriously."

Viv heard irritation underneath her words. *She's not that happy with her boss*, she concluded.

Sutton opened the door. "Come to think of it, he hasn't returned to the stage. No mentalist shows scheduled on the books. I suppose that's a big change."

"Interesting," Viv replied. "Maybe he's really going to retire this time."

"Or maybe he's lost his nerve." Sutton's jaw tightened. "I hate to think a month of introspection took away his bounce. But honestly I have my own life to worry about."

After closing the door, Viv wondered if she'd gone too far. *I know he'd hate me asking her, but I'm curious. And a bit concerned*, she admitted. A loud knock came from the front door.

Maybe Sutton forgot something.

But it was Rex and Kevin who stood on the other side. "How about a neighborhood walk?" he asked. He sounded chipper, his usual self.

"I need to grab a hat," she said.

10

____

REX REDONDO

Dressed in his disguise, Rex took one last glance in the mirror and groaned. *I look like my dad with this terrible hair.* He patted and primped and checked his pocket. The warmth from the watch was intensifying, burning a hole in his pocket. He couldn't wait to return it to Wally's bungalow. Then he'd put the watch back. *No harm, no foul.*

The heat of the metal case had surprised him. He worked with the watch the evening before, hoping to inspire a few images. He carefully examined it by pulling at the chain, clicking the fob to open then close the gold cover.

Stories played in his mind. How a man might use the watch back in the day without cell phones. He imagined being just such a man as he twisted the clasp, revealing the face. He closed the cover, shoving it back in his pocket. Unable to bring up inner images, Rex tried again.

This time he twisted the stem to see if he could set the time. It twirled between his fingers, but the hands didn't move. He sensed an emotional connection between the timepiece and the owner. *Wait.* He stopped himself. *Maybe more than one owner.*

Holding the watch in his hand, he closed his eyes. The object warmed, sending a jolt from his palm, to his wrist, and up his right arm. Used to his body's response to the process, he waited for his inner vision.

The images began to spin. Three in a row. To the left was an old man. He sat in a recliner. He had thinning gray hair, his hand on a TV remote.

The middle image showed a younger man with dark hair. He wore a cop's uniform. Ribbons on his chest pinned over a dark blue shirt. His chin was set and looked similar to the old man's. *Maybe his son...*

The third cylinder kept spinning. Rex focused on the motion. Even when it slowed and stopped it lacked detail. Just the outline of a man's head and shoulders.

He opened his eyes.

"Bork," Kevin called from the other room.

"Not now, buddy. We're on assignment. Going under-cover." Rex slipped the pocket watch back into his pocket. His thigh felt hot where it lay against his skin.

Interesting, he thought.

"Bork," came Kevin's reminder.

Rex found the dog standing by the door with a dangling leash in his mouth.

"Life is hard. Sometimes you gotta wait." Rex opened the door. "Let's check on Viv's disguise. I bet she looks fantastic."

She met him on the pathway. "You look..." He had trouble hiding his disappointment. No low-cut, tight-fitting dress. Just something with big designs that flowed to cover her body. "Nice," he added. His heart wasn't in it.

"Got a problem with my ensemble?" she asked.

"That dress covers you up, and what about the bangs? I have to have a word with Sutton. This was not my fantasy."

"You expected what? A naughty call girl or a slutty maid?" She blushed.

Now look. You've made her embarrassed.

He lowered his gaze to open the car door.

Vehicles lined both sides of the street in front of Wally's bungalow. Rex circled the block before he found a spot around the corner.

"Did you see that?" Viv asked.

"What do you mean?" His gaze lingered on the back of her neck, exposed by the shorter hairstyle.

"The landscaping." Viv's voice rose. "The rocks are gone. Turf's been rolled out. Look at all those new plants. Agave and aloe right there." She pointed. "And the trim's been painted. Oh, and someone filled those pots on each side of the new front door. Lots of freshly planted flowers."

"Overnight," he mused. "That took some work. Maybe Jax called a designer. I've heard of businesses like that. But again, he'd have to plan all of these changes long before Wally passed.

"There's a crowd. That's good. Less chance of being singled out by Jax," Rex assessed.

One step over the threshold and a woman with a big smile handed him a brochure. She was dressed in a bright pink business suit with black three-inch heels. "My name is Gloria. Welcome to my open house. Have a look around. I'd be happy to answer any questions."

Rex picked the first phrase he remembered. "We've been doing a lot of juice cleanses lately—Palm Springs has good juice spots, right?" He groaned inwardly, realizing his mistake.

Gloria's eyebrow rose as if she didn't understand.

Viv did her best to cover a smile. "Don't pay any attention to him. My partner's first instinct is his stomach. Once he's had lunch the fast will be over and then he'll make more sense."

Fortunately another woman came through the open front door. Gloria shifted her attention. "Welcome to my open house. My name is..."

Rex walked away, feeling ill at ease. He directed Viv to stand closer. Dismissing his gaff, he glanced over the living area. The shabby couch and recliner had been replaced with neutral modern furniture. Sage green and terra cotta accent pillows filled the sofa. A walnut coffee table held three stacked oversized books. Rex recognized the name of the local photographer on the front.

The television had been replaced with an art print of a desert landscape. Underneath, the shelf the photographs had been removed. He whistled under his breath. "Quite the transformation."

"I'm heading to the kitchen," Viv said, then stopped abruptly. "Let's wait until they leave."

As the couple inspected a drawer, Rex looked at the new stainless-steel appliances. The pot of utensils was nowhere in sight. The walls had been painted a light gray to coordinate with elegant white placemats. Dishes and matching napkins, painted in desert hues, were placed in a setting for two.

"The energy here is so *low-key*, but like, in a good way." He quoted from another of Sutton's cards.

Viv rolled her eyes. Once the couple moved aside, she opened the refrigerator door. What a difference. Inside, curated containers with matching lids were lined in a row. One container held carrots and celery. They'd also been arranged in even rows.

Viv spoke quietly. "Look at all those vegetables. This isn't just a house. Anyone who falls for the staging is falling for a healthy lifestyle."

Rex felt flustered. He knew how to improvise during his show but this was different. He wasn't in control. He felt at a loss to contribute to the conversation. Mostly because he didn't care about vegetables.

Viv shut the refrigerator door quickly.

"I want to see the bedrooms." Rex took her by the arm.

Standing in the hallway, Viv's eyes were wide. "What's the matter with you?"

"I'm not selling the persona," he admitted. "I feel really uncomfortable. The staging for one. I don't like the..." He ran his hand over his wig, searching for the word.

"Go ahead. You're going to say 'vibe.'" Viv smiled. "You don't like the vibe," she repeated.

"When I read the room, I feel anxiety. Like something's not right. The first time we were here it felt entirely different. Wally Walker's personality fit the space. I knew we were in the home of an older guy who'd recently passed away. No conflict.

"But now I feel like we're in the home of an older guy who's been covered up. As if he were inconvenient. No longer relevant to the sale."

Viv nodded.

He cleared his throat. "Let's check out the office. Maybe the paperwork is still there. Our trip won't be for nothing if we can take some quick photos." The pressure of returning the pocket watch weighed heavily. He needed to get rid of it before Viv noticed.

He followed her out of the kitchen and down the hallway. Once in the office, Viv reached behind him to close the door and push the lock. "We need some space," she explained.

His gut clenched. "The old furniture is gone." He pointed to a sleek desk and a modern chair. *Why don't you just admit what you did*, he chastised himself.

The newly appointed office looked personal yet generic. A small bookcase held a fake cactus and a few neatly arranged books. Titles were three years old, taken from the Los Angeles Times Bestseller list.

A daybed with neutral cushions and a fluffy comforter had been placed under the window. The office no longer looked like the den of an old guy living alone with his memories. This space functioned as a home office and a cozy guest suite.

"Nothing in the closet." Rex closed the door. "I wonder where they stored Walker's stuff. Maybe they called a junk guy and had it hauled away." He tapped his pocket again. He felt a burning sensation over his thigh.

He gritted his teeth.

"How are we going to get, you know, our client's information, like his social security and bank statements without the papers?" he asked. "Sam Spade never had this kind of problem," he mumbled under his breath.

A knock sounded on the door. "Open up," called a man's voice.

Viv released the button on the knob. "Oh, sorry. Must have locked by mistake." Jax pushed his way into the room. She kept talking. "This house would be so perfect for hosting our next sound bath circle," she quoted from a Sutton card.

Rex patted his pants pocket. *Ouch. I'm going to have a blister if this keeps up.*

"Bath circle. Right. Love me a bath circle."

11

____

VIVIENNE ROSE

Viv felt mentally off-balance. Rex's unfocused recent behavior made her wonder: *what happened to the liar-liar-pants-on-fire impromptu storyteller guy I've come to know and love? So much confidence. Where are you, Rex Redondo?*

Maybe I need to up my undercover game. For one, I need to distract Jax. I don't want him to recognize us from the other day. "What a beautiful backyard," she said, using a bright voice as she turned toward the window.

To her surprise more turf had been added. Looking luscious and green, trimmed neatly around the concrete patio. Potted plants and a fancy outdoor kitchen contributed to the allure. *They're obviously selling a lifestyle with this home.*

Behind the grass was a gravel area that included a walk-in shed with French doors open to the yard. Aware that Jax wasn't paying attention, she turned. To her relief the realtor didn't seem that interested. Instead he scrolled on his phone.

Rex looked at her like a deer in headlights. So she dove

in with conversation. "You must be the realtor." She pitched her voice slightly higher than her usual register as part of her disguise. When Jax said, "Um hum" but didn't look up, she tried another approach.

"Maybe we're done here," she said crisply. "We have other homes to view."

Rex's eyes sparkled with admiration. Jax finally put his phone away.

A voice called from the hallway. "Got your text. I'm coming."

Gloria hurried into the room, her face flushed with exertion. She extended a hand toward Viv. "Hello there. My name is Gloria Ramirez. Welcome to the open house."

"We met," Viv said sharply. "When we first arrived."

"That's right. So many faces. Did I give you a brochure? I must have. Tell me more about yourselves. By the way, I'm sure the bids will start coming very soon. So no time to dawdle." She smiled brightly.

"Show me the list of bidders," Jax insisted, looking over her shoulder.

She held up her phone. He grunted approval. "More than I thought. All of them way over asking price." He turned to Viv. "If you're interested in this place, you might want to make an offer now. Send me a text. Here's my card. Gloria will fill out the paperwork. She's my assistant."

"I'm your partner," Gloria retorted. "And the stager," she added. "Doesn't this place look amazing!" She whirled around on one high heel.

"We noticed," Rex finally said. "You're talented."

Jax's chin dropped. He was back to texting. Gloria blinked her eyes with appreciation. "Here's my card. I can help you with any real estate project in Palm Springs. I'll stay with you for the entire process, even escrow. And if you want to flip the property quickly, I'll give you a discount on the staging and landscaping. Don't you think the turf is to die for?" She slipped the card into his hand with a conspiratorial wink, nodding toward the backyard.

"That freshly laid sod will be dead in two weeks without irrigation on a timer. I can see there's no sprinkler system in place," Viv said dryly.

Gloria's smile drooped. But then her lips perked right back up. "My brother is a landscaper. If you want artificial turf he can give you a deal. Give me your contacts and I'll connect you both."

Rex shrugged. "Quite the operation you have here. We aren't ready to make an offer just yet."

Viv noticed that he was inching toward the desk. His fingers walked toward the far side and then slowly moved over. *Is he looking for a drawer? He seems unusually interested.*

"No drawers," he commented. "Too bad."

Gloria pushed back with a redirect. "Nowadays many home office desks are designed to be multifunctional. You can see on the side that there's a strip where multiple devices can be plugged in. Keeps the surface looking clean and orderly. You have a cell phone, right? You can put it right here in the built-in dock and then slide it onto this shelf. I can include the desk with the house." She smiled brightly. "A little incentive."

Rex rubbed his hand over his hair. Then he stared at his palm.

Viv wondered if he was testing the security of his wig.

"Still no drawer." He rubbed his palm against the leg of his cargo shorts.

"I'd suggest you add a hundred grand over asking for the house. I'll toss in all the furniture for free." Gloria moved right into a bid proposal, disinterested in his fixation on the desk.

When he looked confused, she narrowed her eyes. The tone of her next statement sounded like a threat. "You better prepare for a bidding war. This place will be going, going, gone."

Tired of the charade, Viv cut to the chase. "I heard the owner just passed away. Do you have the legal authority to be selling this home so soon?"

Jax looked up immediately. This time his phone slipped from his grasp. He caught it midair. Viv's direct inquiry had his attention.

"This home happened to belong to a family member. I'm the executor of the estate and have full legal authority to deal with his property," he explained.

Viv felt a jolt. *He admitted his relationship to Wally again. I think that's important.*

"My business partner is just curious," Rex explained.

Jax shifted his gaze toward Rex. He blinked. "Do I know you..."

Rex shook his head. "We're developers and we're on the lookout for good deals. Short-term rentals have proven lucrative in Palm Springs." He handed one fake business card to Jax and another one to Gloria.

"Do you have any other real estate that you can show us?" Viv chimed in. "We have to get back to Beverly Hills right after dinner. We may be able to make an offer on multiple properties—if the price is right."

"Oh, we have properties," Gloria insisted. "Why don't I give you a call right after we close up the house? I can send you listings." She glanced at the card Rex handed her. Then she smiled slyly. "Nice to meet you."

12

———————

REX REDONDO

Rex sat behind the wheel of the rental car waiting for Viv to buckle her seat belt. His inability to return the pocket watch made him feel on edge. He was even more concerned that she would find out.

Finally she asked, "Is everything okay?"

"I'm good," he lied. But then he had another idea. *I can fix the drop-off failure right now, before she finds out.* "I have to go back in the house," he announced.

"What for?" Viv looked surprised. "Our cover might have been blown. Why do you want to risk being noticed and remind Jax?"

"I want to look more closely at the backyard. Did you see that shed? Maybe they've stored Wally's belongings in there. I could have a look around for more clues."

The corner of her mouth tightened. "I think the shed is a staging device. It's been designed to attract a certain kind of buyer who thinks she requires an outdoor

private 'me space.' It's a thing.

"Influencers post all the time about she sheds. How women long for that special place. Blah, blah, blah. I think

60

it's a throwback to girls having a playhouse while growing up. The lucky ones with fathers who built them their own princess castle to look like Barbie DreamHouses."

Rex was less than convinced. "You realize I have no idea what you're talking about. Barbie DreamHouse. I think I bought one of those for my honorary niece when she was five. But it never made it to the backyard."

"Don't be so literal," she chided. "Women like their own space. Just ask Virginia Woolf. A room of one's own has become a she shed."

He suddenly felt curious. He had to ask. "Is that what you want?"

"Not really. I live with Miss Kitty. My house is a big she shed."

"Okay," he agreed. "Back to my plan. I want to check out the shed before they close up the open house. Would that be possible?"

"I'll wait for you. If we both go in it will cause unnecessary scrutiny. Pat your wig down first." Viv pulled down the visor.

Rex adjusted his hairpiece. "Not enough glue," he muttered. Once he stepped to the curb, Viv leaned back to close her eyes. "Stay out of trouble," she called.

Rex waited for two people to step away from the door toward the street. The woman waved a brochure, talking rapidly as the door closed behind them. *Time to make my move while Jax and Gloria are buttoning up the inside. It will only take me a minute to slip through the side gate to the backyard.*

The gate closed behind him. He felt his thigh tingle. *Not a perfect drop-off solution but better than letting it burn a hole in my pocket.*

He leaned against the side of the house, making sure

neither Jax nor Gloria had stepped out the back door. A quick glance revealed Jax in the kitchen with his back to the sink. He held his mobile to his ear. Gloria called out, "Hurry up. I have another appointment."

He darted toward the shed. Fortunately the French doors, propped by containers overflowing with flowers, were still left open. String quartet music spilled out. *Like Bridgerton*, he thought.

I wouldn't mind living in a she shed, he mused once inside. Styled for versatility, the minimalist aesthetic didn't feel exclusive of men. A chic sofa rested against one wall. An array of decorative pills in yellow, aqua, and neutral tones had been carefully arranged to look tidy but not too casual.

One floating shelf over the sofa held books. He noted three specific titles. One written by Virginia Woolf—*A Room of One's Own. Ahh, I get it. Just what Viv was talking about. If you haven't figured out before that this is a she shed, that book would make the point.*

Two short steps and he stood in front of an apartment-sized refrigerator. He marveled. *Kinda like a young girl's playhouse or an upscale motorhome. Everything scaled to a smaller size.*

He imagined Viv sitting next to him in a deluxe airstream motor coach. *We'd have a blast. Traveling the country solving crimes.* Then he pushed away that fantasy for the job at hand.

He lifted the pocket watch chain cautiously from his pocket. The burning against his thigh still tingled. *I can slip it underneath the rug.* He dismissed that idea, concerned it would be crushed before it got noticed.

How about a kitchen drawer? That would work. Nestled

beside some spoons and forks. It would be found eventually, long after I'm outta here.

He slid the top drawer open. Just as he lowered the watch into the drawer, a voice came from behind.

"Stop right there!"

Rex's stomach clenched. He put on a smile and turned toward the door.

"Hello, Officer," Rex said. He raised his hands in the air. "I can explain everything."

13

VIVIENNE ROSE

Viv opened her eyes at the sound of loud voices coming from the house. She lifted her head from the seat to look out the window. *What has he gotten into now...*

Chirp came a siren's call. She looked over her shoulder through the back window. A light blinked on top of a Palm Desert police cruiser. Her heart sank.

Two uniformed police flanked a man. One opened the back seat door of the cruiser, while the other pushed the top of his head to lower him to the seat.

Oh no, Viv thought as Rex smiled at her.

She took her cell phone out of her purse. "Sutton. Rex has been arrested. Let me know if you get this message."

She laid the phone in her lap. *I can rush over and make a fuss*, she thought. *Or I could stay here and hope they don't notice me. Maybe I'm more help if I stay.*

Rex disappearing behind tinted glass. One officer stared at something in his hand. He called out, "Lieutenant, I have something here." Viv recognized what it was immediately. Rex's hairpiece, looking like a disheveled cat after a late-night brawl.

I guess his cover has been blown. I wish he'd listened to me...

She walked around the car and slipped behind the wheel just as her cell rang. Sutton's ID appeared on the screen.

14

____

REX REDONDO

Rex sat on the edge of the metal-framed bed, which groaned under his weight. One glance at the stained mattress made his stomach clench. But the view of the metal toilet with no lid and the matching metal sink made him feel worse. A single bulb hung from the ceiling. *It could be worse*, he thought, trying to be optimistic, but his gut clenched in protest.

This is a first, Rex thought. He'd been arrested one time before, by Officer Farrah. But that didn't count. Because she was trying to get him out of the way for his own good.

She'd released him before an official booking.

But this—he looked past the bars—*this is a real arrest. I'll tell this story for street cred once Sutton pays my bail.*

He stood, the metal bed bumping against the bolts on the wall. He moved near the bars to look down the hallway. *Nobody here.* He sat back down on the mattress with a sigh.

Resting a palm over his thigh, he felt lingering heat. *I bet I have a burn mark from that watch.* A high-pitched ring started in one ear. A sure sign that his nerves were on hyper-alert. A quick shake of his head made his temple throb.

Viv must have seen me. I wonder if the cops arrested her too, as an accomplice. He felt instant remorse. The very thought of her in such a circumstance made him groan.

His mind raced. *I wonder if she got her phone call. But who would she contact? They might play us against each other, like on TV. I suppose she could call Sutton.* The brusque voice of the booking officer came to mind.

"Make your call," he insisted as they took his fingerprints.

Rex shook off the earlier incident and patted his head. His palm came back sticky. *Oh yeah. The hairpiece. I forgot they took it for evidence.*

I must look terrible in that photo. He glanced around the cell. *No mirror. I'm such a fool. Can't even keep my disguise in place.* He dropped his head to his hands.

"Mr. Redondo…" A police officer stood on the other side of the bars. "Sutton Drew has posted your bail."

Rex stood, feeling slightly lightheaded. He shoved his hands in his pockets and pursed his lips to whistle. *Nah, maybe that's too casual.* Instead he made up a story.

"Getting arrested happens to me a lot in my line of work. Good to know my assistant was on her toes. What was Ms. Drew wearing? I bet you got an eyeful…"

"I think that's an inappropriate question," the officer snapped. "You need to treat women with more respect."

Rex walked through the door toward the main desk to the sound of familiar laughter. It was Sutton. She seemed to think the officer in charge was funny; a smile lingered on his face.

"I'll call you," the officer said. Then he turned to Rex. "Here you go. Bail's been posted. There will be a hearing. You've got your cell phone, wallet, and some loose change. By the way, we're keeping the rug as evidence."

"You mean his hairpiece?" Sutton chuckled. She wore skin-tight red pants and a low-cut black tee. The cop's eyes traveled from her hair to her shapely calves and back again. Normally the attention Sutton commanded didn't bother Rex. She could handle herself. But right now he felt disgruntled. *Shouldn't the focus be on me?*

"Let's go, boss." Sutton used her businesslike tone. Then she turned to the cop. "I'll take him off your hands. Have a nice day."

Rex nursed his bad mood on the drive home. Once Sutton pulled into their driveway, he slammed the car door and stomped inside. Kevin greeted him with tail wagging.

The bad mood instantly lifted. Rex scratched behind the dog's ear as he spun around.

Mood snatcher. How can I possibly embrace my dark side when Kevin's around? I'm a criminal now. He doesn't even care. He stared at the dog's upturned face and then reached to give him another pat.

He heard the electric garage door close from behind. Sutton walked past without comment.

"I need a drink," he demanded.

He wanted to get his feelings out in the open. That would require picking a fight.

Being demanding usually worked.

"IPA coming up," she calmly replied. "Should I give Viv a call? She's probably worried. I'll invite her over for a beer."

The thought of Viv pulled him up short. He didn't want her in the middle. But he didn't want to give in quite yet.

Sutton spoke quietly. "Hey boss. Stop acting so crabby. Getting arrested isn't that bad. Most of your detective heroes end up in the clink at one time or another. By the time you hire your lawyer, all of the charges will go away."

He knew he was being handled, his emotions massaged by the best. But his mood had lifted despite his best intentions.

"True," he admitted. "Sam Spade was always in trouble. Mickey Spillane was nobody's nice guy when it came to breaking a few laws. I could be the inspiration for a new TV drama."

Then he frowned. "You know what's really bothering me. It's that dratted hairpiece you made me wear. I looked foolish. The arresting cop thought I was hilarious."

Sutton handed him a beer. "The price of doing business." She turned away before he could get in the last word.

15

____

VIVIENNE ROSE

Viv was uneasy with the silence. Rex had been quiet since she'd arrived. Usually forthcoming, even if he prevaricated, he'd not answered her questions. So she tried again. "What did the police arrest you for exactly?"

He put down his empty beer bottle. "Let me look up the exact wording. I'm still vague on the language." He scrolled. "The code's complicated." He cleared his voice.

"I'm charged with violating Grand Theft Property Penal Code number 487 (a) PC. The item had to be valued over 950 bucks to make it stick."

"Does it matter that you stole something from a private residence? I mean, it's not like you took an Amazon package from a doorstep or lifted a pricy item from a boutique. Plus you returned the pocket watch. I thought Jax was satisfied. I can't image why he had you arrested a day later."

"Jax was hard to read. But he's filled with revenge, obviously."

A surge of impatience was Viv's first response. *Is he telling me the entire truth? Enough of this beating around the bush. If I push harder, we'll be arguing.*

Over the years Viv had learned to navigate men who lied and who got themselves stuck in bad moods. Her ex-husband was an expert at turning his discomforts into a verbal fight. But it was never worth the drama for her. *Getting angry only makes things worse.*

Viv now regretted saying yes to Sutton's invitation. Even the beautiful view of the desert night sky and watching the fire glow didn't take away from her need to preserve her peace.

She cleared her throat, adopting a quiet tone. "I assume you went back for that pocket watch."

He didn't answer at first. One quick glance her way and he groaned. "You got me. That's right."

"No wonder Jax called the cops. Once he saw through your disguise..."

"I planned to return it to the office," he said. "But the staging made that impossible. So then I figured I could leave it in the shed in the back," he admitted. "Before I could drop it into the utensil drawer, the cop arrived."

He rubbed at his temple with his finger. "There's something about that old watch. It's literally burning hot in my pocket."

"I wish you'd told me sooner. I'd rather know and not have you lie."

"Don't you want to know how I accomplished the trick? Instead of chewing me out about lying," Rex complained. "I don't suppose now's the time to take a bow..." he added in his little-boy voice.

"I'm curious," Viv ignored the tone, "why you think the temperature of the pocket watch matters."

He tapped his fingers on his knee. "I felt the heat as soon as I held it in my hand. Then when I slipped it into my pocket, it burned really hot. I've experienced heat before in items that I pick up. A warning sign. There's something about the watch that I'm not understanding. In a show I'd know what to do, but in this case I'm not sure. So I took it back. To figure out. Not to keep.

"Once I got home, I used the watch to activate my senses. You know how I get insights that way. I asked questions about who owned it. When and where."

"And what did the watch reveal?"

"Three images, well two actually. Wally Walker for one and another cop who looked like he could be related to Wally, maybe his son. The third image was vague.

"At one time or another the watch belonged to each of them. I felt certain about that. The metal case burned with sentiment. That's the best way I can describe it.

"Then I had a brief thought that the watch had been handed down, like something you'd give to the next generation." His voice trailed off.

"Any inscriptions or dates?" she prompted.

"Not that I could tell." He touched his thigh and winced. "I can lower my pants and show you my leg." She saw a flash of white teeth in the dark.

"Not necessary." Viv held up her hand. "I'll take your word for it. Is that common? For one of your objects to scorch you like that."

"I've had metal items glow when I'm holding them. That's more common. They can even grow warm or very cool. But that watch! It left a burn on my skin. And then the funny thing is, once I started talking to it, asking questions, it cooled. My take is that someone who owned it desperately wants to get something off his chest. An untold story maybe."

Viv felt a tingle up her spine. *Is this some kind of mentalist voodoo talk? No wonder he lies.*

To her surprise he dropped his face to his hands. "I would have explained sooner but I didn't want to make you mad. Once I got the read, I knew I had to return the watch. A perfect opportunity arose with the open house. The disguises made it easier. I figured the realtor would be on the lookout for Rex and Viv, but in a crowd we'd go under his radar. I would slip away and return the thing where I found it. Then I wouldn't have to admit to you what I'd done."

Viv took the last sip of her IPA. Now that he'd told the full story she felt much better. *So that's why he rushed away and left me in the car. I get it now.*

He turned toward her. "I'm just embarrassed," he finally admitted. "That I lied. That I was caught. I tried to pick a fight with Sutton."

"Want another beer?" she offered. "That was quite a tale."

When she returned, he'd laid his head back and closed his eyes. The flames cast a light across his face and his breath came slowly. She suspected the arrest had taken more out of him than he wanted to admit.

She sat down to enjoy the heat against her legs. The crackling of the fire and the rustling from the eucalyptus trees overhead brought her a sense of peace. The beauty and the quiet of the desert never failed to calm her nerves.

Rex opened his eyes and sat up. He reached for the new beer. He drained the contents, words coming out slightly slurred. "I guess I dozed off. After Sutton bailed me out, I intended to get righteously buzzed and go to bed. But now I'm glad I told you everything."

"Sutton said they kept your hairpiece," Viv commented dryly.

"Not my finest moment," he admitted. "I feel a little protective of my style, you know. The silver fox image. I guess I didn't realize how much until that cop started laughing."

"I saw everything from the car. But I don't suppose I'd have felt any different if it had been my wig." Viv stood. "Time for me to go."

"I'll walk you to the door." He yawned.

She patted his shoulder. "You head off to bed. Kevin will see me out."

____

16

REX REDONDO

Rex felt his shoulder being shaken. "Boss, get up. There's a guy at the door. He says you've met and he wants a word. Really persistent."

Rex rolled over. "Go away." He buried his head in the pillow.

"It's already ten o'clock," she insisted. "He's sitting in the kitchen waiting for you, drinking your coffee. If you want any, then get dressed." Rex heard the bedroom door close.

He swung his legs around to sit on the side of the bed. *No way I'm facing a stranger without a shower.* He ignored Kevin's scratch at the door. On his feet, he stripped off his pajamas.

"I know you." Rex entered the kitchen freshly shaved and awake. Brad May, the kid from Mojave Mesa, leaned toward Kevin, a huge grin on his face. *Why's he drinking my morning coffee?* Rex wondered.

Sutton's eyes twinkled with amusement.

"How did you get past the security gate?" Rex asked

Brad. "Or did she"—he directed a thumb toward Sutton —"let you in."

"I slid behind the car ahead of me," Brad explained, his voice filled with pride.

Sutton pointed toward the empty coffee carafe on the counter. "Make some more," she said. "Ya snooze, ya lose."

Rex muttered under his breath. To his disappointment neither Sutton nor Brad paid attention. They were too busy flirting with each other to notice his disapproval.

"So the boss told me to mind my own business after that," Brad was saying. "She says your boss couldn't be a serious detective if he has to take a class to qualify." Brad had a way of nodding with superiority that irked Rex, even from his view in the kitchen.

Sutton's peals of laughter didn't help. *She used to laugh like that with me. Not so much lately. She's gone very serious and become quite demanding. Now look at her flirting with a boy years younger.*

What about her job—to make breakfast and provide me with amusing morning news while I eat. A hiss and a gurgle caught his attention. "Coffee's ready," he announced, expecting Sutton to leap to her feet. When she didn't, he felt even more aggrieved.

Refusing to serve them coffee, Rex returned to the table to find Brad with a silly grin on his face. He'd folded his arms on the table and his face flushed slightly pink, he kept talking. "So that's how I found the address. It seems your boss is on my boss's list."

Rex raised an eyebrow. "What list and what's the name of your boss?"

"Janis Jets. Lily Rock Constabulary." Brad winked at Sutton. "She takes note of the private detectives in the area.

Up the hill and here in the desert. Redondo and Rose were at the top of her list."

Rex sat down, holding up his empty mug. "More coffee..."

Sutton finally looked over. Her eyebrows lifted.

"Want a refill?" she asked Brad.

"Sure. You make great coffee. Just as good as Thyme Out. That's the bakery from up the hill," Brad explained.

Rex yawned. He didn't care about Lily Rock or Brad's stories.

Brad, oblivious to Rex's boredom, kept explaining. "The bakery owner collaborates with a local to make seasonal blended coffee. He usually has a specific bake that pairs with the choice."

Sutton returned to fill Rex's mug. Without waiting to see if he approved, she turned to refill Brad's cup instead.

"What's for breakfast?" Rex noted Sutton's annoyance in the tightening of her chin. He was satisfied that he'd touched a nerve.

"Are you trying to be a pain this morning?" she asked. "No more fussy Rex, okay? This is a new day."

A tap dance of irritation got on his last nerve. She'd called him out in front of a stranger. They had met at the crime scene, but that didn't matter. He wanted to shout *don't forget I'm the boss.* But the words stuck in his throat.

This isn't the first time we've gotten into the weeds, he reminded himself. Emotional hills and valleys of their rela-tionship over the years couldn't always be avoided. But they'd managed to negotiate an understanding with a good deal of humor. Rex didn't want to upset their apple cart over breakfast. Not in front of Brad May, who would tell the story to his boss..

"Looks like you're the fussy one to me," he retorted, directing a glare at Sutton.

He turned to Brad. "Women. Can't live with them, can't live without them." He dropped a slow wink waiting for the kid to agree. This was bro code for "step up and join forces" like any decent male would do.

But Brad ignored the remark and the wink, his eyes only for Sutton.

To give her credit she looked amazing. Not because she was even trying. No wig. No low-cut top. She appeared effortless and natural. Her clean brown hair curling softly, framing her face. Straight-leg jeans, slim fitting but not too tight. The blue silk shirt brought out the green in her eyes.

"I'll make something to eat," Rex mumbled. He pictured a television game show. *Point for me, not for the kid. I gave him a chance. Me, an older, more experienced man. He thinks he knows better. A feminist probably. Don't forget, kiddo. I'm the silver fox.*

He buttered a slice of toast, his mind ranting trying to explain this sudden and unexpected situation. *Us men have to stick together. We have traditions that mold and shape our emotional territory. Bad moods, for one. How else can we control the women in our lives? Time for me to show Sutton what's what. Or she'll be running the show. I'll start by taking over the conversation.*

He returned with a platter filled with toast, butter, and strawberry jam. Sliding it to the center of the table, he sat down. "So what brings you to our house?" he asked Brad.

"I was telling Sutton"—Brad reached for a slice—"that my boss had actually met you before. It was an investigation a year ago. She was called in unexpectedly."

"So a detective from Lily Rock shared her private information with her assistant." Rex wanted to call into question anything about Janis Jets. He didn't care if Brad was upset.

After all, his recent experience in the slammer had hardened his resolve. He knew firsthand how the police operated. A shudder traveled up his spine. The smell of the toilet and sink in his cell. He'd never get that out of his mind.

I survived, he reminded himself. *Now that I've been inside, I know things. More than this kid with his sticky fingers reaching for another slice of my buttered toast.*

Brad hurried to defend his idol. "The boss didn't exactly tell me in so many words. I have access to her personal information because I work at the constabulary. We've been together for years. She trusts me. In fact, she's the one who asked the town council to fund my education. She gave me free time in the morning to take the PI class. She even..."

Rex blocked out the rest of the explanation. He'd had enough. He didn't care what Brad had to say. As the kid kept talking, insisting that his boss was the best and that he was the best because she was the best, well that was music to Rex's ears.

Success. He's on the defensive now. Rex didn't bother to hide a smirk.

He reached for a slice of toast, applying jam liberally to one side. The louder he crunched, the more the kid kept talking.

Well played, Redondo.

Brad finally simmered down, his words sputtered as he inhaled deeply. Maybe because there was no more toast, or maybe because he realized that Rex set him up, he leaned back in his chair.

Finally Brad asked a question. "Have you heard

anything more about Wally Walker—did he die of natural causes?"

"I haven't heard a thing." Rex brushed a crumb off his lips. "I've had more important leads to follow."

"He's been kinda busy." Sutton spoke up. "Got himself arrested yesterday."

As Brad's gaze turned toward him, Rex took a moment to reflect on his natural right to be the center of attention. When he arrived in a room, people usually stopped talking to stare. Mostly because of his looks, the silver-fox image he carefully cultivated. They had no idea that he took over with a combination of mental acuity, keen insight, and deep intuition. Any mentalist worth their good reputation knew how to do that—work the room.

Any pro would tell you, don't start a show until everyone in the audience has their eyes on you.

Rex took his skill set everywhere he went. He even applied his talent to picking up women in non-mentalist situations. Once he had everyone in a room focused on him, he'd have a clear opportunity. No matter who the delicious female came in with, they'd leave on his arm.

I use my power for good, not evil, he'd remind himself. *Just take a look at the kid now.*

"Really. What happened?" Brad's eyes opened wide with admiration.

Now that's more like it. Rex felt so much better, having shifted the power dynamic. He took a moment to appreciate the kid's look of surprise. Because up until now, he'd been behind. He'd allowed himself to compete.

Sutton raised an eyebrow in his direction. To his embarrassment he felt even more pleased. This sense of accomplishment, and her acknowledgement of his ability.

Are you losing your edge? his inner voice questioned.

Nah, I was hungry and woken abruptly. Now that I'm back in charge, I can let all that go.

"Tell me about the arrest," Brad repeated, putty in Rex's hands.

"Ya see, kid, it was like this." Rex began his story slowly. Having explained to Viv the night before, he had all the details, real and imagined, ready. When he got to describing the jail cell, he embellished a little. He even made up someone else. "The guy next to me was a seasoned criminal." He nodded, taking note of the kid's wide-eyed stare.

Sutton seemed less convinced. She glared over her coffee mug.

Feeling the attention of half his audience drifting, Rex shortened the story. *I'll leave out the psychometry details and I won't show them the burn on the leg.*

You can't handle the truth popped into his head. His favorite scene in the movie *A Few Good Men. I'm just like Jack Nicholson. Strong. Virile. In charge.*

"Where's the pocket watch now?" Brad asked.

Rex's jaw clamped shut. *This kid is so irritating. I'm not giving away my best clue.*

"The cops picked it up and kept it," he said. The truth but not the whole truth.

"That sucks," Brad admitted. "Do you have another suspect?"

"Viv and I work alone," he said. "We'll let you know when we feel like it."

"But we're in the same PI class." Brad pointed out the obvious. "We can be a team."

"Walker could have died from natural causes. So far as we know, that's what the police think." He turned to Sutton for confirmation.

"I suppose," she said matter-of-factly. "But the actual facts never stopped you before..."

17

VIVIENNE ROSE

Viv finished her last doula consultation with her stomach growling. She looked at her phone. A text from Rex.

Lunch at Just Desserts?

Give me twenty minutes.

Parking her car at the end of the block, Viv stepped onto the curb. She felt better than the day before. An early morning swim helped and then getting back on track with her clients. Staying available when parents had questions proved to be her best practice. Every returned call, text, and email might alleviate unnecessary anxiety.

Plus she liked having a day when her exercise and work could be accomplished early. Then she felt free to enjoy lunch with Rex. A wonderful extravagance that she knew she'd earned.

"Right this way," the host said.

Viv was surprised when she reached the table. She'd expected to find Rex and Sutton. But instead it was the boy from Mojave Mesa.

Rex rose, pulled out her chair, and answered her unspoken question. "Remember Brad May? From our class..."

"Hello." She smiled.

By the time they ordered, Viv's curiosity got the best of her. "So did you two run into each other?"

"Kind of," Rex said. "Brad was having breakfast with Sutton when I got up this morning."

The young man in question lifted a water glass. "Tracked him down." He sounded pleased. "I don't know if I mentioned it, but I work at the Lily Rock Constabulary."

Viv reeled back her curiosity, realizing he'd want to talk more about something that really didn't interest her. She sensed that Rex already knew the details and would be bored having to hear them again. She could find out later if necessary.

"We're talking about suspects," Rex said. His eyes had a bit of the old twinkle.

"But do we have a murder? I think that comes first," she reminded.

"Always suspect foul play until you know different, my boss says," Brad stated. "She's the senior constable in Lily Rock."

"Is there a junior constable?" Viv quickly suspected that Brad had a tendency to exaggerate on behalf of himself and his small town.

"Not yet. Maybe when I get my class done, they'll find the money."

"I see. That's your goal, to become a police investigator."

Brad looked shocked. "Do you think? I'm nearly thirty. So you think I could be a *real* cop?" He sounded genuinely surprised at her suggestion. *He's not that confident,* Viv thought. *Maybe he's been thrown some challenges in his young life.*

Viv acknowledged a need to regroup. Brad's immaturity struck her as genuine. If he wanted to do some investigating with them, it wasn't a terrible idea. She could tell by his wide-eyed need to please that he saw her as someone to impress. Aware that she might need to assume the role of guidance counselor, she slipped right into the persona.

"What other career have you considered?"

Before he could answer, the server brought her whole wheat cheese and veggie sandwich. He set it on the table, along with Rex and Brad's food.

With his attention drawn to the huge burger sitting in the middle of his plate, Brad forgot the question. While he chewed, she turned to Rex. "I admit, Mr. Walker may have been murdered."

"It's still a possibility," he agreed.

"Did you notice the plastic pill container on his desk?" Brad swallowed and took another bite.

"At the crime scene," Viv said. "I did notice."

"We saw another pill container by his recliner in his living room," Rex said.

"It was gone when we returned," Viv added. She stopped to admire the efficient way Brad had consumed his half pounder in less than five minutes. "Want the rest of mine?" She pointed to her vegetable sandwich.

He gulped his water. "No thank you. I'm a carnivore."

Rex glared. "Anyway, when we went to the open house, we realized that Wally's bungalow had been cleaned out. A professional stager removed all of his belongings to prep for a quick sale."

"Mr. Walker most likely had medical issues," Viv added. "That happens to most of us as we age."

Rex pulled his plate closer, poking the corned beef on rye with a finger. "We need to find out more specifics about Wally's health." He lifted half the sandwich to his mouth, taking a bite and quickly returning the rest to his plate. He swallowed and closed his eyes as if relishing the taste.

Viv saw him squint with a slight shake of his head in her direction. *He's holding something back and wants to tell me later*, she realized.

Viv lifted half of the whole wheat sandwich and took a bite. Cucumber and fresh sprouts crunched between her teeth. She swallowed and dipped her fork into the kale side salad. "Never too many vegetables," she commented aloud. She hoped she'd distracted Brad from Rex's odd behavior and Rex from defending himself unnecessarily.

Brad leaned closer to Viv. "So what would it take for me to become a police officer? A lot more classes?"

Basking in the young man's direct gaze felt slightly intoxicating. *Nothing wrong with that*, she concluded. She wasn't so old that she didn't appreciate a good conversation with a younger man.

"You can go online and read the requirements," she told him. "Or better yet, just ask your boss."

He shrugged in disappointment. "I suppose."

Rex winked at Viv and then pushed back his chair. "I'm checking out the pie bar," he said.

Viv began to object, but he brushed her off. "I love pie. All kinds. Especially ones filled with fresh fruit..."

She couldn't believe what she was hearing. A distinct memory of him saying, "I hate pie. A waste of calories," came to mind. *What's he up to*, she wondered.

Brad took the opportunity to launch into another story about Janis Jets. She watched Rex make his way toward the indoor cafe. From where she sat, she could see him take a seat near the register. Holding a menu, he looked over the top toward the display case.

Finally a young woman in a white apron stood across the counter. She smiled and he grinned.

Not pie, Viv concluded. Rex has other ideas. If I'm not mistaken, that's the woman who burst into tears over Wally Walker's death.

18

REX REDONDO

"What's your favorite?" Rex often did this with servers, asking their opinions about food to gain their trust.

The young woman smiled and spoke in a singsong girlish voice. "I love the apple. There are two varieties. One with the traditional lattice top, the other is a single crust French apple with a crisp brown sugar topping. Oh, and the lemon cream. That's a good pie. So refreshing on the tongue." She showed him the tip of hers to make a point.

He put down the menu. "Do you have a way for me to sample a bite?" He softened his gaze, hoping she wasn't going to think his interest was personal.

"Let me see what I can do." She turned away, giving him a chance to admire the big bow over her curvaceous posterior. It was as if the apron tied at the back were begging for him to pay attention.

Rex caught himself with a self-conscious exhale. He detached his glance to look at the rest of the people sitting on stools. He wasn't surprised to find it lined with men. *A great way to chat up the waitress. Free refills on coffee. A great view too.*

The server slid open the glass display case, where single slices had been arranged on the bottom shelf. She took three samples, each with a plastic fork. Placing them on a plate, she slid the glass back.

"I'm not supposed to do this, give free bites. But for you... Finish with the lemon cream," she suggested.

He avoided looking down the gap between the apron's bib and her low-cut blouse and instead picked up a fork. Eyes closed, he stifled a gag. "Delicious," he lied. *So sweet and gooey. But Rex, ol' boy. You have to sacrifice for the sake of the investigation.*

With renewed courage, he swallowed the last sample. Turning his head, he coughed into his napkin, spitting out the lemon cream.

"What do you think?" the server asked.

She's kinda sweet. Caring about my pie preference. He folded the napkin into a ball and shoved it into his pocket.

"Each one has its own distinct flavor," he commented.

An interruption came from farther down the counter. "Can I have a check?"

The waitress looked over and said, "I have to help another customer, be right back."

Rex felt fairly confident that she never suspected he was anything other than a guy who loved pie. He'd done a good job of playing into her expectations. But now he had to make things more personal. Especially if he wanted information.

Turn on your inner glow, Rex old boy.

He'd had great success charming women in the past. No matter what age, women sensed he was a viable male and interested. He'd learned over the years to use this way with females both professionally and personally. Actors did the same. They turned on the charm, or the charisma, or the inner light for the camera.

She returned. "I can sneak one more bite but just for you. Don't go telling your friends, okay? I'll get in trouble with my manager."

"I'm good," he told her. "Never tasted such great pie." His tone projected enthusiasm while he smiled into her eyes.

By now he could feel Viv's glare boring into his back, staring from the outside patio. She was already suspicious and most likely bored to tears with Brad's endless chatter about Lily Rock.

He felt a ping in his ear, followed by a throb in his temple. He turned his head to close his eyes. The cylinder rolled, producing three fresh images. All pies. Cherry, lemon, and apple. With a flicker they disappeared.

The double lattice-top apple looked brighter than the others. The image, sharply focused, would be his choice. "Could I have a slice of the apple with the lattice top?" He pointed over her shoulder toward the display case.

Her eyes brimmed. She brushed the back of her hand to wipe away the tears. "Just a minute."

She placed the plate in front of him. "Anything else?" she asked quietly.

He felt her unhappiness and knew it was genuine. "Do you have a special connection to apple pie?" he asked.

"Yes," she said. "A favorite customer, he used to sit right where you are now. He'd come in every morning for breakfast. He'd always take an apple pie slice to go."

Rex was done with the pretenses. "Was his name Wally Walker, by chance? I read in the news he recently passed away." The stab in the dark with the name of a random local felt a bit lame. He waited to see her response.

"How did you know!" Tears trickled down her cheeks. Ever the gentleman, Rex handed her a clean paper napkin from the dispenser. "It's okay, honey. Let it out. Go ahead and tell Uncle Rex."

She blew her nose and glared at him. "You're not my uncle," she said tartly.

He hastily retreated. "I didn't mean it like that."

She stuffed the napkin in her pocket. "I've done nothing but cry since I heard about Wally's death. He was such a great guy. Left big tips every morning. I've been saving that seat for him for at least a couple of years."

She picked up a cloth and began to wipe the counter. "Are you going to eat that piece of pie here or take it to go?"

"If I can get a coffee I'll eat it right here."

"Sure enough, hon." She edged toward the row of coffee carafes.

Rex felt the intimate conversation window shut as quickly as it opened. She'd disappeared into her waitress persona, pushing him back to just another customer status. *That's okay*, he thought. *I'm laying groundwork here.*

When she returned with a full mug of coffee, he smiled gratefully. His inner voice began to coach. *Go slow, old buddy. This might take several more pieces of pie before we establish a connection.* He felt his gut clench at the thought of all that crust and goo.

"On second thought, I'll take the pie to go. I'm actually here with friends."

"Okay," she said.

One long swig of coffee later, he stood to pay, leaving a ten-dollar bill before picking up his container. He wanted her to remember him favorably as a good tipper.

She stuffed the money in her apron pocket. "Thanks. Come back soon." She smiled.

Rex made a point of looking at her name badge. "Mia Porter. I will see you soon. And you're most welcome."

19

VIVIENNE ROSE

Viv eyeballed the to-go box as Rex sat back down at the table. "Thought I'd bring home a piece of pie," he said nonchalantly. "We can share it later."

"Seems like you got along really well with the waitress," she commented dryly.

"Name's Mia Porter. She was very kind. Gave me a free sample." He glanced toward Brad, who scrolled on his phone. He leaned closer to Viv. "Mia mentioned another favorite customer who loved apple pie. Wally Walker. She seemed kinda sad when she said that, like he was on her mind."

Viv's eyes grew wide. "Do I need to pick up another piece of pie, you know, for later? Ask more questions about her favorite customer."

"I got what I needed." He patted the box and then added, "For now."

Brad looked up from his phone. "I gotta go. The boss needs me." He hurriedly stood. "Have you heard when our class will start up again?"

"Not a thing," Viv answered.

"I hope they begin next Monday. Now that we're a week late, we'll run over into the holidays. My boss won't like that. Lily Rock has a big share of crimes to solve then. You'd be shocked."

"Is that so?" During Rex's foray at the pie bar, Viv had certainly grown tired of acting interested in Brad's Lily Rock stories. She was ready for him to leave.

Apparently he forgot he was in a hurry, because he kept talking. "We had a fire one year. And then a nutcracker that killed a woman. Oh, and a clown strangled by his trick lasso. I bet Palm Desert isn't that exciting."

"Oh, we have our share of crimes to be solved," Rex drawled.

Finally Brad got the message. "I'll see you next week. Like I said, I'm needed." Viv breathed a sigh of relief...until Brad circled back to the table. "How much do I owe you for lunch?" He reached into his pocket.

Rex took out his wallet. "Don't worry about it, kid. We've got this."

Brad's relieved smile made Viv feel guilty. *Stop being impatient. He's still young.* Viv waited for him to disappear past the exit before she turned back to Rex.

"So Mia Porter is the same woman I saw crying. The other day," he reminded.

"When I mentioned Wally's name, she teared up. Apparently he was a regular morning customer. He loved apple pie. Took an extra piece with him on the way to work. I got the feeling that she felt an emotional attachment to Wally. It felt genuine, but you never know. Could have been because he was a big tipper." Rex looked thoughtful.

"Do you think that you reminded her of Wally?" Viv asked.

"Grief must have blinded her," he reasoned. "Wally

looked decades older than me." His wounded expression, the lowering of his bottom lip into a pout, nearly made her guffaw.

"You're pulling my chain, right? Saying Mia thought I was like Wally. You forget I got Mia to open up. I've got innate charm. I can still woo the ladies."

"Ya think..." Viv teased.

"I turned on my superpower that apparently has not gone dormant despite my years. You could say I'm like a good aged cheddar. I'm sharp and better with each bite." He sat up straighter to preen.

She began to giggle. "That's you. Old cheese."

"Okay, stop laughing. If you must know, I made the apple pie connection by using my highly tuned intuition."

"I didn't know you liked apples," Viv said.

"Apples are okay. But I detest apple pie. So sweet and slimy with all the syrupy sugar. But Mia didn't know that."

"So what prompted you to ask for a slice of that particular variety?" Viv asked.

Rex tapped his forehead. "The images. Right in a row. From left to right. Cherry. Lemon. Apple. The apple stood out. Brighter and bigger. So I knew I'd lead with that one."

"Good hunch," Viv said.

"Turned out to also be Wally's favorite," Rex added. "The double lattice, not the single-crust French. I'm an expert now. On pie."

She patted his hand, feeling slightly contrite. "So what's next—has the investigation stalled?" she asked.

"I'm done for now," he said. "Exhausted, if you must know. But I think Mia will be an invaluable lead. I'll check in with Sutton. She's doing a deep dive on Wally Walker on the internet."

"How do we pick up the interview with Mia then? Order more pie? Thanksgiving is months away," Viv said.

Rex answered quickly. "We have to go back and get in her business. In a nice way, of course."

"Sounds familiar." Viv remembered that he'd done the same with her when they first met. It had taken months but he'd won her over in the end. Proximity had been in his favor. Living next door gave Rex access to the daily ins and out of her life. Bringing Kevin over for meet and greet also helped. Even Miss Kitty grew to appreciate the overzealous Bernedoodle.

"But not today," she said. "Going back to the counter too soon will make you look like somebody who's too interested. How about tomorrow morning? She told you she saved a seat for Wally. If you show up at the same time it will feel like you're destined to be her next favorite customer."

He groaned. "That's really early."

"Getting up early is good for you."

Viv did not apologize. Just like a newborn, adults require a sensible schedule, beginning with an early wake time. This was something she'd told her families for years.

"I suppose," he sighed. "Early morning it is." He pulled a card from his wallet.

Viv knew she was right. In the end, a life well lived required a few simple rules.

The next day Viv settled herself onto the stool at the pie bar.

She yawned behind her hand as Rex inspected the breakfast menu.

"I got a good parking place," he said. "What are you having?"

"Oatmeal with dates, flax, blueberries, and low-fat milk," she instantly replied. Rule number two. Consistent eating patterns, including breakfast, she said to herself.

"No pie or cinnamon roll?"

"I dare not. I start my day with a sweet overload, I'll feel worse and worse as the day goes on." One advantage of age, she'd realized, is to know yourself in small important ways.

Mia Porter held her pad and pencil. First she glanced at Viv but then spoke to Rex. "Back so soon? Can I get you juice and coffee to start?"

"Mia. Such a pretty name," Viv said.

"My grandmother's," she replied brightly. "What can I get you?"

By the time Rex and Viv ordered, an easy conversation had developed among the three. Viv felt as if she'd been handed the script of older-woman-making-conversation-with-waitress-at-a-cafe. Fortunately Mia played right along.

Give and take, superficial chitchat, and to Viv, excruciating. Small talk exhausted her. As soon as Mia left, she spun to face Rex.

He'd propped his feet under the stool, his knee bouncing impatiently. She suspected he had something on his mind. "Is this going as planned?" she asked.

Rex held his palm over his knee and pushed to make it stop. "Going fine. Sorry about the jiggling." He leaned closer. "I'm kinda nervous. I sense Mia has shut down. Hiding behind the waitress role. We won't get anything from her at this rate."

Viv suspected that Rex was most likely lining up ways to manipulate Mia, bring her closer, getting her in touch with her feelings.

She'd observed Rex's agitation and thinking patterns since they got together. The way he planned and pondered.

And then pulled a rabbit out of his hat. Not exactly a rabbit, but more of a revelation. Much the same as his on-stage performance.

Mia returned with their orders. Rex had gone all-in with bacon and eggs and a side of toast. "Here's yours," she said to Viv, sliding the bowl of oatmeal closer to her.

"I won't need sugar," Viv told her. "I eat my porridge plain."

Mia acted as if she didn't hear. She turned away to offer a menu to another customer. She returned to ask, "How about honey? I know it's considered to be healthier." She made a note on her pad of paper.

"I'm good," she insisted. "But before you get our check, I want to tell you something in confidence."

Mia looked up, her eyes wide with interest.

"We're private investigators and are concerned that your customer, Wally Walker, may have been murdered. Naturally we're talking to everyone who knew him and we'd appreciate an interview with you."

Rex's chin dropped. She felt him inhale.

Color drained from Mia's cheeks.

Viv nearly regretted surprising Mia with her statement. She wasn't too concerned about Rex. He knew it was her habit to cut to the chase and ask hard questions without beating around the bush.

Mia leaned closer. Her bottom lip trembled. "Let me help those other people and I'll be right back." The intensity of her hushed voice caught Viv by surprise. Hair raised at the back of her neck.

She took her first bite of oatmeal. "The direct approach," Rex drawled. "Your go-to move. Nice work."

Viv relished his praise. Rex may get images, but she didn't let grass grow under her feet.

20

REX REDONDO

"Will you be taking anything to go?" Mia didn't mention Wally Walker.

Her glare gave Rex a start. But then he caught sight of the possible explanation. A man stood on the other side of the register. He wore a suit and tie, a light blue shirt covered by a navy-blue blazer. He glared right at Mia. *Probably the manager*, Rex reasoned.

"How about apple pie?" Viv used an uncharacteristically loud tone. "We'll take two slices to go. We love a good dessert, don't we, honey." She batted her eyes at Rex.

"Got any cheesecake?" he grumbled. "That's my favorite."

"Not today." Mia shot Viv a grateful glance. "I'll get the pie and be right back."

The manager growled and then moved on. When Mia returned, she placed a Just Desserts to-go bag on the counter. "I'm so happy someone hired you to check into Wally," she whispered. "He was in trouble. His grandson wasn't speaking to him. And some other woman kept pestering him to list his bungalow. Plus something about his past. Did anyone else you interviewed mention..."

The sound of her voice convinced Rex that she was more than eager to discuss her relationship with Wally. Viv had been right—his beating around the bush approach would have wasted valuable time.

Viv's so... He searched for the right description. *Cool and calm and really confident. No wonder people don't mind chatting her up.*

"Something in Wally's past haunted him," Mia continued. "On the morning before he died, he tried to tell me but got really emotional and had to leave before he could finish the story. I sent him away with the usual bag of goodies and his vitamins. And then I never saw him again." She blinked to hold back tears.

"Did Wally bring his medicine with him for you to sort?" Viv asked.

"Yes he did. He had some trouble getting the pills and supplements straight, his morning prescriptions and the ones he was supposed to take at night. I was happy to help," Mia replied.

"I've got my eyes on the manager," Rex cautioned. "You two keep talking."

"Put your number in here." Viv slid her phone across the counter. "That way we'll keep in touch."

Mia gave Viv a grateful nod. She slid the phone back across the counter. "Thanks for coming in. Don't forget your to-go order. Have a nice day."

Later that morning Rex sat in his office to make a few phone calls. The first was to Seraphina Morales's office receptionist. "Yeah, this is Rex Redondo. Put me through to Dr. Morales."

"Is this personal or professional?" she asked.

"Kinda both," Rex admitted. He wasn't sure. His enrollment made him a student. But his investigation was more professional. And then everything was personal to him. And everything professional. No boundaries, his retreat counselor had told him. "That's the root of all your problems."

"I'm a student," he blurted. "I was enrolled in Wallace Walker's Introduction to Private Investigation 101 class. I want to talk to Dr. Morales about a substitute teacher. I have someone to recommend."

"Please hold and I'll put you through," came the crisp voice.

Seraphina greeted him warmly. "Hello, Mr. Redondo. My assistant mentioned that you may have a recommendation for a substitute lecturer."

"In my pervious employment," Rex began to explain, "I was a military Intelligence Officer. I thought you might want a good reference, from someone with experience. I do have a worthy recommendation. But I'd prefer to talk face-to-face," he explained.

"I'll have my assistant make that appointment for an hour from now, before lunch. No time to dawdle. See you soon." She clicked off.

Rex felt slightly offended. She'd not bothered to ask if that time was good for him. *I suppose she assumed that I'm retired and don't have other appointments.* He'd have preferred to go right over to Mojave Mesa, but now he had time on his hands.

When he worked at the casino, he always had something to do for the show. Practice slight-of-hand moves. Do research. Watch videos of other performers.

His counselor told him time might weigh heavily once he cut back on work.

"You're a lot better," Chaps admitted. "But the down times will be challenging. I want you to pay attention to your feelings instead of running away."

"I'm healed. You did this. Just admit we're done here." Rex wanted a clean bill of health from Retired Chaplain Little. He liked things neat and tidy that way, especially when it came to chinks in his otherwise impenetrable armor.

"I wish that were true," Chaps said. "You'll always have the Afghanistan memories and you may from time to time need to reframe and put them back where they belong."

"I'll be fine," Rex assured him.

"Not too busy," Chaps warned. "Your challenge isn't to take on more. It's to do less and feel slightly bored like the rest of us."

Rex hadn't discussed any of this with Viv. But he hadn't booked any more gigs. He'd waited to see if she would even notice. He'd been home barely a day and sure enough, Chaps was right. He felt restless. *Just like some old retired dude. Going from one meal to the next. Before you know it, I'll be watching years-old golf tournament programs on television for recreation.*

Then his leg would fidget. He'd scroll on his phone. After a bit he turned to social media. With one click he found his favorite French bulldog named Huey. He laughed aloud, no longer bored, as the dog took a flying leap right into a swimming pool over and over again. *Gotta be better than sports reruns*, he consoled himself.

. . .

"Right this way, Mr. Redondo," the receptionist greeted him in her black pencil skirt and white silk blouse. High black heels made her legs look long and shapely. She reminded him of Bunny Watson played by Katherine Hepburn. A '50s movie: *Desk Set. Look at me, remembering her.*

He shifted into a Spencer Tracy imitation, pretending to pull a hat over his eyes, shoving a hand into his pocket. Rex couldn't remember the name of the character that Tracy played but he retained certain details. *Deadpan, calm, and methodical. That's me.*

The assistant pushed open the inner office door and nodded for him to go through. Rex assumed a sense of unfamiliar calm.

"Mr. Redondo." Dr. Morales rose from behind her desk. She came around to offer a handshake.

"I won't take much of your time," Rex said. Normally he'd sneak into her head to pick up clues. But not today. Today he was Spencer Tracy. *I'm calm and methodical. Oh, and deadpan*, he reminded himself.

"Do sit down," Dr. Morales offered.

"I'll come right to the point," he said. But then he got distracted. He couldn't help himself. Like the time before he felt drawn by the array of awards and photos. *Surely they mean something.* He looked at the groupings on the wall. His gaze lingered on two familiar faces. "Isn't that..."

"Yes it is." Dr. Morales didn't seem surprised. "I'm standing with Ronald Reagan. A friend of the family. We both lived in Palm Springs, the Thunderbird Heights community."

Old Rex would have been impressed. But Spencer Tracy not so much. Rex held his face in a deadpan expression. *My cheeks hurt. From not smiling*, he concluded.

"Bottom line up front." Rex used a common military

expression. "I'd be happy to lend you my assistant, Sutton Drew, to become a temporary substitute for the Introduction to Private Investigation 101 class. I assume you are still understaffed." *Look at me. Got it out in one sentence. Talk about methodical.* He coughed into his hand.

Morales's eyebrow shot up. "What are her qualifications? Besides being your assistant?"

"Ten years serving in Afghanistan as an intel officer. Boots on the ground with a vast knowledge of surveillance, and she's an expert at electronic data collection."

"I see."

Rex enjoyed the surprised look on Dr. Morales's face. *She's impressed,* he concluded. *This is a win-win. Sutton will be a catch for the community college staff. She'll be on the inside for the Wally Walker investigation. Well done, old boy.*

I wonder if I can ask for a finder's fee, like a headhunter.

Before he could suggest his idea, Morales spoke. "She'll have to apply herself. With the appropriate CV and references."

"I'm giving you the reference. My word should be enough, along with Sutton's background clearance from the FBI. It was good enough for the United States Marine Corps, don't forget. Stop stalling. Let's get her behind that desk by Friday," he snapped.

"Goodbye, Mr. Redondo." Seraphina Morales stood. "I'll take your recommendation under advisement. Nice to see you again."

On the elevator ride down, Rex realized that the interaction with Dr. Morales had brought up unexpected conflicts. *She got under my skin. Refusing my recommendation out of hand. Not just mine. She's turned down Spencer Tracy. Now that's just wrong.*

21

VIVIENNE ROSE

That afternoon the desert sun softened into a warm golden glow as Viv offered Mia an iced tea. Viv extended a basket of freshly baked chocolate chip cookies toward Mia. She kept frozen dough rolled into a ball in her freezer for precisely this kind of drop-in-at-the-last-minute occasion.

Mia accepted the cookie with a smile. "It's good to eat something other than pie." She took a bite. "These are delicious."

Without rushing into a conversation, Viv took her time to appreciate the view. Especially the feel of the slight breeze across her cheeks. The surface of the pool rippled. "The air smells fresh," Viv said.

"You're so lucky to live here," Mia sighed.

She felt her jaw tighten. Mia had unwittingly touched a nerve. She'd always been uncomfortable in the gated community and with her newly constructed home. It took a lot of convincing from her son to get past those reservations. Mostly because she saw herself as open and hospitable. A gated community made her wonder if that was really the case. And she knew she could afford the upscale community, but others could not. Her doula colleagues had made that abundantly clear.

"Next time why don't you bring a bathing suit? I often take another swim this time in the afternoon. Because it's so calming."

"Really? I'd love to do that. Or are you just being nice?"

The frank way she asked made Viv like her even more. "I'm not that nice," she assured her. "I can be quite direct, in fact. That often puts people off. Like right now. Tell me about your relationship with Wally Walker. Start at the beginning when you first met."

Mia set her glass on the table. "We first met a couple of years ago. He'd sit in the same place and order apple pie. One to eat in the diner, the other to go. After a few weeks I'd stop to chat when I wasn't waiting on other customers.

"Honestly I've been worried about Wally for months. His health, for one. He was type 1 diabetic and had used insulin for years."

"Injections?" Viv asked.

"And tablets," Mia added. "After we got to know each other, he'd sit at my counter in the morning once a week and count out his pills while he ate breakfast. He'd dump all the bottles from a backpack. My manager hated that he made himself at home at the pie counter. He thought Wally would put off other customers. But once I explained how he was such a good customer, how he came every morning, even on weekends, my manager backed off."

"I see," Viv said. "Did you know what prescriptions he took?"

"Not really. But he'd get mixed up sometimes. Four months ago there was an incident. He passed out in class. Something about A1C and insulin. They had to call the paramedics. The next day he came in with all of his pills.

He lined them up on the counter and asked me for help sorting them out."

"It's not unusual for a man in his late seventies to need help with medications. But most turn to a family member or a health aide."

Not the waitress at the pie bar, Viv thought to herself.

"Wally wasn't close to his family," Mia explained. "He talked about his grandson and how he was a big-deal realtor. But they didn't get along."

Viv had no trouble believing the father and grandson story. She'd observed Jax firsthand. "I met him," she said.

"Then you know." Mia nodded. "Not like his grandfather. Everyone loved Wally. I heard that old students would stop in to chat after his class. He'd bend their ear with stories from his time on the force. He served for nearly thirty years as a Palm Desert cop. People would stop at the pie register and recognize him. I think he sat there to be noticed."

"Sounds like the opposite of Jax," Viv agreed. "He's transactional to his core. I'll give you this if you give me that, based on money. He wouldn't bother with stories or chitchat unless there was a payoff."

Viv offered another cookie. "What about Jax's father, Wally's son. Does he live in the desert?"

Mia sighed. "That's another story. Very sad. Jax's father, Wallace Jr., got shot in the line of duty ten years ago. He's a big hero in Palm Desert."

"Wally must have been very sad but at the same time very proud."

"He never got over the death of his son. Wally didn't talk about him much, but he drank."

"Plus took pills," Viv reminded.

"I felt kind of guilty. Every morning I'd have a glass of

orange juice and a mug of coffee ready for when he showed up. Then he'd order a three eggs over easy breakfast including bacon and pancakes on the side. That part was okay." She frowned and then looked toward the pool. The corner of her mouth tightened.

"He used to roll the bacon in a pancake and eat it like a wrap. So cute. Anyway..." She focused on Viv. "After his food I'd bring him a Bloody Mary."

Viv couldn't hold back the shock in her voice. "Not with alcohol..."

"I tussled with him at first. Told him he might get stopped on the way to his class, pulled in for driving under the influence. That would be the end of his teaching job. He'd say, 'Nah, baby. I can handle my liquor.'" She used a dry voice to imitate the older man.

"When I asked my boss if I was obligated to fill his order, he said it wasn't any of my business. If a diner wants a Bloody Mary, who was I to say no. Plus lots of people in Palm Springs drink over breakfast. It's kind of a thing."

Viv's mind whirled. "Sounds like Wally was self-medicating.

Mia leaned back in her chair. "I tried to keep the pills organized in the weekly plastic case. It was the best I could do. He did have a couple of episodes..."

"Episodes?"

"The college had to call 911 at least two times. Maybe this last incident—they got there too late."

Once she said goodbye to Mia, Viv spent time in her kitchen tidying up. Miss Kitty wove her way around her ankles, softly purring. "I know. It's dinnertime." She held the cat in her arms for a cuddle.

Miss Kitty leapt from her arms onto the floor with a loud, "Meow." Viv dabbed at the scratch on her hand. "Okay, food it is. There's no need for violence," she scolded.

Viv hung the dish towel while Miss Kitty waited impatiently. She stalked away, her tail waving. Viv followed and then stopped at the sound of a scratch coming from the front door. Kevin waited on the doorstep.

Rex stood by his side with a six-pack of his favorite IPAs dangling from one hand. "Beer time. I have much to report." He walked past Viv with Kevin at his heels.

"See you in a minute." Viv closed the door. "Miss Kitty wants her dinner first."

"Bork." Kevin stopped to sit. He strained his neck to glance around the corner and wagged his tail. Viv chuckled.

"Oh okay. She's in her catio. Door's open. Don't make a nuisance of yourself. She hasn't eaten and is in a crabby mood."

Kevin dashed away before she finished the sentence.

"Miss Kitty. You have a visitor," Viv called. *Won't she be surprised.* She rubbed the scratch on her hand. *She deserves a little inconvenience...*

A sharp high-pitched yowl, followed by two excited barks came from down the hall.

22

REX REDONDO

Rex reached over and tapped Viv's beer bottle with his. "Here's to you, beautiful. And our investigation." She scowled when he said "beautiful." *She's not one for the offhanded compliment*, he reminded himself.

Instead of apologizing and making a bigger deal of his mistake, he looked toward the dark and foreboding horizon. The sparkling light cast from the swimming pool created a sharp contrast to the night sky. He took another sip.

"I talked to Mia," Viv began.

"I dropped in on our favorite community college president," he said.

"Did you approach her?" He could feel her curiosity from the tone of her voice.

"I thought I could help with the personnel shortage. You know, recommend a qualified part-time professor for Introduction to Private Investigation 101. Time's a-wasting. We need to get to work on that investigator certification."

"Who did you recommend?"

Rex heard the sliding glass door open from behind. Sutton Drew stood next to his chair but didn't speak. At least not with words. Her body language was another matter. Feet planted firmly on the pavement, she looked as if she was bracing herself. There was a set to her lips, pressed into a thin line, that looked unforgiving.

"Ah, there she is, my noble assistant." He held up his beer in greeting, hoping to shift the mood.

"How dare you pimp me out without asking!" Sutton's voice, knifelike in the dry desert air, caught Rex off guard. He was used to a warmup with Sutton. He'd been successful in the past, derailing her anger with his humor. But this time she was having none of that.

He held his hands up in a placating gesture, his mind whirling. *What's gotten under her skin? I haven't done anything wrong.* He cleared his throat, directing his gaze toward Viv.

"I was just telling Viv that I got you a new job. I thought you'd be the perfect person to substitute at Mojave Mesa. You're good in front of people and you have the right background. Plus you could get intel for our investigation."

That should do it, he congratulated himself. *I've complimented her, so she's bound to feel better.* He was convinced that he'd avoided an argument with his good news.

She'll forget about whatever she's annoyed with because I've done her a solid. Had he been paying more attention, he'd have noticed how Viv's eyes widened and she nearly dropped her IPA.

Sutton hovered over Rex. He felt her need to intimidate so he instinctively rose to his feet. "Let's celebrate. Have a seat. I brought extra beer."

Later when he'd tell the story, he'd explain that it was dark that night. "I didn't see it coming," he'd say, knowing full well he did.

When Sutton's closed fist connected with his jaw, a

sharp pain shot up the side of his face. He staggered back-ward, arms flailing. A foot got caught in the chair, causing him to lose his balance. Once airborne he hit the water with a wide-eyed splash.

Rex resurfaced, his head pounding. Sutton glared down at him.

"What the hell, Sutton," he gasped.

"You're not the boss of my entire life," she screamed. "You should have talked to me first. You don't get to pimp me out for employment. Expect my resignation forthcom-ing. I'll be packing my gear. I'm done." She pivoted on her heel and stalked toward the house.

Rex lifted himself out of the pool, water cascading onto the pavement. His clothes stuck to his skin as he wiped moisture from his eyes. As Sutton disappeared around the side of the house, Rex turned to Viv.

"I know what you're thinking. It's obvious she's overre-acting. I wasn't pimping her out. What a horrible thing to say." His hurt feelings were nearly as painful as his jaw.

"You think she overreacted?" Viv sounded incredulous.

"Yeah, that and...I seriously underestimated Sutton's right hook."

Viv returned from the house with an ice bag. Rex sat in his chair with eyes closed. He touched his fingers to his jaw. Feeling that he'd been unreasonably attacked, his mind raced, fueled by pain and indignation.

Sutton's my assistant, he rationalized. *On my payroll. I send her on jobs all the time. Gathering intel is something she does every day for my mentalist show. It's literally the definition of her job.*

Of course he'd never written a job description for

Sutton. Over the years their relationship had been negotiated by his need and her acceptance. He liked it that way. Because he was in charge.

The memory of Sutton's indignant voice pushed aside his reasoning. *"You don't get to pimp me out."*

Ridiculous, Rex fumed. *What ever made her think such a nasty thing, let alone say it aloud in front of Viv. I'm embarrassed for Sutton. She let her emotions get the best of her.*

"My actions are perfectly justified," he told Viv, holding the ice bag to his jaw. "You'd think Sutton would be happy. Adjunct professor at a community college is a coveted job for most people." He pressed the ice against his jaw and groaned.

"That will help with the bruising," Viv advised in a calm voice.

But I want to look bruised, Rex thought. *Then I can tell everyone how I was unfairly accosted by my own employee.* Playing the victim had a certain allure. He liked feeling that he'd been abused. But there was a downside. He'd have to admit that a woman got the best of him.

When Viv stayed silent, staring at the pool, he began to feel uneasy. He turned his head to read her expression. But then he got distracted. Her beautiful toned legs stretched out in front of her.

"I may go to emergency. Of course I'll need to make an appointment with my dentist for early tomorrow. My TMJ is already acting up." He hoped she'd take his cue and start fussing. That's what he needed now.

When she offered no word of sympathy, he tried again. "I may require surgery—for the jaw."

"Or," Viv finally spoke, "you could stop talking. Rest your jaw. That might help."

He huffed back into his chair and closed his eyes with

another loud groan. *Women. They don't understand.* Awareness of a show tune came to mind from *My Fair Lady*. He pictured the actor Rex Harrison. "Let a woman in your life. Your serenity is through."

That's my problem. I have two women in my life and neither one is bringing the love. Rex hummed under his breath, hoping Viv would pick up the clue and laugh.

When he finally opened his eyes, he realized that Viv was no longer there. *She must have gone inside*, he thought. Before he could hoist himself to his feet, he heard the door slide open.

She reappeared with a fresh IPA. "If you've stopped complaining you can try to explain again. Here, take a sip." She held out the beer.

Rex dropped the ice bag to the ground. Wounded to his core by Viv's lack of compassion, his heart ached to be understood.

"I did nothing wrong," he said. "Isn't it obvious? All on her. Calling me a..." He stopped short of saying the word because he couldn't bring himself to use that despicable phrase again.

She raised an eyebrow. When she didn't agree, he felt more agitated, assuming he hadn't made himself clear. So he kept talking.

"I tried to get Sutton a job. A new surveillance job. That's she's well-qualified for." He let his annoyance sound in his voice.

"So you said," Viv replied calmly.

"She has the skill set Mojave Mesa needs to fill the position left by Wally Walker's untimely death. That would be a win-win for us and for them. Oh, make that a

win-win-win." Rex began to shout. Now that he was on a roll, he couldn't stop himself.

"Sutton would get prestige and more cash. We would be back in class. Mojave Mesa could get back on track." He held his hand to his jaw with a deep groan.

Talking hurts.

"I see," she said quietly. "That's your perception of the situation."

She obviously didn't see. Otherwise she'd be more indignant. And solicitous. That's the least he expected. He tried again. "I don't understand why Sutton got so mad. It hurt my feelings."

He felt like he'd finally pulled a rabbit out of his hat. His hurt feelings. Who wouldn't be compassionate after such a heartfelt confession? *Women always want me to tell them my feelings. And now I have. At the very least she'll be kinder.* He'd finally given up any hope of fussing.

Viv looked over briefly and then looked back to stare at the pool. Without her approval he felt lost. So he touched his jaw to remind him of his pain.

For a moment he felt confused. *Why isn't she opening her arms wide to comfort me?*

The silence felt suffocating. His thoughts on his pain made everything feel worse. Especially when he realized, *Is Viv mad at me too?*

Now he clamped his mouth shut. No use making things worse than they already were. Especially if Viv was going to take her shot. *I'm a broken man,* he groaned inwardly.

"You might want to consider Sutton's point of view. She told you why she's mad. Pretending you didn't hear isn't doing you any favors. Did the splash in the pool erase your memory?"

Rex felt utterly defeated. The word "pimp" was the only thing he remembered. He'd forgotten what else Sutton had said. But he wanted to get Viv on his side so he tried to answer.

"She said I tried to pimp her out. That's just insulting. I've never underestimated Sutton's independence or her ability. I pay her to work for me. I don't get paid for her work."

"From your point of view that makes some sense," Viv admitted. "But your logic didn't save you from an unexpected dip in the pool nor a sore jaw. Try again," she added sternly.

He clamped his jaw and then groaned. "I don't have to explain again," he growled.

"Then I will," she reasoned. "Sutton did not ask you to find her other work. Unless she hired you as a headhunter. If that were the case, she'd be paying you. Have you ever thought of that?"

I hate it when she uses that doula voice. I'm not her client. She is not playing along. I expect her to support me when I'm hurt, not treat me like a child.

"I'm heading home." He rose to his feet. He forgot to groan, indicating his firm commitment to making a hasty exit. He hoped she'd come after him and apologize.

But when his hand rested on the sliding door, he knew that wasn't going to happen.

Then he heard her chair scrape as if she were standing. He'd smile if it didn't hurt so much. Relief filled his chest. *She doesn't want me to go. She'll call me back and make up.*

But then he groaned. Her voice, with unmistakable clarity, was not an apology. Instead she said, "Don't forget to take Kevin."

23

____

VIVIENNE ROSE

The next morning Viv stood in front of the mirror. She used her forefinger to wrap her hair into a curl. Then she took her finger away as the tendril bounced next to the side of her face.

While she worked with more strands, she considered Rex's exit the night before. *Maybe I was a tad harsh,* she thought. She wrapped another curl. *But he was so obviously wrong and then tried to play the victim.*

Viv was never one to appreciate self-pity. She'd made it a point to avoid those who indulged. She'd learned to counteract her own disappointments with action. Her distaste was that strong.

In the past she'd been told that she lacked compassion. She'd lost a friendship or two over the years because she didn't, as she would say, kiss the boo-boo. It took some time for Viv to realize that was not the case.

After all, she was the first to cuddle a newborn in her arms, reluctantly handing it back to the parents. She hugged her son when she saw him. She even missed the intimacy with Rex. She felt for people and their circumstances. But she had her limits, self-pity being the red flag for her to push back.

But Rex's quick departure and his insistence made her reconsider. *Rex is dramatic and a bit much with his demonstrative emotions. He is a stage performer and that comes with the territory. But maybe he's even more so since his recent rehab in Hawaii.*

A place of disquiet lurked in the back of her mind. Since his return he'd not mentioned a date night. Or staying over. Or even invited her to spend the night with him. *I'm not sure where I stand. Maybe I'm distancing myself for a good reason.*

Viv fluffed her hair. She ran her fingers through the soft mass of gray curls. *I like this look*, she concluded. *Not too tidy; definitely not too prim.* She applied a thin coat of mascara over her top and bottom lashes. *I look my age but not by mistake.*

Glancing toward the top drawer, she reached inside to pull out her journal. *I need my own pep talk*, she decided. Over the years Viv had written affirmations that helped her during difficult times. She repeated the first one that caught her eye.

"I confidently claim my years." Then she added her own twist. "Because no one gets out of this alive."

Viv brewed a fresh pot of coffee and then sat in her office to listen to her messages. Her last call was to a mom who was not ready to return to work.

"I don't want to leave him," the mom had wailed in her message.

Viv listened but did not linger over the mom's feelings. "Dry your tears," she said. "Remember, baby needs you but your work is also important. It will take a few weeks but eventually the routine will provide stability for you both."

After finishing the call Viv felt satisfied. She'd given a list of practical suggestions about pumping ahead and then storing the breast milk. "Baby's diaper bag requires two fresh outfits and several extra diapers," she warned. Then she finished the call with a few more practical suggestions about where to buy disposable diapers at the cheapest price. "I'll send you a link for coupons," she'd told the mother.

Viv knew that all of these suggestions were far more useful than focusing on what could not be changed. The new mother's employer wanted her back to work. She'd been paid for eight weeks of leave. If she wanted to keep the job, she had to show up. "The more you plan and prepare, the less anxious you'll feel," Viv stated firmly. "And I'll let you in on one of my secrets."

"What's that?" the mother sniffed.

"If you feel anxious, count your blessings. Name at least five things that make you happy. Start with how fortunate you are to have a healthy, happy infant. By the time you get to blessing number five, your anxiety will be gone."

"Really?" The mom sounded doubtful.

"Let's do this together," Viv suggested.

As they named the blessings, the mother's tone shifted. She sounded less teary and more grounded. Viv ended their conversation by saying, "Call me in a few days to let me know how things are going."

She closed her laptop. Now that she was done with her doula calls, she was left to consider Rex. Even if they weren't heading down a more intimate path, they'd decided to be private investigators. As partners they had to practice resolving disagreements.

Once they were talking, the first thing she'd say is that

his relationship with Sutton wasn't any of her business. The punch and splash... That was between Rex and Sutton. *I was only an observer.*

I've only known them for a year or so. Maybe that's how they are together. Fighting and making up. I want no part. I'm no one's audience. I didn't pay for a ticket to anyone's self-made drama.

Viv lifted her cell.

TEXT Let's have lunch.

When Rex didn't respond she felt disappointed. And then sad. *Not a good sign. If he can't negotiate a disagreement without a silent treatment, I may need to reconsider being his business partner.* Stonewalling was not something Viv tolerated.

But Rex had pulled away and gone quiet before. Despite how Viv disliked being treated that way, she knew he was trying. *I can use the quiet to my advantage.*

Instead waiting for a return text, Viv took action. *I'm going to take a swim. Later than usual but still important. And then I have an idea.*

Her energy shifted.

A quick underwater turn and her body resurfaced. Stretching one arm out, she continued her swim. She turned her chin to take a quick breath. Face back in the water, her left arm reached, her breath taking on a steady rhythm.

She embraced the rush. *Feeling pushed aside is a human thing,* she told herself. *Now that I know what I feel I can move around the obstacle and investigate myself.*

She felt her mood lift. Her inner voice took on a happier message. *Rex will reach out when he's ready. I am capable of navigating his moods. I'll use our disagreements to claim my own space. Plus everyone gets into disagreements over time. It's how you get past them that matters.*

After a shower and change into dry clothes, Viv picked up her phone. She felt refreshed and eager to continue her own investigation. *I may not see images, but I get hunches. The realtor and the stager were not on the up and up. I'll start there.*

She looked at her screen. Still no response from Rex. She smiled, no longer feeling sad.

Opening her phone, she clicked on Contacts. Gloria Ramirez's name popped up. *I can move ahead with a line of questioning. What reason will I use for making contact...*

Wait a minute. Gloria gave me several avenues. Her brother the landscaper, for one. I could call and get a referral because I'm redesigning the backyard landscaping. Of course, I'm not. But she doesn't have to know.

And then there's Gloria herself; she's a stager. All that mid-century furniture showed a certain talent for form and function. Viv found Gloria's business cards in her wallet. She's also a licensed California realtor. On the back Gloria had a website for her staging business.

A plan already formed in her mind.

I'll play into her passion for home design. Make up a backstory. Then we meet up. One thing will lead to another. We'll chat. Be friends. And I'll shift the conversation to Wally Walker.

She lifted her phone to make that call.

24

REX REDONDO

Rex awoke with a start. His stomach rumbled and he felt hot breath on his cheek. He lifted one eyelid.

Kevin stared at him, swiping Rex's mouth with a warm tongue. "Who let you in?" he mumbled. *Where's my coffee?* was his next thought.

He sniffed and then coughed in his hand. *Not coffee; is that dog poop?* Rex sat up. A mound of poop lay in front of the closed bedroom door. "Kevin!" he roared.

"Bork." The dog jumped off the bed. He scrambled to hide underneath. Only his tail poked out.

"Bad dog." Rex hated messes. Up until now he hadn't had to deal with Kevin's house-training. "Why didn't Sutton take you out!" Then he remembered the night before.

He couldn't open the door without making a bigger mess. With a mound of toilet paper, he picked up the poop. Then he dropped the smelly mess into the toilet and flushed.

A smudge on the carpet remained. *But at least I can open the door.*

Convinced he was no longer in danger of a scolding,

Kevin appeared from under the bed. He wagged his tail in appreciation.

"I am not your butler," Rex scolded. When Kevin refused to duck his head or act one bit contrite, Rex felt irritation rise. His jaw tightened. He groaned. He realized the unthinkable. *Now I have to let Kevin out. Before I get dressed. Not to mention before my first cup of coffee.*

His stomach turned over. To his sensitive nose, even the lingering scent of dog poop was offensive. He opened the door as Kevin raced past, barking with delight. Rex followed. He found the dog standing in front of the sliding door. Kevin pawed at the glass, making Rex's teeth stand on edge.

Sutton locked the dog door so he can't get out.

They'd had an extensive discussion about that very door in the past. The dos and

don'ts of keeping it locked during the night. All of this brought on by a scorpion that scooted right through the open dog door and made a home under a pillow on the sofa.

Sutton convinced Rex they needed to lock the door after that, especially at night. She said she'd take Kevin out early in the morning. That was their agreement. Since then Rex paid no attention to Kevin's potty needs. *Why would I? Sutton's got this.*

With a look of longing toward the kitchen, he ignored the dog door and opened the slider to let Kevin outside. "Hurry up, you mutt." A quick glance toward the fence that separated Viv's house from his brought up regret.

I wonder if she's swimming this morning.

The thought of observing her effortless strokes as she pulled herself through the water felt positive. Better than waking up to a dog in his face and the smell of his poop.

But then he touched his jaw. "Ouch," Rex exclaimed.

Placing two fingers over his ear, he pushed. *Man, that hurts.* The pain and

Sutton's punch came back. *She clocked me. And she quit. And now I have this Kevin thing to deal with.*

Impatient to put the day behind him, he hadn't bothered to look in the mirror when he got home. *What if there's bruising. What am I gonna tell people...*

I had some work done. That would be better than saying my assistant, friend, and war buddy sucker punched me for no reason.

He opened his jaw, appreciating the pain, relishing his story. Gone was the glimmer of happiness, replaced by the encroaching bad mood he'd taken to bed the night before.

Kevin pawed at the glass. Rex let him back inside. The dog raced to the kitchen, sliding to a halt in front of the pantry.

"I suppose I have to feed you," Rex grumbled.

He dumped kibble into Kevin's dish. "What about my breakfast?"

He took inventory of the kitchen. Dishes lay on the counter from their meal. Stale muffin crumbs were already being attacked by a line of ants. He squished three and wiped his fingers on his pajamas. Rinsing his hands under the faucet, he noticed a stain in the sink. *Probably blueberries. How does she remove the color...*

Rex cleaned the coffee carafe and made a fresh pot of coffee. *I have skills,* he told himself. *I can make my own coffee.*

He listened to the perking, realizing he didn't have his cell phone. One glance at the blank screen made him sigh. *Sutton usually plugs it in for me,* he lamented. The charging cord lay right next to his phone. His list of things to do had doubled.

The dawning of Sutton's abandonment hit him full force. *I've only been awake for half an hour and there's catastrophe around every corner. I have to get her back. Not just for me but for Kevin.*

25

VIVIENNE ROSE

Gloria Ramirez tapped the keypad with her security card. She lifted the roll-up metal door to the storage unit. "Here you go," she told Viv. "I keep all of my furniture and staging decorations in one place. Why don't you look around." Gloria stepped back to let Viv pass.

Earlier that morning Viv had executed her plan with a call to Gloria. Her backstory intact, she made meeting up with her sound plausible. "I'm thinking of getting into real estate investment on my own," she'd said. "Flipping properties, renting to tourists for weekends. I'll need a stager and I thought of you right away."

It had taken only minutes for Gloria to confirm an appointment.

Viv had no trouble finding the single-story facility. One of the more recent constructions, it sprawled over flat land, painted a warm desert beige to blend into the surroundings. Gloria's business name, displayed near the entrance, added to a professional impression.

Inside Viv looked around. There was one area for living room furniture, another for bedroom sets, a separate section for artwork and wall hangings. She noted illustrated desert designs with colors that she'd seen in offices all over Palm Springs.

Shelves contained decorative pillows. Rolled rugs lay underneath, and lamps were stacked at the top. Yellow, brown, orange and a lot of beige, Viv realized. Everything could be used again with various properties because the color scheme was the same.

"Sit down." Gloria pointed to a coffee maker and refrigerator on a side table. She sat behind her desk. "We can have a cup of coffee and look at some listings to get started."

Gloria opened her tablet. "Here's an excellent bungalow," she said promptly. "I can take you over this morning for a look."

Viv felt off balance. She hadn't expected her to move so quickly. "I like to hear more before I visit," she explained.

Gloria typed. Viv knew this was the time to bulk up her backstory.

"I'm already targeting three properties," she explained.

Gloria's eyes lit up. Viv glanced to her right. "I can see you have a realtor's license. So do you want to represent me in the purchases? Then we can talk about staging."

Gloria closed her tablet, her fingers trembling with excitement. "Well that makes a big difference. Of course I'll represent you. Three properties, you say. As a matter of fact you've assessed correctly. It's time to bring in a professional." She continued, "I know every house in Palm Desert and we can get a viewing before they've been publicly listed. Now that's an advantage." The bright gleam in her eyes was replaced by a calculating sharpness.

There's the zealous businesswoman right there, Viv realized.

"Once we make a bid, there's an excellent chance that

the seller will take the offer. It saves them time and trouble and the wait."

Viv assessed quickly. *Okay, you've hooked Gloria. Now you have to spin the story before she realizes you have no intention of buying property.*

Time to start asking about Wally Walker.

26

____

REX REDONDO

Rex showered and dressed with trepidation. It had only taken a few dishes, the stain in the sink, and a dog poop accident to derail his mood and maybe his entire day. That made him feel weak, something he hated.

Kevin sprawled out in his basket. Nose on paws, fast asleep. Rex caught himself more than once looking for Sutton. Right now he looked toward the front door, expecting her to come inside, glowing from her early morning run.

Images pinged his memory. Sutton laughing, wearing her tight yoga running pants and a bright pink crop top. How he loved her smile, and of course, the way she'd made his life effortless. Radiant and the picture of health, Sutton inspired him. Prone to a slothful lifestyle, he'd drag himself out of bed just to keep up with her.

Surely she isn't still mad...

The more time that went by, the more he wasn't sure that was true. *I'll have more coffee and send her a text. I don't suppose I know how to make scrambled eggs. That's a bit of a problem.*

Once I apologize she'll come back, he reasoned. *Then she'll admit she acted irrationally. That she's feeling overly sensitive for some female reason. We'll hug it out and she'd make me a conciliatory pot of coffee.* He didn't see why this couldn't happen sooner rather than later. But then he'd begin to doubt. To reassure himself that he was right, he'd come back to the same conclusion.

Any rational man would be upset. I'm the one who should be mad.

His jaw tightened, sending a pain up his temple. Reenergized by his indignation, he dumped the cold coffee into the sink, ignoring the stain.

As the fresh coffee dripped into the carafe, Rex looked toward the dining room. Except for the kitchen, everything else in the house looked spotless. Another reminder of Sutton's diligent housekeeping. *Who's going to clean...* He felt a moment of panic.

He lifted his loose pants. They kept slipping. *I forgot a belt.* He poked at the shirttail of his Hawaiian shirt. *Pants up, shirt down. I hope that covers me.*

Holding his pants with one hand, he walked down the hallway and opened Sutton's door. She'd left the mattress bare, no sign of pillows or linens. She'd removed her leopard-skin area rug.

Inside the closet he saw a row of empty hangers. Nothing on the shelves. No sign of her hats or shoes. He looked under the bed. Not even a fur-ball.

The final straw was a quick glance in the bathroom. The counter had been cleared and wiped down. Not a cosmetic bottle, or a candle, or any of the usual makeup remained. He ran his finger over the surface, detecting a slight smell of disinfectant.

. . .

An hour later Rex unplugged his phone from the charger and sat down on the edge of the bed. He'd composed a short text to Sutton. But before he could send, his phone pinged with a text from Viv.

TEXT Let's have lunch

The offer set off a number of reactions. Unlike Sutton, Viv wanted to reconnect after last night's fiasco. She reached out halfway. She'd most likely be responsive to his grand apology. Reminded of its effectiveness in the past, he had every reason to believe Viv would be impressed.

He applied the grand apology to every misunderstanding with a female. How he didn't mean to upset her, followed by an appropriate excuse. Then he'd follow up with flowers. And if that didn't make it go away, he'd resort to jewelry. Making certain that it came from an expensive Palm Springs boutique, so that she could check on the price later.

Then makeup sex and back to business as usual.

His bad behavior would become a thing of the past.

Some women were a bit challenging. He had a backup arsenal for those unusual occasions. A resistant female would require an unleashing of his superpower. He'd wrap his mind around the distrustful female's spirit, just like she was a mark in a mentalist show.

He'd look into her eyes with a mesmerizing stare, all the while releasing his inner warmth to break down her reserve. With a slight tilt of his chin he'd send a message accompanied by a look of admiration her way. She'd see that he couldn't get along without her, the message all women desired.

By the time he was done she'd be giggling because she'd forget what had made her mad in the first place.

Of course his relationship with Sutton had always been

complicated. When they disagreed, they tended to let bygones be bygones. And there was never a hint of makeup sex. Because she reminded him of the sister he'd always longed for, not someone he'd casually date.

Rex stared at Viv's text. He wanted to put on contrite Rex, initiate the grand apology, but now he felt less confident. Sutton had ruined him with her desertion. He no longer trusted his instincts.

I should text back, he told himself.

But Viv is different, his inner voice warned. *She's not an employee or close like a sister. And she's not a young woman easily swayed by my charm.* None of what he'd done in the past, no matter how successful with others, would work with Viv.

Even though she'd opened her arms to him a few months ago. He'd been ill then. A bruised jaw wouldn't be the same. She'd be less inclined to give him another break. Viv didn't like repeat offenders who acted out their bad moods to get their way.

Texting back would be admitting failure and setting himself up to take responsibility. And that bothered him as much as being abandoned.

He touched his jaw, feeling the sharp pain.

The intense confusion brought up a feeling of overwhelm, and then to make matters worse, he could taste the bitterness of despair on the back of his tongue. He'd used the two women in his life. Without Sutton he couldn't talk about Viv. And without Viv he couldn't talk about Sutton. What a mess...

"Bork," came from the living room.

"What do you want?" he called in a loud accusing voice. *How can I focus on me when that dog is interrupting?*

Rex heaved himself to his feet. Both knees twinged. He flopped back on the bed. *I feel old.*

"Bork," Kevin called again.

"I'm coming," he muttered.

The dog's nose was pressed against the sliding glass door. He pawed at the glass. Something in the backyard had caught his attention. "What's so interesting?" Rex came closer.

Miss Kitty strolled past the firepit. She didn't look over, ignoring Kevin. "What's she doing in our yard?" He turned to the dog. "Did you invite her?"

"Bork, bork." Kevin paced in front of the sliding door in frustration. Miss Kitty did a 180 to stroll past again. This time she came right up to the glass, though she still refused to acknowledge his presence.

Rex tapped with his knuckles. Miss Kitty skirted across the patio. She leapt up on the table and turned to face them both, lifting a casual paw for a thorough lick.

"She's taking over your yard, Kevin," Rex explained. "Flaunting herself, treating you with indifference. That must be annoying, letting a cat have that much power over you." He bent to pat the dog's back.

"I know how you feel, buddy."

Tempted to open the door and release Kevin to a chase, Rex hesitated. Instead he closed the curtain to block the view. "Sometimes out of sight, out of mind is the best course of action," he advised. "Come on, Kevin. I'm taking you for a walk. You're not going to win a fight with Miss Kitty. She's way out of your league."

He opened his front door. An old movie and its theme music came to mind. *Gone with the Wind.* He'd never liked the film. The story was overly sentimental and oblivious to the suffering of everyone who wasn't a plantation owner. Some considered it racist despite the accolades.

Rex whistled "Tara's Theme." *A good tune*, he had to admit. *I wonder why it's popped into my head now. Probably because of Viv. The actress who played Scarlett O'Hara. Her name was Vivien Leigh.* The memorable scene, right before intermission came next.

"I'll think about Viv tomorrow," he explained to Kevin. "Tomorrow is another day."

27

VIVIENNE ROSE

"I can print up a contract right now," Gloria insisted.

Viv didn't like her time wasted. She prided herself on getting to the point. She needed to acknowledge the contract but get past the offer. "How about you send the contract to my email. I'll run it past my attorney." Viv adjusted her tone to sound encouraging, hoping to cover up the mixed emotions brought on by her fake story.

Gloria's eyes narrowed. *Rex would call that a tell*, Viv observed. *She's lost control and knows she's being put off.* The realtor pushed herself to her feet. She spoke in a tart voice. "Of course. It's time for you to go. I have other clients."

Realizing her mistake, Viv stayed seated. "I'll try to call Mr. Rocco right now. Maybe I can get approval quickly over the phone." She reached for her cell.

"I suppose," Gloria sighed. But instead of giving Viv space for a private conversation, she made her way around the desk to hover nearby. Close enough to listen in.

Might as well make this convincing; the phone call to my nonexistent lawyer. Viv kept one eye on Gloria as she held the phone to her ear. "This will just take a minute," she assured the realtor.

"Hey, Sally." Viv pitched her voice to business efficient. "How are things? Is he in?" She smiled at Gloria as she improvised.

"I have a quick question before I get on his calendar." Looking up at the ceiling to avoid Gloria's narrow-eyed gaze, she feigned impatience. Viv had pulled the name Joe Rocco out of thin air since she didn't actually have an attorney. Plus she knew he'd sound familiar to locals because of the advertisements on bus benches all over town.

"Joey." Her voice adopted a warm tone. She tittered at an imaginary joke, then added a full laugh, followed by a giggle. "Okay then, lunch soon." She ended the call and stood to face the realtor eye to eye. Viv wasn't as tall but she held herself in a way that didn't invite pushback. "My attorney is taking an early lunch. He promised to call me back. But we both know what that means. Three martinis and he'll forget. But I'll be sure to follow up with his assistant for an appointment." Her lips curved into a faultless fake smile.

"Since I've taken so much of your time, why don't we have lunch? We can discuss our plans and get to know each other better." Viv picked up her purse. She kept talking so that Gloria would be encouraged to follow without protest.

"I know property taxes are a consideration." Viv didn't turn to look. She wanted to appear confident. When the click of high heels met her ears, she felt a surge of satisfaction.

Gloria won't reject my lunch offer. It would be a missed opportunity.

. . .

"I eat here all the time." Viv nodded at all the people seated on the patio of Just Desserts. Most of the crowd dressed business casual. She'd seen them use expense accounts to woo customers. The rest included locals, the retired crowd. Only a few were tourists. The servers sat most of them at the pie bar.

Once seated, Gloria buried her head in the menu. Viv kept chatting. "My business partner Rex, you remember him? He frequents the pie counter. That man loves himself a slice of French apple." The lie flowed off her tongue, her previous guilt replaced with a small sense of excitement. *Maybe it's because I'm paying for Gloria's lunch. She may not be getting a contract, but she could order a good burger.*

"Is that so." Gloria buried her face back in the menu.

When the server arrived, she was the first to order. "I'll take the Caesar salad, no dressing."

"Not even on the side?" he asked. "Or if you're worried about the calories, I can offer a low-fat in-house raspberry vinaigrette that people love."

"No dressing," she snapped. "No bread either. I'm gluten-free." The server made note of her order and turned to Viv.

"The Havarti and veggie sandwich," she said. "Gluten included." She winked.

He held back a smirk.

Being a regular customer had its advantages.

Once he walked away, Viv unfolded her cloth napkin and reached for her water glass. She didn't intend on saying anything more. *I'm the buyer; Gloria needs to step up and make her pitch.* Viv assessed her situation with her usual attention to detail.

I have time in the game but no money, and I haven't

signed a contract. So come on, Gloria. Convince me that you've got a property all set up.

Gloria turned her fork over between a manicured forefinger and her thumb. She put the utensil down to wave at her face. "Hot today."

"It's heating up," Viv replied in her most noncommittal tone. She relaxed her jaw to form a benign smile.

"So you come here often?" Gloria asked.

Viv lowered her voice. "My companion Rex is the frequent customer. The pie passion I mentioned... He hangs out at the counter every morning and orders a slice to go."

"I have a property that you might be interested in," Gloria blurted. She lifted her phone. "I can check out the listings while we wait for the food."

As the realtor scrolled, Viv kept up her pie bar chatter. "I heard that Rex isn't the only male who appreciates a good slice. One of your clients, Wallace Walker, used to come in every morning. He became quite close with Mia, the server."

Blood rushed to Viv's head. She felt giddy having finally broached the subject she'd come to discuss.

Gloria pretended not to hear Viv, still searching on her cell. Finally she laid her phone back on the table. "I'd rather do the search on my office computer. The WiFi isn't good on the patio. You were talking about Wally..."

Viv held her breath as Gloria continued.

"He mentioned to me once that he came to Just Desserts every morning. Even on weekdays before his class at Mojave Mesa. I was very close to him, you know."

Having successfully shifted the topic, Viv felt relieved. She'd managed to lure Gloria away from business. Now she might forget about the contract, allowing Viv to get the answers she was looking for.

She switched to a sincere tone. "Were you friends with Wallace Walker? I had no idea."

"He and I go way back. I took a class at Mojave Mesa. In my late teens. It was an elective. He was the most popular instructor on campus then. They called the class a "Mickey.""

"What does that mean?"

"Named after Mickey Mouse. It means not serious. An automatic A if you showed up. Wally wasn't a hard grader. He liked to share his cop stories, not read term papers or grade tests."

Viv expected to hear more sadness at the mention of the dead man's name. Maybe a tear or a trembling bottom lip.

"I made it a point to stop by and say hi to Wally over the years. It was easy to catch him before that early morning class," Gloria said. "But then we got closer. That didn't lead to much."

"Did you have a falling out?" Viv was genuinely curious.

"Not until lately. We were good until then. We reconnected. I'd stop by his mid-century bungalow. I really helped him out. He'd get confused about his meds so I'd put them in the little pill organizers every week. And then he'd forget old food in the refrigerator, so I'd clean it out for him.

"I even brought groceries. He was always trying to lose weight, keep his diabetes in check. Wally visited several specialists. I'd arrange for the appointments. It took hours.

"I bet he talked to you about selling his bungalow." Viv's eyes narrowed.

"No matter how hard I tried to persuade him with all the ways he'd thrive, he was reluctant. Even when I told him how great senior living was and how lots of my clients love it. I brought him a contract and he agreed to look it over. But he always had an excuse. He'd lose the paper or have another problem he had to look into. This time it was that principal, his boss at the college. Boy, was he mad at her."

"Dr. Morales..." Viv's voice trailed.

"She targeted him. It became her life's mission to get him to retire by the end of the spring term. He was furious. I tried to smooth the way, you know, explain how he'd be able to live his remaining years in comfort.

"He had two pensions, if you count Mojave Mesa. He received a good monthly payment from the cops too. If he listed his house and used the proceeds to upgrade his lifestyle, well, he could afford a nice comfortable life."

"Did you recommend one of those deluxe retirement communities in Palm Desert?"

"That was one option. I told him he'd be waited on hand and foot."

"He must have been encouraged by your interest."

Viv felt strangely defensive of Wally Walker. Especially after hearing the lengths Gloria had gone to sell his bungalow. Only a couple of years ago she'd had to make a similar decision. Her son encouraged her to downsize and move to the Desert Tortoise Estates. Lucas had no financial gain helping her with the decision, unlike Gloria. But the entire experience had unsettled Viv for months. On the other side she realized the benefits, but not when she was making the decisions to dismantle her home.

"Every time I brought up a move, he just got angrier," Gloria continued. "And then when the principal started pressuring him to retire, he blamed her for all of his unhappiness.

"He was obsessed. 'That woman can't tell me what to do.

I'm a police subject matter expert." Gloria shifted her voice to a gruff imitation of the older man.

"I learned my lesson and didn't mention his retirement again. I didn't want to give him a heart attack. I'm not a monster," Gloria said.

"So you were waiting him out," Viv replied.

"That's what good realtors do. We keep a file and we keep coming back. 'No pressure,' I kept telling him."

Viv felt the bitter tang of distaste on the tip of her tongue. *I'm not the only liar at this table.* She took a sip of water.

"One day I stopped by his classroom with a couple of fancy retirement brochures. I was going to explain again how I would get him a great price and a quick sale on his house. I found him slumped over his desk fast asleep.

"I had to yell, 'Wake up, Wally!' He finally raised his head. I brought him coffee from the vending machine. Then I lectured him about his food and what he'd eaten that morning.

"He claimed he'd done everything right. Tomato juice and eggs. But I could see the bag from Just Desserts." She shook her head. "What could I do? Lead a horse and all that. Wally wasn't gonna change. He kept drinking and eating sweets. An insulin resistant nightmare.

"I felt discouraged but I didn't give up. The following week I brought him printouts of three well-priced condo listings. Before he could get himself worked up, I explained again how he could retire and buy a smaller place. Downsize like other seniors. How he could afford to hire help and even have meals delivered.

"I did my homework," she insisted. "I even listened while he took dozens of trips down memory lane. All about moving to Palm Springs with his bride. How they raised their son. His commendations with the Palm Desert police. Wally was so proud. He cried as he told me how his son got killed in the line of duty. And then his wife passed from cancer. He had a grandson, that was some consolation. Turned out I knew Jax already. He's a real estate legend. Sells more real estate than any other realtor in the desert."

"There's a quote I heard that made a difference to me," Viv offered. "'Life is long enough when lived well.'"

Gloria rolled her eyes. She dismissed Viv with a shrug.

28

REX REDONDO

Rex sauntered through the open door of Dr. Morales's office. He found her talking to a familiar man. *That's the custodian,* he remembered. "Am I too early?"

"Oh no," Dr. Morales said. "I'm having a word with Eddie before he's off the clock. A maintenance issue."

"See you later," Eddie mumbled. He stopped to look Rex up and down. "Nice outfit. Love the shirt." Then he disappeared into the outer office with a chuckle.

"Please close the door," Morales said, staring at Rex. She blinked her eyes as if warding off the glare.

Everybody wants to be me, Rex thought. *I'm rocking this shirt.* He waited for the principal to settle herself before he took his seat. Since he had to pick out his own clothes that morning, it didn't hurt to be admired. He tugged on the waistband of his pants. *I never did find that belt.*

"How can I help you, Mr. Redondo?" Dr. Morales asked.

"It seems I was remiss. When I was here before I recommended Sutton Drew and I failed to talk to her first." He rubbed his sore jaw. He wanted Morales to notice the bruise. Then he could tell her how badly he'd been treated.

When she didn't acknowledge the obvious swelling and discoloration, he felt annoyed. Dropping his hand to his lap, he made an effort to hide his disappointment. A kind word from an attractive female would have been welcome. He sighed.

"I see," she stated calmly. "I did call Ms. Drew right after our talk. She didn't sound unhappy to me. In fact I had the idea she might be interested in taking on the position.

"She would be ideal for the job. So much younger than the previous instructor. She'd relate better to potential law enforcement students. We have a certificate program specifically designed to train young people to qualify for the rookie exam." She warmed to her topic, her cheeks growing pink.

"The State of California has very specific guidelines when it comes to funding community colleges. There's a Student Centered Funding Formula—SCFF for short. They allocate according to the key metrics."

Rex felt a buzzing in his ears. Probably because he really didn't care about the boring details of academic life. He forced himself to pay attention but it took an effort.

"I know the metrics are important," Seraphina continued.

"Not really," Rex mumbled under his breath. But she kept talking, undaunted by his lack of interest.

"We get the most funding for the FTES students."

He felt trapped. He knew that any indication he was confused would only make matters worse. She'd just explain more. That was the way with a lot of teachers. They assumed they were interesting and that more explanation was always better.

"That would be the Full-Time Equivalent Students," Seraphina added.

She's not gonna stop. Rex resisted slapping his hand against his head in frustration. *I didn't come here for this.*

Dr. Morales barely paused for a breath. "Mojave Mesa keeps track of all the FTES students by assessing their student success outcomes."

Due to his years in the military, Rex was no slouch when it came to acronyms. Finally he'd found a place to speak up and derail the conversation. "The Student Success Outcomes. That would be the SSOs." Rex smiled. He assumed the persona of a student who'd been listening, hoping she would finally stop.

But she didn't crack a smile. It was obvious to him that Seraphina Morales took her job very seriously as she just kept explaining.

"This is serious business, Mr. Redondo. The state tracks students who transfer to four-year colleges or who get technical certificates by taking two-year programs. You people"—she glared at him—"the second career folks. The truth is that I make very little money on you. You take up space for younger learners."

Rex felt his face flush with indignation. "Hey, I'm going to be a PI. Doesn't that count for something? I have an unused GI Bill benefit. I did serve in the military."

"Thank you for your service," she stated automatically. Only now did she shift gears. Probably because she was afraid he'd been insulted.

"Of course, we all loved Officer Wallace. He had quite a following over the years. But he'd become somewhat of a dinosaur, especially with his health issues. I've had trouble keeping his 101 class open due to decreasing enrollment. Sad, really..."

She doesn't look sad, Rex thought. *More relieved, if you ask me.* He rose to his feet. "Thanks for letting me drop in," he said. "You'll stop chasing Sutton Drew now, right? That's why I came."

Her phone buzzed. She didn't answer Rex. "Yes," she said into the receiver.

Her face drained of color. "I'm so sorry to hear that." Her voice trembled. "Can you share any of the details? ... You can't. Not at this time. An ongoing investigation, you say. I'll put the word out." She placed the phone back.

"That was Lieutenant Darius James from the Palm Desert police. There's some discrepancy in Wallace Walker's toxicology report." She looked away. "He may have intentionally or accidentally overdosed. There were so many substances in his blood they have to do more tests."

"Intentional like suicide?" Rex asked.

"They're not certain. Lieutenant James will keep me up to date. I assume it will be solved fairly quickly and in the news." Tapping a stack of papers on her desk, she added, "I have more work to do. Your 101 class may have to be postponed indefinitely until all of this is figured out."

Rex felt a growing sense of certainty. Dr. Morales was disappointed at the news; she'd wanted Walker's death to be off her plate. She only cared how he died if it interfered with the college class. She most likely was worried about how the FTES would impact the SSOs. Or if she had to cancel the Introduction to Private Investigation 101 class and lose some of her state funding.

Despite Morales's obsession with her job, he'd been encouraged with the report from the police. Ever since they'd discovered Wallace Walker, he had his doubts about the cause of death. Now it seemed he might have been right. Especially with the inconclusive toxicology report.

Even though his reason for talking to the principal was to correct any assumption about Sutton, the information he now had made his and Viv's investigation even more valid. He could tell Sutton once again that he meant no harm, and they could go back to where they were...

He slid his hand into the deep pocket of his cargo shorts. The image of the pocket watch rose in his mind. The tips of his fingers felt warm.

Dr. Morales watched him carefully. She was obviously waiting for him to leave.

He averted his gaze, paying attention to the words pinging his thoughts. *The finger warmth—is that a clue?* His chin jutted forward. *There's something about that watch. I'm convinced that it will be the most important piece of evidence as to who murdered Wally Walker.*

Dr. Morales walked around the desk and opened her office door.

He didn't need another reminder. On his feet, he stopped to ask one more question. "Will the investigation postpone the memorial?"

She frowned.

She's not even thinking about a service. That's obvious.

For the first time that day Rex felt better. He'd caught Morales out, exposing her less-than-compassionate nature when it came to Wally's death. When he felt his fingers tingle, he realized something more.

Seraphina Morales wasn't above killing someone who got in her way. She was ruthless when it came to running her school. The funding was a major incentive in keeping the institution award-worthy. Wally Walker's refusal to retire only got in the way.

He walked toward the elevator, pleased with the morning's work. He'd taken full responsibility for Sutton's feelings by talking to Morales and removing his assistant's name from the list of potential substitutes.

Plus he'd listened to the principal yammer on about her job without yawning. That took some discipline. Once he reconnected with Viv, he'd be in perfect harmony with three diverse women.

Taking charge gave him a new bounce to his step. He tugged on his shorts. *That's a good morning's work, Rex ol' boy.*

His fingers reached up to take a quick tug on his earlobe. Just like one of his favorite film detectives, Philip Marlowe.

It was time to take their investigation to the next level.

29

VIVIENNE ROSE

The server refilled their water glasses. Fresh ice tumbled from the pitcher as Viv circled back to the conversation. "So when you listened to Wally's story, he finally agreed to sign a contract and begin a search for a new condo."

Gloria held up a finger. "I have to take this call." She turned her head to speak quietly into the phone. The interruption gave Viv a chance to think.

Gloria's story, the intensity about Wally, hit her in personal ways. Identifying with him as a senior, for one. What about the other coincidence...how both Mia and Gloria helped Wally with his pills. Gloria's motivation was obvious. She wanted a sale.

But Mia... Was she hiding behind her I'm-just-an-innocent-waitress-who-cares-about-the-elderly persona? Or did she also have a financial motive...

Plus there was that brief mention of Wally's problems with Mojave Mesa; Viv wondered if his tenure was closing despite his pushback. If he'd been targeted as redundant and treated unfairly by Seraphina Morales, she may have decided to remove him by force.

As soon as Gloria ended her conversation, Viv spoke up. "So you were saying about Wally..."

"It doesn't matter now," Gloria sighed. "I have to get back to the office. Another staging request."

"Wally's property will sell quickly. Once you find the right buyer. There will be a whopping commission." Viv watched her face for a tell.

"I'm not into it for the cash, Wally was a friend," Gloria insisted. The flush on her cheeks indicated otherwise.

Viv wasn't letting go. "Wally must have had a trust. That will speed things up. Once you sell, and you will with that bungalow, the payment will come quickly. It's not as if you have to go through probate. Or do you..." Viv left the question hanging.

"Not me," Gloria stated flatly. "I suppose you might as well know. It's not a secret. There was a trust but it doesn't matter. He died before he could sign our agreement and Jax jumped to list the place before I could object. He's the next of kin. The executor."

"But you did all the work," Viv exclaimed. For a brief moment she felt empathy for the realtor. She'd been in similar positions, outdistanced by a competitive colleague.

"Wally double-crossed me. He kept the paperwork and told me he'd sign. But he never did. And then he died before I could follow up. Jax couldn't wait to tell me. He called the same day. 'You can help me plan the memorial,' he insisted, as if that's all I'm good for. He actually laughed and hung up.

"Jax will be the one laughing all the way to the bank." Bitterness dripped from her words.

The server arrived holding two plates. "Salad no dressing no gluten; a veggie sandwich with cheese, mayo, sprouts, and whole wheat." He placed them on the table. "Will there be anything else?"

Viv shook her head in response, but she needed sustenance. Gloria's obvious lust for a sale had made her feel empty. She took a bite of her sandwich to savor the crunch of fresh cucumber and the creamy texture of Havarti cheese. The thickly sliced whole wheat sourdough only added to her satisfaction. She focused on each bite, using the time to consider Gloria's revelations.

Raising a fork, the realtor poked at the arugula and other greens on her plate. She selected a single leaf and lifted it to her lips. Viv knew other women like that, who paid attention to each bite. They called it mindful eating.

Viv also knew you could tell a lot about a person when you observed their relationship to food. She related to a good meal as a form of comfort. But Gloria viewed her salad as a necessary evil.

Viv took another bite.

After finishing half of her sandwich, Viv called for the server. "Do you have a box?" She'd gotten what she needed from the realtor, distasteful as it was.

When the server returned with a small container, she reached for the bill. "I'll pay for lunch. Unless you want to write it off as a business expense."

Gloria put down her fork. "When do you think you'll be talking to your attorney?" Apparently the three bites of lettuce gave her more energy, enough to return to her potential real estate sale. She sounded less bitter and more professional.

Viv pretended to check her phone for a message. "Not yet. I'll let you know as soon as I hear."

A look of disappointment clouded Gloria's eyes.

After paying the bill and bidding Gloria a brisk goodbye, Viv sat behind the steering wheel. She took a moment to decompress. *This has been a difficult morning,* she concluded. *I had to pretend to be someone I'm not. I invented an attorney who I've never consulted. In fact, I think he's in jail. I've had lunch with a greedy and desperate realtor. Who took advantage of an old man. She might have contributed to his death, with her interfering of pills and doctors' appointments.*

I wonder how many other old people Gloria has stalked. Wait a minute. Maybe she thinks I'm her next mark. I always forget I'm old. Maybe not as many years as Wally but certainly getting up there.

I thought aging would be different, Viv realized. *I assumed that people would respect me more for my wisdom and maturity. I ignored the fact that many see dollar signs because of my financial security. Just the other day I read an article about generational wealth. How younger people resent not having their share.*

Not everyone is Jax Walker. I suppose Gloria may have felt envious. I wonder if she even owns her own place. It has to be difficult to get other people into houses that you may not be able to afford.

Her thoughts turned to her own son.

My Lucas had some money from his grandparents. He will most likely have children and pass on some of the wealth to them. But that's not the case with everyone, she reminded herself.

Viv glanced over to the passenger seat to look at her cell phone. She picked it up, hoping to see a message from Rex. She dipped it back in the seat. *Such a stubborn man.*

When it pinged, she quickly picked it back up, hoping he'd finally responded. But no. Mojave Mesa Community College left a voice message. She didn't bother to listen.

Aware of her fluctuating feelings about Rex's silence, Viv wondered if she needed to reach out again. *I could break my rule and give him a call. I've had to do that with my doula staff in the past.* The sound of her voice often broke down emotional resistance. *Once they hear my concern the ice is broken. Because it's hard to stay distant when someone really cares about you.*

She felt her stomach tighten. *One text,* she reminded herself. *I'm not chasing him,* she reasoned. But she stopped herself. *Rex has to step up and admit his own feelings. I'll wait him out.* "Boundaries," she said aloud. *I learned that the hard way.*

By the time she drove into her garage, she felt less conflicted. The electronic door hummed closed. One step into her kitchen and she glanced to the window sill. *I'm like Wally. I forgot to take my vitamins this morning.* Viv reached for the blue container and popped the lid. She tossed the tablets into her mouth thinking, *One of the best parts of living alone is that I never come back to someone else's mess.*

"Meow," Miss Kitty greeted her.

"You're the best," she mumbled, burying her face in Miss Kitty's fur.

After cuddling her cat and offering treats, she sat down at the dining table. Email from two new parents and one expectant mother needed attention. She opened the most urgent, thinking about Wally Walker.

I wish I had an answer to getting older. Other than dying, she admitted.

Her lower back twinged. She reached around to rub her hand over her muscles. *I'm getting older. No doubt about that. No sense in lamenting. All I can do is move forward one step at a time.*

As she rubbed, she continued to think about Wally. *It feels like he ran out of time. He never got to retire or downsize. He was stuck in the past. He'd relocated once. Maybe that was too traumatic and he didn't want to repeat the experience. Of course, he was younger then.*

Wally was past retirement age. Way past. I suppose it happens to more people than I realize. Not a very fitting end to a man who served as a police officer and professor for all those years. He was beloved by his students and friends. But now his grandson rushes in to claim his inherited wealth.

Her inbox flashed on the screen. Time to get to work.

30

REX REDONDO

Rex was ready to apologize. He couldn't wait to tell Viv. Maybe he'd take Kevin along. The dog was always good for a laugh. That would break the ice. *Put on your big boy pants and make this apology one she'll remember*, he told himself.

To his consternation, his progress on the short walk next door was delayed by his pants. Every step, he had to stop and adjust because his cargo shorts kept slipping. Keeping them in place was made even more difficult because of the bouquet of flowers he held in one hand. Plus his other hand was gripping Kevin's leash.

"Sutton's to blame for all of this," he grumbled.

I could be wearing my alligator belt if it weren't for her. He'd not been able to locate any of his belts that morning, let alone his favorite. *I bet she gave it away to the Goodwill. She never liked real skin wearables.* He felt the pants slip, settling precariously low on his hips.

"Take this," Rex ordered. Kevin obediently opened his mouth to carry his own leash. Rex yanked with one hand, only to have the pants return to the same place when he was done. "Gravity," he mumbled.

. . .

A car honked. The new homeowner association's president leaned out an open window. "Looking good there, Redondo." His eyes scanned Rex's shirt and shorts. He smirked. Before Rex could say thank you, he sped away.

"Whatever," Rex said, shifting the extravagant bouquet of hibiscus to the other arm. With a final tug to his shorts, he knocked on Viv's front door.

When she didn't answer right away, doubts settled over him. Normally a confident man, Rex had not considered the possibility that Viv wouldn't be delighted to see him. Up until now.

I should have responded to her text as soon as I got it. What if she's mad? She has no idea I'm showing up with flowers and an apology and another murder case to solve. Maybe she's doing something else...

This carefully conceived plan of wooing Viv with a smile, a gift, and a murder felt absurd. *What was I thinking.*

The door opened slowly. "Meow." Miss Kitty peeked at Kevin. Kevin dropped the leash.

"Bork." The dog danced on all four paws.

"Hello." Viv's voice, carefully measured, didn't give away her mood. "To what do I owe..." She stopped mid-sentence to look him up and down.

Her eyes settled on the bouquet. Then her gaze dropped to his feet. She burst into laughter. "Who dressed you this morning?"

He'd not expected her to laugh at him. Far from it. *I suppose this is infinitely better than being shooed away and rejected,* he decided in a moment. "What do you mean?" He yanked his cargo shorts up with the free hand. "I just forgot my belt."

"And your good sense." She waved her open palm in front of him. "Nothing goes together. The flip-flops, for one. Lime green! Holdover from a Jimmy Buffett concert. They clash with the shirt. And those shorts. Don't turn around," she warned. "When they fall to your ankles, I don't need to see your other business."

Rex's face heated up. He lifted his foot to step across the threshold but she stopped him. "Don't move. If you're not careful you'll be exposing all of your manly goods right here on my doorstep. How did you wear that outfit in public?"

"Well that's the thing," he explained. "Sutton's left me for no reason and I can't find my belt collection."

Viv gave him a doubtful stare.

"Once I'm inside I have lots to tell you." She didn't look convinced, so he kept talking.

"Wally Walker's death has been categorized as suspicious. Probably an overdose."

Now her eyebrows rose.

"And your cat." He pointed to Miss Kitty, who sat primly by Viv's foot. "She's been observed trespassing."

"Is that so." Viv looked up. When her glance returned, her eyes sparkled. "Come on inside. Hold on to your shorts. I'll take the bouquet."

She closed the door behind him. "But before you sit down..."

He knew what she was after. This time he didn't pout. "Okay, I'm a jerk. I'm sorry. And I want to make up." He added a genuine thousand-watt smile for good measure.

Viv nodded curtly. "Good. Have a seat. I'm going to put the flowers in water."

Kevin stormed past Rex, nearly knocking him over. He raced around the corner, making his way to the catio and Miss Kitty.

31

VIVIENNE ROSE

"I overreacted," he began as they sat at her kitchen table. He stroked Miss Kitty, who abandoned Kevin to sit in his lap. Viv braced herself. She knew he took pride in making a thorough apology. The first admission was the most difficult. After that Rex Redondo loved to spin the story, humbling himself to best effect.

This time she cut him off mid-sentence. "You know you've relied on Sutton for too long. You can't even dress yourself," Viv stated flatly.

"No excuse for sucker punching me," he grumbled.

"You have to see this from her point of view. She's not just your employee. She's also a colleague and friend. You two go way back. She must have seen you at your best and your worst. Why would she punch you now and not before? I'd ask myself why this situation was different."

Rex rubbed his chin. "Do I have to do this? Be all introspective about Sutton. Isn't that why I pay her, so that I can make demands and not have to be nice?"

Viv's eyebrows flew up. "Do you hear what you're saying?"

She felt disappointed. She'd hoped he'd be further along and willing to take some responsibility for disregarding Sutton's perspective.

Viv wanted to double down on him to make him see. Wag her finger in his face. A rapid knock from the front door prevented her from a further scolding. "Who could that be?"

Miss Kitty jumped from Rex's lap. Viv followed her cat to look through the peephole, then opened the door.

Brad May stood on her doorstep, holding his cell phone in one hand and a squirmy dog under his other arm. "Yip-yip." The round bundle of fur landed on all fours at her feet.

Miss Kitty hissed, lifting a paw to swat at the intruder's nose.

With one motion Brad lifted the dog in both arms. "Watch out. Tater Tot's a pure breed."

"You'd better come inside," Viv suggested.

Miss Kitty darted away and hid under the sofa.

"Tater Tot," Viv said. "He's not brown. Why the name?"

"He's a Frenchie and was named by the boss for his shape, not his color. Looks like a baked potato. Want to hold him?"

"Oh, no thanks." Viv shook her head. "Miss Kitty would never forgive me. But I know someone who will make friends. Another man who loves dogs." She pointed toward the kitchen.

"Yip-yip." Tater Tot jumped to the floor. With one quick leap he launched himself onto Rex's lap.

"Hey, little fella." Rex scratched between the dog's ears. "Do you smell my dog?" Then he turned a fierce look of distrust toward Brad. "How did you get here?"

"Okay, so my boss got notice from the Riverside police about our investigation." Brad pulled out a chair.

"Go on," Viv encouraged.

"The Lily Rock Constabulary has special access to official channels. Wally Walker's name popped up on their newsfeed. He didn't die of natural causes." Brad sounded triumphant, as if he'd announced a winning lottery ticket.

"We know," Rex said. "Cops suspect a deliberate overdose, maybe suicide."

"That's terrible." This was the first Viv had heard.

"I've been talking to Gloria the realtor, and she knew Wally really well. She never mentioned that he was depressed."

"This case is complicated," Brad said softly.

Rex grumbled. "Not to us. Viv and I are professionals. We've been investigating and have come up with more suspects than you or Janis Jets. She needs to mind her own business. So do you.

"Plus you're not even a cop. Just because you can nose your way into the database and get some answers, that doesn't mean you can do the hard work. The interviewing, for one. I've already talked to the principal, Dr. Morales. She's a bit dodgy. I suspect she might be a person of interest. I don't think she even liked Wally. Wanted to get rid of him. That woman is cold as ice, especially when it affects her bottom line."

"And I've just interviewed Gloria Ramirez," Viv added. "She revealed damaging information to me about Wally's grandson, Jax. Both Gloria and Jax have motives."

"That's new," Rex admitted.

"I'm not done," Brad insisted.

"That's enough, kid. Let the lady speak," Rex admonished.

32

REX REDONDO

By the time Viv finished telling about the conversation with Gloria, Rex felt himself swell with admiration. *She got good intel without my help.* Then he felt a niggle of relief. *She must be taking the investigation seriously. Plus we're not talking about my apology anymore. Nice work, Redondo. Once again you've refocused and survived.*

He hid a grin. Ready to compliment himself more, he stopped. *Hey, wait a minute. Maybe I have Brad May to thank for arriving unannounced. He made things easier and served a purpose.*

Nah. Viv and I have got this. No need to give the kid credit. Plus it's time for him to go home and mind his own business.

Unfortunately Brad still talked animatedly to Viv, who leaned closer with unwavering interest. *She's already brought him lemonade and cookies,* Rex grumbled to himself.

On a double-down inner rant, he sat back to appreciate his own mind at work.

He's too young to be interesting. I admit he has a certain charm. But I hate the way he makes her laugh. Plus those big worshipful eyes. Spare me.

At the first pause in the conversation, Rex moved things along. "Time to go," he announced, using his most authoritative tone.

Brad shrugged. "Have a nice day," he said, not looking over at Rex.

"You, not me," Rex clarified. "I'm sure you have things to do in Lily Rock. And take this overpriced boutique mutt with you." Tater Tot hung limply across Rex's lap.

"Not yet," Viv insisted. "I think Brad's onto something. You most likely didn't hear." She glared at Rex and then back to Brad. "Tell him what you told me, honey."

Rex flinched. *Honey? Really...*

Brad lifted Tater Tot from Rex's lap and hooked the leash to his collar. "I need to take him outside for a walk. Come on, buddy. Let's go."

As soon as the door closed, Rex turned to Viv. "What other information? Did I miss something?"

"He started to tell us about the toxicology report," she explained. "It would be helpful to know just what exactly killed Wally."

"I think that would be important," he admitted. "But after the kid spills the details, it's time for him and the lumpy dog to go home."

Viv looked skeptical. "Do you wonder how Brad got past the Desert Tortoise Estate's security guard?"

This is more like it. Time to consider pretty boy's motives. "Huh. That's a good question. Is he stalking you?" Rex asked. "Or maybe he's a possible person of interest in our murder?"

"I don't think so." Viv looked skeptical. "Maybe he yearns for my granny vibe. A comfortable old lady to bake cookies and offer the occasional coddling when his spirits require bucking up."

"Granny vibe..." He was surprised. Obviously Viv had no idea what she looked like to him. From his perspective she made every other woman her age seem dull. She was a hip businesswoman. Sexy as hell with her laughter and coastal grandma look. Plus the homemade cookies... A bonus.

Tater Tot scrambled around the corner. A perfectly executed flying leap landed him back in Rex's lap. He turned twice and slumped into a ball, his eyes closed. Despite himself, Rex liked the Frenchie. He scratched in front of his stubby tail.

"I was thinking," Brad began. "Maybe I can send you that report. I'd have to break a few rules, but it would save time and be more helpful to our investigation if we all have the information in writing."

Rex sighed. There he goes again. *Our investigation. Nobody invited you...*

"That would be helpful," Viv agreed. "But before you go, how did you get past the security guard? This is supposed to be an exclusive gated community."

"I'm a cop. I showed the guard my ID."

"Almost a cop," Rex corrected. "What ID?"

Brad shrugged. "It's not an actual badge. Just my constabulary keycard. But the guy didn't look that carefully."

The kid has his own slight-of-hand move.

Before he could express his distrust, Rex felt his fingertips burn. He looked away, waiting for an image. Janis Jets. She wore her navy blazer and her hair back, eyes crinkling with laughter.

The cylinder stopped rolling and the image vanished.

He knew instantly why Jets laughed. Because he was stuck with her assistant. *She foisted him on us!*

Brad glanced at his phone. "I've got the report right here. Wally had a lot of chemicals in his system, mostly prescription drugs. He was overweight. That was obvious when we saw the body. His BMI was thirty-three."

"What does that mean?" Viv asked.

"He qualifies as obese."

"He didn't look that fat," Rex insisted.

"It's a medical number, not what anyone thinks," Brad explained.

"So why is his weight important to us?" Viv wondered aloud.

"According to this"—Brad held up his phone—"toxicology found several substances in his blood. Weight loss drugs. Amphetamines. Sleeping pills." He slipped his phone into his pocket. "I'll send you the report later."

When he didn't move to leave, Rex could barely contain his impatience.

"Why don't you stay and have dinner with us?" Viv asked.

Damn. She just can't help herself.

"No thanks," he announced in a hurry. "No thanks. I have to get Tater Tot back to Janis or she'll be upset."

"I can go out to dinner," Viv replied.

Brad popped out his cell. "I know a great place up the hill. Why don't we drive together, it would take about an hour to get there. The Refuge has amazing food."

Rex instantly realized his mistake. He'd thrown them together without meaning to. Now Brad would have the pleasure of Viv's company while he ate alone.

33

VIVIENNE ROSE

Viv waited in the truck. When Brad stopped at the constabulary to drop off Tater Tot, she used the time to think about their conversation. The hour-long drive had given them more than ample opportunity to get to know each other better.

Brad managed to tell his entire life story, which wasn't that surprising since he was not quite thirty years old.

Viv had tuned out when he got to the part about being the Lily Rock weed dealer. She took a moment to look in the backseat at Tater Tot. Encased in a dog harness, he rested on the plush seat cover, fast asleep.

As Viv half listened to Brad, she watched the road. One treacherous curve after another had her catching her breath. Like most young men, he drove over the speed limit, causing her to reach for the security of the arm rest on the door.

"So you plan to drive up and down the hill for class once we start up again. That's a lot," she told him, once the road straightened.

"I like the drive," he admitted. "I feel like I'm getting away. All the curves and the views."

She sensed an unexpressed longing in those words. Maybe an important insight. "What are you getting away from?"

He gripped the wheel and stared at the road. Since he'd been quite talkative up until now, his hesitation spoke volumes.

"I've never lived away from Lily Rock," he explained. "It seems like my friends will always see me as Brad the bumbler and former weed screwup." He sighed. "Tell me about you. How did you meet Rex?"

"Rex and I met just over a year ago," she explained. "We're total opposites. But he wasn't easy to get rid of, despite my intentions. He pursued and we ended up being friends. Of course, we're also neighbors. That makes things a bit tricky."

"Are you guys, like, more than friends?" Brad's tone shifted to playful, a slight quirk at the corner of his mouth.

"Sort of," she said. *If that one time on the cruise counts.*

Viv stopped talking. Brad's question brought up some hurt feelings. Since the one-night stand Rex hadn't even asked her for a date. *Maybe he backed away because I didn't meet his expectations...*

The Tater Tot drop-off complete, Brad slid behind the driver's seat. "The boss was worried. But now she's reunited with her fur baby, so I'm free for dinner."

"Am I dressed well enough?" she asked.

"We're very casual on the hill." He nodded toward his distressed faded jeans and flannel shirt.

Viv took in the uneven hair that hung over one eye. *Almost a man but still a boy,* she thought.

Brad's truck bounced over uneven dirt. "The Refuge is at the end of this road. I hope you like Italian. I get a locals' discount, so dinner's on me." He looked over as if to see if she was impressed.

Twenty minutes later Viv selected the pumpkin ravioli while Brad ordered a Caesar salad and an individual pizza. They barely had time to chat because an stream of people stopped by their table to talk to Brad. He introduced her each time, obvious pride in his voice.

"You know everyone in town," she said.

"Nearly." Brad nodded. "Lily Rock residents all know each other. I'm almost considered an Old Rocker."

"But you're not old." She smiled.

"Old Rockers are unofficial town council people who have lived here forever. At least what seems like forever," he explained.

"I see." Viv watched his face for clues. "Is that okay with you—to be considered an Old Rocker?"

"I used to think so," he admitted. "But now I'm not so sure. I feel restless. But I'd miss everyone if I left town."

"Found family," Viv said. "The people you've grown to love and who love you. My son lives up north. It took him time to adjust. You can make new friends."

"I suppose I could find another Lily Rock..." He was interrupted by an older woman wearing a denim jumper, her long braid swinging across her shoulder. She stepped up to their table.

Hello, dear." She bent to kiss Brad's cheek, then offered a hand to Viv. "I'm Meadow McCloud, the Lily Rock librarian. I believe we met once before."

"We did meet. When your daughter was pregnant. I came up to do a doula consultation. How is she? I believe her name is Sage. And the baby is Star?"

Meadow beamed. "They are both thriving. What a joy to be a grandma."

Brad gestured to the waiter.

"You're paying?" The waiter sounded surprised.

"I have a job, you know. I can afford this." He took the bill and gulped.

"Ya sure?" the man asked. "I gave you the Lily Rock resident discount. You've never taken advantage before."

Brad took money out of his wallet and laid it on the table. "Your tip's included," he said.

The waiter didn't count his money. But his chuckle was audible as he walked away.

Meadow gave Viv a quick hug. "It's so good seeing you again. I hope you'll come back soon. If you need a place to stay, I have a guest room. You can find me at the library most days and you're always welcome."

"Such a nice woman," Viv remarked as she left.

"She's the best," Brad admitted. "And she makes a killer Christmas cinnamon roll. You can come up this year in December and see for yourself. Meadow used to invite everyone to her house in the old days. But now Sage has taken over. She's the hostess and there's always room for one more."

On the drive down the hill Brad was less talkative. Viv had more time to reflect. Especially on Wally Walker's unexpected shift from Palm Springs to Palm Desert. His timing felt peculiar—right when his career was beginning to take off.

Unlike Brad, Wally had not acquired a found family. He and his grandson didn't get along. Mia and Gloria helped him out. Viv wondered if they invited him to

Thanksgiving dinner. Or was he only considered a steady customer and a good tipper to Mia? And Gloria just saw dollar signs, more interested in selling his bungalow. Not exactly found family. More like a business target.

Brad rounded the next turn, tires emitting a squeal. She held onto the armrest as thoughts of her own son Lucas came to mind. He didn't live close by but he called once a week. He listened well and shared his life. They had an easy give-and-take. Despite the distance she knew their family connection was solid.

No grandchildren, but she didn't mind. Lucas was enough. His vibrant life as a professor brought him status and a good salary. He dated important women who often traveled to conferences with demanding jobs of their own. No wonder he wasn't interested in settling down.

Lucas didn't need her that way. She and Rex were a perfect match. He didn't have close family and they'd managed to become friends despite their differences.

34

———————

REX REDONDO

That evening Rex sat nursing his second IPA. Somehow the time had gotten away from him. The connection between Brad and Viv firmly established, he felt like a third wheel. Once he excused himself and walked home, he missed Sutton even more. Especially her greeting when he walked through the door.

Kevin bounded from outside, tail wagging. *That's something,* he thought. Yet even the dog's greeting wasn't enough to displace his loneliness. Kevin nudged his knee, a sure sign that he wanted dinner.

Rex filled his dish with kibble. Then he wondered if he was doing it right. *Sutton told me to make him sit before he eats. I suppose I can do that.* "Sit," he said in a firm voice.

Kevin cocked his head to the side. He didn't sit.

Even the dog doesn't take me seriously.

Don't tell him twice, Sutton's voice insisted.

Rex glared as Kevin finally lowered his back haunches to the floor.

"Good boy." Rex put Kevin's bowl in front of him.

The dog leapt to his feet.

Kevin finished in less than a minute. He sent Rex a look of longing that made his chest tighten. The dog's nose quivered. Then he leaned over for a sniff of his flip-flops and shorts.

Rex explained, "Another dog. That's right. I held him in my lap. His name is Tater Tot. He liked me best. Are you jealous?"

I know I am. Jealous. Viv's having dinner with the kid, and here I am talking to a dog like he's a person. He sighed, realizing he was this close to welcoming a bad mood.

If I keep thinking about being left out, I'll launch myself into another pity party.

He made a quick decision. No use sitting around doing nothing. *I'll treat myself to a thick steak at the Roadkill. People know me there. I can catch up with the casino gossip. Then when I get home I'll be ready for bed. No time to feel sorry for myself.*

In his bedroom he tossed the Hawaiian shirt and the loose shorts aside. Being reminded of his dependence on Sutton butted aside any resolve not to feel depressed. *I don't even know what to wear. How did it come to this...*

He sat in the back booth at the Roadkill, still wondering.

Tipping a bottle of IPA toward his mouth, he considered his predicament. *Our relationship in the Marines didn't start with me relying on her. I was the senior officer. We just hit it off, Sutton and me. It wasn't until later...*

After their last tour he'd offered her a job as his live-in personal assistant. Boundaries were clear from the start. This was not a couple relationship. He didn't even step into her bedroom for the first year. After that he always knocked.

When did that change? Rex took another sip of beer.

Bit by bit, he realized. *I let Sutton take over and I rationalized that I paid her a good salary and that was part of her job. The clothes are the tip of the iceberg. It felt natural to let her tell me what to wear. I'd been in the military for twenty years. She just took over after that. But look what's happened. I can't find a belt. It's that bad.*

He remembered the moment when she'd announced, "I can organize your performance wear and the entire closet. Just stay out of the way." Her words held a get-lost-mama-has-other-work-to-do tone. He'd easily complied.

She wasn't like a wife, he insisted to himself. *I made that clear.*

His mind interjected, always willing to make another excuse.

Don't forget, Sutton not only dressed me, she dressed Kevin. The dog had an extensive wardrobe of scarves and collars that coordinated with all the major holidays. He even had one with a menorah print for the Jewish high holy days. Sutton widely celebrated all faith traditions.

This intense scrutiny of his assistant—or was it friend, or was it colleague—made Rex's heart feel heavy. He wiped at his eyes. Finally the truth shoved aside his ego. *It was a lot easier to just take Sutton for granted.*

He put down the empty IPA bottle and rubbed at his forehead. His phone showed no evidence that Sutton had returned a call or a text. He dropped it with a thud on the table.

Rex ordered another beer and looked over the crowded room for a distraction. He caught sight of a familiar face. A guy sitting in a booth all by himself. *A waste of two good booths*, Rex thought. *We could be sitting together.* He narrowed his eyes. *Where have I seen him before...*

I know. That's the Mojave Mesa custodian who told me

to call 911. Rex stood, taking his fresh IPA with him. "Mind if I join you?" he asked.

The man had been staring at his martini glass. His face registered recognition. "I remember you now. You're the adult student. The one who was early for class. With the sexy grandma. I saw you again in Dr. Morales's office. Sure, sit down." He pointed across the table just as Rex slid into the booth.

Rex locked eyes with the man to read his body language and expression. *Depressed. Trapped. Uncertain.* "I'm Rex Redondo. Tell me your name again."

"Eddie Vargas. Wait a minute. You work at the casino. Some kind of mentalist."

"I used to," Rex corrected. This was the first time he'd referred to his old job in the past tense. "But I haven't contracted a gig for a few months. My doctor suggested I take some time off." The truth was he'd had a minor incident on the cruise with Viv, but he knew Viv would call it a breakdown. So would his VA doctor who assigned him a month-long psychological reboot.

When the therapist finally released him it was under one certain condition.

"Don't return to work right away. Deal with the down time. Then we'll talk."

Though Eddie nodded politely, Rex knew he wasn't that interested. He'd overexplained to a complete stranger. He felt tempted to order a third IPA. Right then Viv's disappointed face popped into his mind. She didn't care that he had a beer or two in the evening. But she'd never advise that he use alcohol to avoid his feelings or before he drove home.

"Never mind that whole story," Rex said. "Let's just say I'm taking a break. How about you. Still on the job?"

"You could say that. I've worked at Mojave Mesa for

years, since I was in my twenties. I'm now the maintenance supervisor, so the pay is good, plus I get benefits. But I don't want to spend the rest of my life cleaning up after a bunch of students." He glanced at Rex. "No offense."

"None taken." Rex actually enjoyed being called a student. "You get along okay with the younger kids?"

"I guess I'm pretty well liked." Eddie looked away.

"And Walker, the dead guy. You knew him..."

"I knew Wally really well. We were drinking buddies," Eddie admitted. "He'd use me as a sounding board, mostly before class. A lot of the instructors did that.

"I felt sorry for him. He was like a lot of old guys—he talked about his health. How he felt terrible being type 1 diabetic and overweight. His doctor prescribed a miracle drug. They're called semaglutides. Really pricy. But his insurance picked it up. Did you know he recently lost over a hundred pounds?"

"I only saw him in person that once. He wasn't skinny. But not what I'd call obese," Rex admitted.

"He was an inspiration for me." Eddie glanced past the table edge and patted his gut. "We'd talk about exercise and diet every morning. He planned on teaching for a lot longer."

Rex remembered the conversation with Seraphina Morales. He wondered if she knew Wally's plan. Plus Wally didn't sound like a candidate to take his own life. A sharp twinge came to his temple.

More images, he realized. *Not exactly convenient.*

While Eddie ordered another martini, he focused. Nothing visual. Just the sound of pounding, like a fist on glass. He looked back just as the server slid another cocktail napkin toward Eddie.

"Another IPA?" he asked.

"I'm good for now," Rex responded, then asked Eddie another question. "Did they repair the door to the classroom? I'm hoping our class will be resumed next week."

"It's boarded up." Eddie removed the toothpick from his drink and slipped the olive into his mouth. "Wally must have locked the door from the inside. Bad idea. I warned him before. But he was stubborn."

Eddie guzzled his drink, draining the last bit of gin from his glass. He reached for his check. "Nice seeing you again."

He left without a backward glance.

Rex no longer felt lonely. All the talk about Wally Walker had distracted him from complaining about Sutton. He'd not thought about Viv and Brad either. Plus he'd managed to push away another moody episode.

He was left with the nagging sense he missed something important in the conversation. *Wally Walker recently lost a lot of weight. That must have made him happy. What was the other thing...*

Wally locked the classroom door from the inside, making it impossible for the first responders to get to him in time. Ping! That was relevant.

When Dr. Morales told Wally he should retire, he changed his mind. Life didn't seem worth living if he was forced to retire, Rex reasoned. *I can understand disappointment, losing his job because of his age.*

Rex paid his bill and made his way to the parking lot. On the drive home he tried to recall more details of the conversation. *Wally and Eddie were pals. They both worked at Mojave Mesa for years. They were friendly enough to get drinks after work.*

Did Wally's weight loss mean he stopped drinking? Or

did he return to drinking with Eddie because he was depressed? It feels like alcohol might have been a contributing factor in Walker's demise.

35

____

VIVIENNE ROSE

Vivienne Rose

By the time Brad turned the last curve, Viv had an idea. "We didn't get a dessert after dinner. Let me treat you to the best pie bar in town. They have all varieties."

"French apple," he said. "My favorite. Not with the double crust but with the brown sugar and crumbles on the top. That's a great idea. Are they still open?"

"It's early yet. Make a right turn over there. The place is called Just Desserts. They're open until 2 a.m. I guess pie lovers make good late-night customers."

As they approached the entrance, the fairy lights in the outdoor patio twinkled a welcome. "The pie bar is inside." Viv led the way.

Viv recognized Mia Porter from the long curly auburn hair. Her plan began to unfold. *I'm going to introduce Brad to Mia. I think they'll get along. Close in age and both a little lost. I just have a good feeling about this.*

Her instincts were immediately justified. When Mia

turned around, her eyes lit up at the sight of Brad. He grinned sheepishly, his chin dipped in embarrassment. "Hello there," she said. "Welcome to my pie bar. Have a seat." She glanced at Viv. "Oh, it's you, Ms. Rose. Hello again." Her cheeks turned pink. "Is this...your son?"

Brad could have been her grandson. "This is Brad May," Viv explained. "Not my son, but a friend." She patted the seat next to her. "He's a classmate actually, at Mojave Mesa. He's been telling me that he loves pie."

"French apple," Brad blurted.

"We make the best French apple," Mia assured him. "May I cut you a slice?" She blinked her dark lashes, her green eyes shining.

Viv could feel their energy and attraction to each other. She intervened to turn down the heat. "You're working a long shift this evening."

"I took the late shift today," Mia said, keeping her eyes on Brad.

I used to be like that, Viv thought. *More open and flirty. That spark is gone. Replaced by the steady energy of experience.*

Brad and Mia hit it off. They didn't even notice her step away from the bar as she headed toward the register. She paid the bill with cash. Without a glance backward, she made her way to the exit.

I'll text him later, she thought. *He won't even notice that I'm gone.*

TEXT Still up? My date stranded me. Any chance of a ride home? I'm at Just Desserts.

Within seconds she received a thumbs-up emoji. Ten minutes later an SUV pulled around the corner. Rex leaned over to open the passenger door. "How was dinner?" Rex asked, a huge smile on his face.

"A long drive," she said, hopping in beside him. "My companion ditched me for another woman. Thanks for picking me up."

"What happened?" He pulled away from the curb.

"I hooked him up with our favorite pie bar waitress and now they're planning a future that doesn't include me."

"A future?" He sounded surprised.

"Oh, they're going to get together," she confidently added. "I know that much."

"So I'm the mentalist and you're what, a matchmaker?" He sounded happy. At least more than he did earlier.

"Not always," she admitted. "But this instinct served an ulterior motive. I'll call Brad in the morning. He'll be sure to spill everything he knows about Mia. We're confidants now."

"So wait a minute." Rex's voice held a note of caution. "Do you actually think Mia's a suspect?"

"I do," Viv admitted. "Brad will be oblivious to that because he isn't thinking with, you know, his brain. At least not right now. But he'll pump her to learn her life story. Then there will be pillow talk. That's what they called it in my day. He'll share all the details because he can't help himself. And then I'll figure out if Mia is a person of interest."

"Don't forget, we're partners. You need to keep me informed." Rex sounded wary. "We're neighbors in crime. Now that Sutton's gone, I hope we can rely on each other more."

Out with one partner, in with the new, Viv thought. *Am I to be his Sutton substitute?*

She remembered Brad and Mia at the pie bar. How

sparks flew as soon as they caught sight of each other. The need for later-in-life companionship felt quite different. No longer controlled by the energy of youth.

Stop picking at every word. Take what he said as an invitation. He wants to see more of you...

She reached across the console to rest her hand on his knee. He placed his hand on top of hers.

"Your place or mine..." She squeezed her fingers more deeply into his firm thigh. All her sadness disappeared when she heard a sigh that meant yes.

The following morning Viv scooped freshly ground coffee into the carafe basket. "How did you sleep?" Rex asked in a low voice. He wrapped his arms around her waist.

"Quite well. How about you?" She turned to offer a quick kiss. "You brushed your teeth."

"I used my finger." He waved it in the air. "You seem like the kind of woman who appreciates good dental health."

Viv chuckled. "I'm a flossing and brushing connoisseur, or at least my son thinks so." Dark roast sputtered the last drip into the coffee pot. She pointed. "Grab two mugs and I'll meet you at the table. I've already spoken to Brad and I have news about Mia."

"So he got lucky last night, just like me." Rex raised an eyebrow.

She responded with a pert tone. "I didn't get the intimate details about all of that. I was more interested in what he learned about our favorite pie waitress."

Rex groaned. "I was hoping for more."

"The less talk about sex the better." Viv grinned. "Not to be encouraged."

"Is that so..." Rex placed the mugs on the table. "But

before we talk about Brad, I just want to say thanks. I pushed off a bad mood all day yesterday. You fixed all of that!"

They sat at the table with full mugs and a basket of warm muffins between them.

"Apparently, Mia—" Viv began.

"Hold on to that thought!" Rex jumped to his feet. "I forgot about Kevin. I didn't let him out last night or this morning. Be right back."

He left his napkin and mug on the table.

A few minutes later Rex returned, his smile sheepish. "I forgot." He stared down at his bare feet, over Viv's pink bathrobe. "I'm not dressed."

She laughed so hard she spit coffee. "I was wondering if you'd notice."

"I'll get dressed and then check on Kevin," Rex called from the hallway.

She blotted spilled coffee from the table, still chuckling.

"I'll text you after I clean up the mess," he shouted a minute later.

She detected panic in his voice, which only made her laugh more. It wasn't until later that she realized she'd been unable to share Brad's report.

36

REX REDONDO

Rex unlocked his front door. When Kevin wasn't there with his tail-wagging hello, he suspected the dog was hiding, due to a guilty conscience. He sniffed. No wafting of dog poop met his nostrils.

Did Kevin leave me a gift... One glance revealed an open dog door.

A conversation with Sutton came to mind. They'd just gotten the puppy when she warned him, "We have to lock Kevin's dog door at night to keep out the snakes."

He remembered instantly questioning his decision to live in the desert.

"What about daytime?" he'd asked.

"Not as big of a threat." She'd dismissed his fears without any more explanation.

Sutton's eyes had gleamed. She seemed to enjoy upsetting him. "Don't forget there are coyotes. One could easily make his way indoors and attack Kevin. Oh, and the scorpions. They've been known to set up residence, lay some eggs, and pretty soon you have an entire colony."

Rex felt his skin crawl. He'd deflected by changing the subject, picking on her choice of words.

"Isn't a family of scorpions called a nest?" he asked.

"Colony, nest—who cares? Do you want a nest of scorpions taking up residence under a sofa cushion?"

Rex shuddered. He had a deep aversion to crawly things. They made him feel skittish. The tiniest of spiders, let alone a snake, sent him running. As for coyotes, the thought of Kevin being attacked made his stomach drop.

He'd finally relented. "Okay, you win. I don't want rattlesnakes creeping in at night."

Now that he realized the door had been left unattended, he looked around, hair raising on his neck. *Where would a rattler or a spider hide?* He felt quite certain a coyote wasn't inside. Otherwise he'd have been met at the door with quite a different greeting.

He stopped to listen. No hiss. He shuddered. On his knees, he looked underneath the sofa. Just a few Kevin hairballs. Oh, and a corkscrew from a recent bottle of Prosecco. He heaved himself to his feet.

What about the pillows? He picked up one cushion, rising it tentatively between two fingers. He listened again. No hiss, no rattle. He made a thorough search under each cushion before he realized the obvious. If a coyote had snuck in, it could have attacked Kevin and dragged him back to the den.

Rex looked over the remainder of the living room for signs of a struggle. The oversized leather chair. The drawer in the coffee table. Behind the floor lamp and under the potted palm. All potential strike zones.

He pulled on his ear, feeling frightened and exasperated.

"Damn Sutton," he mumbled under his breath. "There's

too much to remember about dog doors and cushions. All the details I never had to bother with before."

All concerns about Kevin had been replaced by the now familiar inner voice of trying to make his feelings seem reasonable. It turned out that being abandoned by a personal assistant was time-consuming.

He caught himself mid-rant and took a deep breath. Rex heard the words of wisdom from his therapist. "When your mind goes on overdrive, think of something more pleasant."

About last night, for instance. How Viv held his hand in bed after making love. That felt so comfortable and complete. Her naked body under the warm comforter...

If he had to assess last night's performance, he'd call it an eight. A flush of embarrassment crept up his neck. *Don't be so modest. You know last night was definitely a nine.*

As a man of the world who dated lots of young women, he liked to think he always brought his A game. Once Viv had captivated him with her womanly wiles, he knew she'd be a challenge. Older and wiser than his usual conquests, he knew she'd made him work harder.

Even naked she was slightly aloof, holding her finger over his lips when he wanted to ask for directions.

"Shush," she'd said. "Just feel. Stop analyzing."

Once he got quiet, he had risen to the occasion. *A good time was had by all,* he thought with a smirk. With thoughts about last night, he'd done a good job of shifting his focus. Fears about Kevin's abduction dismissed.

Rex slid open the glass door to the backyard. "Kev-in," he shouted.

Still no sign of the Bernedoodle.

Maybe I should call Viv. She can come over and help me out. She'll know what to do. Plus she's a good listener. I'll get to rant a bit about how Sutton left me defenseless and that I'd been nearly attacked by a vicious snake or a huge coyote.

I admit not precisely the truth. But to be bathed in her concern would be worth the telling.

A sharp jab to his right temple drew his palm to his forehead. He recognized the warning. Images on the way. He closed his eyes.

Finally the cylinder stopped spinning. Two images this time. The first of Kevin asleep on his bed. The second an orange pillow. Rex opened his eyes. *I'll check my room.*

He found the dog curled up in the middle of his bed. Next to Kevin was the orange pillow. *Lazy mutt...*

But then the orange pillow moved. Rex flinched. All his fears returned. He resisted the urge to flee, just as a striped furry snake-like tail twitched on the bed. Only then did he see the orange pillow had fur.

Miss Kitty had curled herself against the dog's side. She waved her tail in the air in greeting.

"Get down," Rex insisted.

Kevin's tail flopped against the comforter.

Miss Kitty batted a paw, seeing an opportunity to play.

It was clear to Rex, neither one had any intention of moving.

Annoyance gave way to instant affection. *Look at those two. Just like Viv and me.* He reached into a pocket to lift his phone and took a quick photo.

TEXT Miss Kitty is at my house.

Now he had a plan. *I'll get showered and dressed. Then I'll make a pot of coffee. Maybe Viv can come over and rescue her feline. We can chat. I'll subtly suggest that a blueberry muffin would be good for tomorrow's breakfast. She'll make that happen. Women are good at that sort of thing.*

Who needs Sutton.

37

VIVIENNE ROSE

Viv stood under the warm shower stream and closed her eyes. She inhaled to appreciate the smell of hibiscus-scented soap. Taking the initiative and Rex's immediate response had done wonders for her self-esteem.

Toes curled into the bath mat, she ran her fingers through her freshly shampooed hair. *I still have, what would you call it... Allure. With the one man who matters.*

She hummed under her breath as she perused her wardrobe choices. When Rex left in a hurry, she felt a bit of relief. This gave her plenty of time to appreciate the morning ritual.

That soft shell-pink sweater and my straight-leg jeans. White sneakers. Holding the sweater in her hands, she pressed it to her cheek. Viv had learned one thing from aging. She might not wear the variety of clothes she did when she was younger, but she appreciated every carefully curated item in her wardrobe more than she ever had.

As she finished applying a layer of body cream, she thought about the investigation. Wally Walker had a number of medical concerns. He'd passed away in his mid-seventies under suspicious circumstances. Sometimes people combined prescriptions and poor lifestyle choices. Maybe Wally didn't realize the ill effects.

What had piqued her interest the most was Rex's comment last night. After they'd made love they lay on their backs holding hands, snuggled underneath the covers. He mentioned that he'd run into the Mojave Mesa custodian at the Roadkill.

Eddie Vargas told him that Wally had been terribly concerned about his increasing A1C levels. His numbers tested higher, paving the way for more potential health risks. Plus the body mass index, the BMI, clocked Wally as obese.

The doctor prescribed semaglutide injections to bring down the numbers. Since Wally was diabetic he was used to injecting himself. He didn't feel that the new medication would be a challenge.

"Insurance covered the cost. Wally was really proud of that," Rex reported. "At least that's what Eddie told me."

Then he'd turned to nuzzle her neck. "But all that stuff is boring. What about us... How did things go for you?" He sounded hopeful. But Viv felt herself bristle. She wasn't one to feed a man's ego with a breakdown of his abilities in bed.

"None of your business," she responded tartly. "If you think you require an evaluation then you weren't paying attention. I'm not a scorekeeper."

Rex turned his head to stare. Shock written on his face. He leaned in on an elbow. "No female has ever passed up the opportunity to critique my lovemaking before. What will I do with you?"

To give him credit, he sounded genuinely puzzled.

"Keep nuzzling my neck if you'd like." She snuggled into his side.

Viv slipped her arms into her robe and cinched the waist. In a hurry to research more about semaglutides, she made her way to her computer. The internet search confirmed much of what she already knew. But she wasn't satisfied.

After reading several articles sponsored by pharmaceutical companies, she watched a video. A man in a white coat with a stethoscope explained. She read a brief bio in the comments to assure herself he wasn't an actor but a certified physician.

One thing remained unclear. According to all the authorities, semaglutides were recommended for those with type 2 diabetes. Wally Walker had type 1. Plus every advertisement insisted that injections weren't enough. That change in diet and exercise were also recommended. She paused the video to think.

Viv knew from past experience that people wanting to lose weight often found support groups. She didn't know a lot about Overeaters Anonymous other than they were everywhere in Palm Desert. She thought one reason for their popularity wasn't just about weight loss support, but that people got bored during the desert hot months. They liked to share their stories.

She found an OA group right at the Desert Tortoise Estate clubhouse. If she hurried she could make a meeting. *I know I can gather firsthand information from people in the group. Since semaglutides are so popular, surely someone will be able to answer my questions.*

As she dressed, she ran a backstory over in her mind. What would Sutton do...

Her pink sweater fell in folds over her body. *This will convince people that I'm trying to hide my body. That I'm on the disordered eating spectrum at least.*

Over the years many of her mothers discussed their postpartum diets and exercise with Viv. The pros and cons of nursing and taking off weight often led to confessions about extreme dieting. A few women actually gained more weight postpartum than they did during pregnancy, leading to any number of distressing outcries.

Though Viv didn't have any particular issue with her weight, she realized she was one of the few. So when the topic came up more often now, she did her own research. Details about binging and purging, obsessive exercise, calories in and calories out gave her the chance to sound informed when she advised her clients.

All of that information and all of the conversations would help her backstory.

She practiced what she'd say to the other group participants in her head, as she fluffed her damp hair with her fingers and then applied light makeup. First a thin layer of sunblock and then her usual moisturizer and light beige foundation. A swipe of mauve lipstick and some eyebrow maintenance followed.

Only one more thing to do, Viv thought. She walked down the hall toward Miss Kitty's catio. "Good morning," she called out. When the cat's customary meow of welcome didn't come, she peeked around the privacy screen. The cat box looked as clean as when she'd last scooped the afternoon before.

"Where are you Miss Kitty—time for breakfast." No cat. Glancing toward the screened doorway, she realized what happened. The mesh at the bottom right-hand corner had been pawed aside, revealing a gap big enough for the cat to slip through. Viv called louder. "Miss Kitty!"

This wasn't the first time her feline decided to take a walkabout. Feeling ignored or bored, she had in the past scratched at the screen. *Who could blame her*, Viv thought. Indoor cats, no matter how luxurious their accommodation, instinctively knew that the outdoors held more adventure. More dangerous but certainly less boring.

Outside, Viv walked around the pool to inspect the shed. Then she glanced toward the fence that separated her yard from Rex's. She called again. When no cat appeared, she walked back into the house.

It's time for the OA meeting. I'd better hurry. She poured kibble in the cat's dish adding a scoop of wet food. Setting it outside, she hoped Miss Kitty would realize she'd been missed.

38

REX REDONDO

Rex lifted his face to the stream of water. Lowering his head, he whistled "Luck Be a Lady Tonight." He turned off the shower and stepped onto the bath mat, bursting into song. He warbled, holding a pretend microphone in his hand.

He wrapped a towel around his middle. *Who needs Sutton*, he told himself. Energized by taking on the new tasks of caring for himself, he actually felt proud.

I'm going to pick out my own clothes. Making his way to the closet, he flung open the doors to examine the contents.

Unfortunately opening and closing each drawer did not reveal his belt collection. He slammed the last drawer shut a with a thump, his impatience showing. *This is a minor setback, Rex old boy,* he assured himself. *Don't forget it's only been two days since you wore a belt.* He turned abruptly. *I know. I left it on my pants when I dumped them in the hamper.*

Voila! He yanked the black leather belt from his slacks, feeling quite proud. *Mission accomplished. I only wear one belt at a time,* he concluded.

Pulling on tan shorts and a blue silk shirt with a collar, he stood in front of the mirror. *You are ruggedly handsome. Just like that TV guy,* he told himself. This mantra was a part of his morning ritual, to help him take on the day. He admired the TV actor who made the line famous, though he couldn't quite remember his name.

He closed the closet door. A quick glance toward the overflowing hamper made him wonder. *Who's going to do my laundry? I could bring my dirty clothes over to Viv's. She can pop in a load this evening while we have cocktails by the pool.* He turned back around to look at himself in the mirror one more time.

Yep. Life is good. Hah, hah on Sutton Drew. I have this covered.

Minutes later Rex rinsed the coffee pot. He'd forgotten to empty it from the day before. *Won't do that again.* He scrubbed at the dark roast residue with a worn sponge. *I'm a quick learner,* he assured himself.

He filled the pot with filtered water as a lump rose in his throat. Whenever he stopped yelling at Sutton in his thoughts, feelings would arise, making him very uncomfortable. *Old habits,* he muttered to himself. *Never mind. I want toast. Where's the bread...*

A drawer search revealed half a loaf of sourdough. He carefully inspected the bread for any signs of mold. Normally he wouldn't look but now that he was on his own...

See? I can make breakfast. I've got this. I don't have to eat at a diner every morning like some old guys.

What about the butter? A frantic search in the refrigerator revealed two IPAs and the familiar covered butter dish. Smudges lined the glass where butter used to be. *So I'll have jam instead.*

He found an old jar of strawberry jam. With a sigh he slammed the refrigerator shut. *I know. I might be able to convince Viv to make my breakfast. Problem solved.*

Once I explain how I feel lonely she'll be making me eggs and picking up baked goods just like Sutton. Then I only have two more meals per day to figure out.

He felt a surge of resentment. *I don't deserve to have my lifestyle turned upside down like this. Pretty soon I'll be going to the market like some old codger.*

Rex spread the red goo on his slightly burned piece of toast. His mind drifted to what he now called the unjustified Sutton attack. He swallowed a bite and grimaced at the bitter taste of mold. He dropped the toast.

Kevin arrived right on time for his morning meal.

"Now you're hungry too. This isn't what I signed up for," Rex groaned. "I'm a mentalist, Kevin, not a..." He paused. "Domestic survivalist!"

He nearly teared up, he felt so unsettled. Feeling hungry and in need of another cup of coffee, he explained to the dog how hard his life had become. "I had to dress myself. Better than yesterday, but look. You chewed the hem." He made note of the puppy teeth tears and sighed.

Kevin barked softly and wagged his tail.

Rex wanted to yell, "But you don't understand," but he didn't. Instead he said, "Traitor," and stood up.

On his way to find kibble he knew he was doomed. *I'll be that retired guy. The one who goes to the market just to keep busy. Who checks each peach to see if it's ripe. And who stands in the middle of aisle trying to remember why he went shopping in the first place.*

Then once I've left the grocery store, the clerk will be saying to his buddies, "That's Rex Redondo. He used to be a mentalist." Used to be. He might as well call me a has-been. That's the worst.

His cell phone buzz. *Maybe that's Viv. I bet she's inviting me for breakfast. I could sure use a scrambled egg and a fresh bagel right now.*

Two texts appeared. He read the one from Viv first.

TEXT Is Miss Kitty still there?

He double-clicked her a thumbs-up. Tempted to invite himself over and bring the cat along, he stopped to read the other text. It came from the Palm Desert police.

TEXT Report to the precinct at your earliest convenience.

This came as no surprise. He'd been expecting to get called back once the paperwork from his arrest made its way through the system. He felt convinced that Jackson Walker would probably press charges and the cops most likely wanted to interview him again.

I'll have to call my attorney, he thought. *What was I thinking lifting that piece of jewelry. I bet it's not worth a dime.* He texted the precinct back.

Will be in today.

By the time he finished tidying up, he'd forgotten about Viv making him breakfast. Kevin stood next to the pantry. "Bork." He wagged his tail.

"Meow." Miss Kitty wove herself around his legs, tail waving in the air. When he didn't acknowledge her presence, she leapt on the table and began to lick jam off the knife.

"Get down. You aren't allowed up there." Rex brushed her aside with his forearm. The cat landed gracefully on her feet.

"I'll feed you," he told Kevin. "Maybe I can find a can of tuna somewhere for your friend."

"Bork," Kevin agreed.

Miss Kitty twisted to lick her tail.

39

VIVIENNE ROSE

It had been a few months since Viv visited the Desert Tortoise Estates clubhouse. Attending HOA meetings had become less desirable, basically due to the dead body they found the first time. Once they helped solve that case, the HOA board all quit. Months of upheaval followed.

Since her fees paid for the upkeep, she thought it her homeowner responsibility to stand outside and take in the condition of the building and landscaping. Adobe-style walls and front courtyard looked tidy. The stark style echoed a common desert architectural design, which was streamlined for efficiency. Even the double-sided glass doors had been wiped free of handprints.

Viv followed two women inside the building. One door in the hallway stood open. The smell of coffee and the murmur of voices confirmed her suspicion. *This has to be the meeting.*

One step into the room, she immediately felt self-conscious. Viv knew she'd invaded a private gathering of people who genuinely struggled with addictions. But what choice did she have?

Personal stories would provide information that might help her solve Wally Walker's death.

She smiled at a woman standing near the coffee pot. Then she took her seat in the last row. Hands folded in her lap, she reminded herself, *No judging. Bodies come in all sizes and types. Just because you've had it easy is no reason to feel superior.*

She'd read that disordered eating did not mean a lack of discipline. The condition was most likely a result of brain chemicals along with subconscious emotional issues.

Four people sat toward the front, in chairs facing the podium. The woman in charge of coffee stepped forward. She wore leggings and an oversized black tunic, her luxurious dark hair swept back in a ponytail. She was what Viv's mother would have called big-boned.

"We have a visitor today," she announced in a calm welcoming voice.

A rush of blood to her face and a shot of adrenaline propelled Viv to her feet. She willed herself to stay calm. "Hello." Before she could blurt out her name she sat back down.

The woman in charge didn't bat an eye. "I'm Abbey and I lead this meeting. Don't worry. Most of us are nervous at first." The warm words did nothing to dispel Viv's discomfort. If anyone were to ask, lying always made her feel uneasy.

But you have to do this, she told herself. *If I want to get to the truth, then I may need to prevaricate.* She liked that word more than "lie."

Be Rex. Tell everyone what they want to hear.

Viv smiled to cover her nerves and stood again. "My name is Viv. This is my first time—I am nervous." She held up her hands. "Sweaty palms. Living proof."

The group chuckled as she sat back down.

The meeting officially began with a reading of the Twelve Steps. Then a younger woman dressed in tight-fitting athletic leggings and an equally snug tank top stood to speak. She seemed especially frail, her legs barely strong enough to hold up her body. When she finished telling her story, people clapped.

Then another participant shared, her words seasoned with anecdotes about food, body image, and recovery. Once everyone else had spoken, Viv knew it was her turn. She fidgeted nervously.

"Would anyone else like to share?" Abbey looked directly at her.

"Not today," Viv mumbled.

Abbey gave a curt nod. "When you're ready." She lowered her eyes to recite the familiar words of the Serenity Prayer. People joined in. Viv closed her eyes in solidarity.

"Accept the things I cannot change" stuck in her mind. Somehow those words held more meaning at this time in her life. *I'm aging,* she acknowledged. *But that doesn't mean I can't still appreciate every moment of my remaining years.*

Once the meeting concluded, Viv followed the same two women toward the back of the room. A table had been set with a large silver coffee pot and a plate of fruit. Abbey approached with a Styrofoam cup in her hand. "Would you like cream or sugar or a sugar substitute?"

Viv took the cup. "Thank you so much. I drink it black." Then she added with a smile, "I'm feeling less nervous." That was actually the truth.

"Nice to meet you." Abbey nodded.

"I've never been to an OA meeting before. I'm here because I want to be more mindful, especially with food." Her explanation brought a smile to Abbey's lips.

"That's a core belief of this meeting," Abbey said. "No matter who you are or your body size, being mindful of food is important for good health. You've come to the right place, Viv." The intentional use of her name made her feel more at home.

40

REX REDONDO

A uniformed officer greeted Rex. "What can I do for you?" she asked.

He noted her name badge. "My name is Rex Redondo. I believe I'm expected."

She checked her computer. "I'll let Lieutenant James know you're here. Why don't you have a seat while you wait."

Rex sat on the opposite side of the room. He glanced apprehensively toward the door that led to the offices and jail cells. His stomach queasy. *Metal and bleach. Not a good combination.*

Though his first instinct was to contact his attorney, he immediately thought better of the idea. He decided to handle the conversation on his own. To make him look less guilty.

Picking up that pocket watch was only what a good private investigator would do, he rationalized. No use labeling his act as stealing. *Why would I need a lawyer to say what I tell the cop myself?*

Just thinking of himself in this new light improved his

spirits. *I'm not retired; I'm going back to school. But that's just a formality.* He could barely repress his desire to whistle, he felt that good.

"Lieutenant James will see you now." A young uniformed officer stood by the door. Rex closed his lips, a tingle running up his spine. His short-lived sense of confidence dismissed as he stood.

You're not being arrested, he assured himself. *In fact, just the opposite. See that cop as your personal escort into the inner sanctum.* Before he walked past the threshold he gave a quick glance toward the two other people sitting in chairs. *I got ahead of these other folks who've been waiting longer. Because I'm a pro, that's why.*

In lieu of his Humphrey Bogart fedora, he tipped his head at the officer in a form of greeting.

"Right over there," the cop grumbled. "The lieutenant's waiting."

He took his time, adjusting his self-talk with each step. *If I didn't know better, I'd mistake myself for Cary Grant in* North by Northwest. *He was so debonaire.*

Now that was a film where Hitchcock showed his true genius. Rex raised his hand to knock on Lieutenant Darius James's office door.

"Come in," came a deep voiced reply.

Rex stepped inside. A quick glance displayed an unusual piece of furniture, something he'd not expected. James seemed like an ordinary cop. But the desk showed him as someone slightly different than the rest.

Made from mahogany, polished and worn, a true antique. I might have underestimated this guy, Rex acknowledged.

"Everyone asks about my desk," Lieutenant James said by means of introduction.

Rex realized then what he'd missed at first. When James showed up at the scene of the crime, he'd assumed he was just a regular beat cop. Maybe one step up from security guard. But now he could see that James was the Palm Desert Police Department detective.

"My grandparents gave me this desk," James continued, "before they moved to assisted living. A real beauty. Made out of pure mahogany. Check out the inlay. And the leather." He ran his finger over the edge. "Smells great, right?" He looked up at Rex. "I love that smell. The real thing, not vegan."

Rex felt as if James were trying to distract him. Talking about furniture instead of why he'd been summoned. He adjusted his face to look interested. "Your grandparents, you say?"

"They had to get rid of a lot of their furniture in the move. Downsized. You must know, being close to the same age."

Rex felt a rise of inner irritation.

"I've heard that downsizing has its difficulties," he agreed. "Fortunately I'm not ready for any of that."

James scowled. "I'm a huge collector of Palm Springs historic memorabilia. But I also have childhood memories. When I visited my grandparents, I'd sit behind this desk. Pretend to be an important executive.

"Always dreamed I'd be a bank manager. But then..." He sighed. "I became a cop."

Rex nodded. He was no longer interested in James, his desk, or his grandparents.

"Why don't you have a seat, Mr. Redondo. We have some details to work out about your recent arrest."

Finally. Rex sighed. Once he was seated, his discomfort

return. *I wish he'd stop staring at me. It's not like I murdered someone or robbed a bank.*

The officer's brown eyes hardened. He reached into a drawer and then dropped a sealed plastic bag on his desk. "This is the evidence we gathered when we found the body of Wallace Walker. I saw you at the scene, remember?"

Rex took a quick inventory of the contents. A cell phone. An empty day-of-the-week plastic pill container. Some coins and a wallet. Underneath the rest was the pocket watch.

Lieutenant James followed his gaze. "Yeah, that's the same pocket watch you stole from Wallace Walker's desk. According to his grandson, it was a prized possession. Wally took it everywhere."

When Rex made no comment, he continued. "A family heirloom. Jackson Walker feels the same about that pocket watch as I do about this desk. You probably don't understand, but tradition means a lot to some people."

Rex knew the lieutenant was doing his best to shame him into talking more about why he did what he did. But he resisted and kept silent.

"Jackson was quite alarmed when you stole the watch. It felt like a violation. Real personal. What kind of a guy are you, taking the treasured possession of a man recently deceased." James snorted.

"Disrespectful. That's what you are. But no wonder. You think you can manipulate and take whatever you want. I've seen guys like you before—all show but no substance.

"That's your opinion," Rex commented dryly.

James kept talking. "Against my advice Mr. Walker has graciously agreed not to press charges. He's had some time to think and now realizes he may have been too hasty. Possibly overreacted. Thanks to our quick police work, he's willing to let bygones be bygones. He's satisfied that justice has been served.

"Good of him," Rex mumbled.

"I wanted to tell you face-to-face that this incident has been resolved without further action, but if there's a next time... You'll be in big trouble, Mr. Redondo. I won't hesitate to arrest you and take the matter further up the chain to a potential guilty verdict."

Not exactly the collegial conversation Rex had hoped for but better than being read his rights or tossed into a cell. Aware that the skin on his thigh had started to tingle, he reached down to scratch at the sensation. The slight tingle turned to an intense burning. He scratched harder.

He happened to glance toward the evidence bag, his eyes widening at what he saw. Inside, the pocket watch gleamed. The inner lining of the plastic coated with condensation from the heat.

A faint acrid scent hit his nostrils—melting plastic. The pocket watch had some kind of hold on him, luring him to investigate further. Rex looked away, not wanting James to notice his interest.

"You got something to say, Redondo?" demanded the lieutenant.

He started talking to keep the cop distracted. "Thanks for calling me in. Looks like I didn't need my lawyer after all. But just so you know, this won't be the last you'll see of me.

"I'm applying for a PI license. It's my plan to take on high-profile cases, which may bring us together sooner than you think. I get why the watch was so important now. That watch...uh, stuff that dreams are made of." Deliberately quoting from *The Maltese Falcon*, he used a gruff Bogart voice impression to make his point.

Before James could respond, a knock came to the door. A young cop poked his head inside. "Lieutenant, you have to come quick. We have a situation in the lobby."

James rose hastily from his chair. "Stay put. I'm not done with you yet!"

As soon as the door closed, Rex picked up a pencil and nudged the bag slightly. The plastic against the watch melted into the mahogany surface of the desk, creating an opening in the bag. He used one finger to lift the chain.

Hot to the touch, he slid it into his pocket quickly. Then he turned the bag over to hide the melted side. *Maybe he won't notice right away*, Rex concluded.

He left the lieutenant's office. *I'll tell him something came up*, Rex reasoned. *Two professionals, one to the other, that happens all the time.*

The back alley revealed a police cruiser. He eased his way past and noticed that no one sat behind the wheel. Rex broke into a run. Down the alley and toward the main street, he didn't waste any time.

As soon as he reached his SUV, he sat behind the wheel. The watch burned against his skin, so he pulled it out and dropped it into a cup holder.

Images flickered behind his eyes as he drove into his own garage. Aware that he might be followed, he pushed the button to close the door.

That watch was begging me to pay attention. Probably a murder weapon. Otherwise why would it glow and burn just for me...

41

VIVIENNE ROSE

Viv focused on Abbey. "I've been considering one of those new semaglutide drugs," she told her.

Abbey frowned.

Another woman added her two cents. "I stopped taking it after the first month. It made me so nauseous."

"Same here," a third woman chimed in. "And I heard you gain the weight back as soon as you stop injecting. What's the point?"

The only man at the meeting spoke next. "Once you start a semaglutide and you lose weight and your A_1C goes down, you may no longer qualify for insurance. They can stop covering the cost. I'd be looking at over a thousand bucks a month out of pocket. No way I can afford that."

"I went cold turkey. It's not for me," Abbey said flatly.

Viv nodded, keeping her expression neutral. "Thanks for sharing. I've heard people say the drug helps with weight loss, but the results don't stick unless you change your diet and exercise routines."

A woman across the circle narrowed her eyes. "Maybe.

But if it's really the miracle drug they claim, I should be able to eat and drink like normal and still lose weight."

Abbey turned to Viv. "Mindfulness. That's the key. Don't even think diet. You'll feel restricted and inevitably have to break out and then the pounds add up again. Isn't that right?"

All heads in the group nodded.

"Plus continuous use of the drug can be dangerous," another piped up. "Even the FDA ones that are approved. If you turn to the compound prescriptions they sell online, they're not regulated."

Abbey's eyes filled with tears. "My sister took the drug, prescribed by her doctor. She's type 1 diabetic and overweight." Her voice quavered. "She lost weight but it knocked her A1C all over the place. She'd be going along just fine, monitoring her blood sugar like before, and then bam. It plummeted. I got called by the emergency room as her first point of contact. By the third time I showed up at the ER, the paramedics told me 911 calls from diabetics had doubled in the last year."

"I read," Viv began, "that the drug is recommended for type 2. Maybe your sister's doctor was just trying to help and overrode the warning." Before Abbey could answer, another woman interrupted.

"Oh, I have an even worse story," she claimed. "My friend didn't want to go through her insurance. She was afraid she'd be turned down since she wasn't considered obese. She got a compound drug online. Now she's looking at a liver transplant."

Is no one going to defend this miracle drug? Viv wondered.

"There are people who take the drugs and have lost

weight, lowered their A1C, and picked up a more active lifestyle," she said, trying to offer another point of view.

"I read," she continued slowly, "that the United States is filled with seniors whose health issues are exacerbated by overweight. Heart problems, clogged arteries, knee and hip replacements. The semaglutides can be game changing for them. In some cases type 2 is eradicated."

"Wait just a minute." One woman glared. Accusing eyes turned toward Viv. "Are you by any chance a plant for Big Pharma..."

"No, I'm not," Viv added hastily. "I read an article in the *LA Times*." Her palms felt moist. She'd deliberately moved against the group's opinion to get more information. But this woman wasn't afraid to push back. *What ever happened to civil discourse?* she thought.

She'd managed to make herself the center of attention, just by offering another point of view. *I wonder if all OA groups are like this. People telling their stories laced with little victories. But when the official meeting is over and they gather around the coffee pot, real feelings and cross talk break out.*

Viv chose not to back down. She adopted a reasonable tone with another question. "Those drugs haven't been on the market that long. Can you really get liver damage from taking them?"

A woman who'd not yet spoken joined the conversation. "Taking semaglutides requires regular blood checks. If you're not following up, things can go wrong quick. I do the private blood tests because my insurance won't pay as often as I need them."

"I admit it seems as if everybody's doing it," Abbey quipped. "The ads on television make the injections sound like magic solutions. Plus they mention unintended side effects at the end in a fast rushed voice which most people ignore."

"Big Pharma rides again," muttered Viv's accuser.

Viv lowered her voice to a conspiratorial tone. "I had a friend," she began. "He recently died. I think he might have been taking one of those drugs."

"So sad," Abbey said in a low voice. "Did he live alone?"

"Seems like a terrible price to pay just to lose a few pounds," Viv admitted. "And yes, he lived alone." Mentioning her friend with the tragic story brought the group to silence. No one wanted to treat her unkindly after that.

She'd gotten what she'd come for. If Wally Walker was taking semaglutide injections, then that may have been the cause of death. She'd heard it not from the online advertising, where most of the information lifted up the benefits of the drug. She'd gotten her information from regular people trying to make sense of their world. "My mom used to say"—Viv glanced around the circle of faces—"'the cure is worse than the kill.' I guess in this case it couldn't be more true."

Abbey was the first to smile. "Come on, everybody. Cheer up. The meeting's over. Time to run three miles and eat a salad."

"Yeah, like that's gonna happen," one woman said with a wink.

By the time Viv arrived home, she couldn't wait to connect with Rex and tell him what she'd learned. Everything was coming together, beginning with Mia's report that Wally was a diabetic. Hadn't she seen firsthand all the pill containers and injection paraphernalia that first time they visited his house? *That's confirmation,* she concluded.

Plus, if Mia was correct about Wally's frequent visits to the pie bar, that would point to a refusal to adjust his diet. If he was injecting a semaglutide, he may have undermined his own health.

Wally could have accidentally killed himself. He could have mismanaged the prescribed drugs and continued his poor lifestyle, resulting in a rapid spike of his $A1C$ followed by coma and death. According to the OA group and the paramedic's account, Wally would not have been the first.

____

42

REX REDONDO

That evening Rex and Viv sat outside gazing into the night sky. "Thanks for returning Miss Kitty." She reached over to tap his IPA bottle with her glass of chardonnay.

"They were quite the pair," Rex admitted. "Kinda cute. She scarfed up the albacore, I can tell you. Not a bite left." He looked up at the stars. "Maybe that isn't exactly accurate. She walked away from her bowl and Kevin finished the rest. He's a very tidy dog." Viv chuckled.

He loved her laugh. Low and feminine. *Maybe now is the time to bring up spending the night and eggs for breakfast...*

"I need to get to bed early tonight," Viv said before he could mention his plan.

Does she mean what I think she means?

"Okay..." He loved where the conversation was going.

"I have to catch up on some doula work tomorrow morning bright and early. I went to an OA meeting today so I got behind."

He felt his heart plummet. Spending the night and the vision of eggs, crisp bacon, and a fresh everything bagel replaced by her work schedule. *Damn. I could almost smell the toasted bagel.*

"I didn't mention that I made a stop at the police department earlier today," he blurted out to avoid any possible overthinking about her prioritizing her work over his well-being.

She looked over. "Are you being charged?"

"Not yet. But I will be soon." He paused for dramatic effect. When she didn't follow up with another question, he added, "Aren't you curious? Because I did something you won't approve of. I'm not sure even I approve." He remembered his therapist's advise. How impulsive decisions based on random thoughts could lead to questionable outcomes.

"So tell me." Viv was finally intrigued. "Why do you think you'll be charged later?"

"I nicked the pocket watch yet again." He couldn't keep the pride from his voice. "When Lieutenant Darius James turned his back and stepped out, I got into the evidence bag. It was begging me, I'm tellin' ya. Calling out my name."

She frowned at Rex and then walked into the house without a word.

By the time she returned with a platter of crackers and cheese, she seemed more composed. "Have a snack," she offered. "I admit I was shocked, critical of your behavior. That impulsive streak has been leading you astray ever since we met. Don't forget you stole my house key."

How could he forget? He'd been instantly attracted to her that night. And then he picked up the house key when she was talking to the cop. Only to read and get insight into her life. No harm was meant. But then he'd put the key in his pocket.

"I told you objects tell me stories. Your key, now the pocket watch. That antique was the only personal item in the perfectly staged house. It stood out. I was ready to let it go, but at the precinct, the watch was literally hot. It melted the plastic evidence bag. Like I said, it was as if it were calling my name.

"Like Wally was trying to speak to me from the other side. 'Take the watch,' he kept saying. How could I say no to a dead guy."

"It would be rude," Viv admitted.

He wanted to be taken seriously. So he disregarded the way she covered her smirk by taking a sip of wine.

"Okay, so I was impulsive. But what do you have? Any more information?"

"I think he unintentionally killed himself," Viv stated matter-of-factly.

"What about Jax? Gloria. Seraphina," Rex insisted. "Weren't you saying earlier that the waitress may have more at stake in Wally's death than it seems?"

"I thought about that," Viv admitted. He sensed she was holding something back.

"Anything else?"

"I got some anecdotal information about Wally's prescriptions. Or what I assume he was prescribed. I didn't talk to an actual doctor. Plus I haven't spoken to Brad. He and Mia obviously hooked up last night. Mia may have told him more about Wally."

Rex felt a moment of inspiration. Somehow the conversation had returned to where he intended. Couples getting along. Before she could tell him more about what she'd learned, he shifted the topic.

"Speaking of hooking up, why don't I spend the night? I promise to leave early so that you can get the doula work done. There's no reason to lose our momentum from our reconnect." He felt breathless explaining. "You could even make me an early breakfast."

Viv burst out laughing. "You were doing okay until the breakfast part. I know you must be missing your fresh muffin, freshly squeezed orange juice, and ground coffee in the morning. Sutton left you high and dry, didn't she?"

Before he could deny, she continued. "Let me make my feelings known right now. No matter how great you are in bed, you won't get a breakfast in return. I have my own eating habits to sustain. Nothing personal."

"But..." Rex sputtered and stopped. No breakfast. Very disappointing. But then he comforted himself with the next thought. *I still get to spend the night!*

43

VIVIENNE ROSE

The following morning Viv texted Brad.

> Any chance we could talk?

She laid the phone down. She respected people's privacy when it came to their intimate lives, and she knew Brad may not want to dish about Mia. *But I have to give him a try.*

A whoosh and then a ding drew her attention back to her phone.

TEXT Give me an hour. I'll meet you at Just Desserts.

She tapped the thumbs-up emoji.

When Rex returned from feeding Kevin, she told him the news. "I texted Brad. He wants to meet at Just Desserts."

Smelling of citrus cologne and looking dapper, he'd showered at home.

"Is that a new shirt?" she asked.

"Found it in the back of my closet." He smoothed his

hand over the front. "I like simple designs, it turns out. I don't know why I kept dressing in loud Hawaiian prints."

The obvious answer, that Sutton picked his wardrobe, didn't seem to occur to him.

"Want to come along to have lunch with Brad?"

"Sure," Rex said. "Another cup of coffee first?" He looked longingly toward the kitchen.

"Meet you in the SUV."

Minutes later, travel cup secured between them, she asked, "Have you heard from Sutton?"

"Not a word," he admitted. "I don't think I'm going to hear from her anytime soon. Maybe never. She has a way of slamming the door in the face of people who piss her off. I guess I should have known that I'd eventually end up on her naughty list."

He angled the SUV into a parking space.

The tone of his voice sounded as if he were resigned to the Sutton turn of events. But Viv wasn't as sure. Her estimation of Sutton was a bit different. *I think she may have a plan up her sleeve.* She hopped out of the SUV onto the pavement.

The host sat them at the pie bar. Rex decided on his usual corned beef sandwich. Viv glanced over the menu just as Mia arrived to take their order. "Hey, you two. It's been a couple of days. What can I get you?" Bright eyes and the quick smile made Viv wonder. *Who put a nickel in her...*

Viv closed her menu. "I'll have the Cobb salad with blue cheese dressing on the side, please. Oh! Save this stool." She pointed to the one beside her. "Brad's meeting us."

Mia flushed, her cheeks pink. "He said he'd be in town

for lunch," she murmured, and then turned to help the next customer.

Rex leaned closer. "So did I read that right? They hooked up?" He winked.

"Mia seems very happy," Viv observed, "like a woman in love."

"Probably lust," Rex commented.

"Speak of the devil." She caught sight of Brad hurrying toward the counter.

Mia slid past, her arms loaded with another order. She smiled at the newcomer.

"What's up, Mia?" Brad sat next to Viv. "Thanks for saving me a seat."

Viv expected him to chat Mia up. But when he ducked his head in the menu, she held back a frown. *Maybe he's not that into her*. A quick glance at Rex confirmed he had his suspicions as well. He raised his right eyebrow in that way he had when he was practically reading her mind.

"What can I get you today?" Mia's tone took a professional turn.

"Double burger with cheddar. Load on the onions and add some avocado. Make the fries extra crispy. And water with lemon." The specificity of Brad's order made Viv flinch. A love interest ordering onion could be considered a smack in the face to some women.

He'd sent a universal signal: I'm not interested.

Mia turned away abruptly. "Be right with you," she called to the next customer.

"So what's going on with you two?" Viv nodded in the direction of the waitress. "I was just telling Rex how well you seemed to get along the other night. Like an instant attraction."

Brad let out a long sigh. "I did like her. But after we, you know, spent the night, she told me something that stopped me in my tracks. Made me realize that I had crossed a boundary. What the boss would call a professional conflict of interest."

"Professional as in you being a Lily Rock Constabulary employee kind of conflict, or is there something more?" Rex sounded genuinely confused.

Brad reached for his water. "She told me things." He lowered his voice. "I think Mia is a person of interest. In Wally Walker's murder." He sounded genuinely disappointed.

The hair rose on Viv's neck. "What does that mean? Do you know something about Wally that we don't?"

"I can't show you the most recent report, but Wally had a lot of conflicting medications and supplements in his system. The boss called it a mishmash of chemicals."

"She's very technical, that Janis Jets," Rex said dryly.

"She's a genius," Brad defended. He looked over his shoulder.

Mia had moved down to the far end of the counter to deliver another order. "So here's what I've got." Brad opened his cell to click on an app.

"Semaglutides," he said. "Looks like they were prescribed by a doctor. He was diabetic. I don't suppose that's a secret. All of this makes sense."

Brad continued, "He also had amphetamines in his blood. More than the usual cup of morning coffee kind of speed."

"People take those to decrease their appetite," Rex mused. "Uppers can raise glucose levels by interacting negatively with his insulin. Something about the risk of DKA."

He did his own homework, Viv realized. *Didn't need Sutton.* "What's DKA?" she asked.

"Diabetic ketoacidosis," Rex explained. "Once blood sugar plummets, coma follows and then if not treated—death."

"Did the reports have anything about what Wally ate?" Viv asked.

"That's a factor." Brad glanced at his phone. "Wally had alcohol and tomato juice in his system. Remains in his gut and intestines when he died. Oh, there was also evidence of apple pie." He looked up. "I've eaten pizza for breakfast but never pie with a Bloody Mary chaser. Was Wally trying to kill himself?"

"Wally may have been an alcoholic. On top of everything else. Could have compromised the effectiveness of his prescription," Viv said.

"Or he got confused," Rex said. "Maybe he was getting the meds from the doctor and the speed from someone else. We know Mia supplied the breakfast."

"And that's why I'm no longer interested in her." Brad slammed a fist on the counter. "Plus she told me something else..."

Viv felt impatient; nibbled to death by ducks. The way Brad kept dragging out the story. "Get to the point," she hissed.

"Yeah, spill, kid. Your person of interest is making a beeline toward us with her arms full of plates."

Mia slid Viv's plate in front of her, followed by Rex's, and then Brad's. Her early spark and high color replaced by a frown. She left a bill and turned away without a word.

Out of earshot, Rex spoke. "She's mad. It doesn't take a brain surgeon to figure that out."

Brad eyed his burger. "Hopefully she didn't spit on my fries."

44

REX REDONDO

Rex, Viv, and Brad stood outside Just Desserts. "I want to hear what Mia told you one more time," Viv insisted.

Brad's square jaw hardened. "Before I go over it again, I want to know that I'm officially part of this team. Since I have the connection with the police reports, I'm a valuable guy. Without me you'd have nothin'."

"Not exactly nothing," Rex disagreed. "Viv did undercover work and got a lot of details about the semaglutides, for one. From people who know how they work firsthand. And I've been doing some research online. Oh, and talking to the custodian. He's a good source of information. He and Wally were old drinking buddies. Bet you didn't know that.

"Plus Seraphina Morales, the Mojave Mesa principal, she could also be a person of interest. She wanted Wally Walker out. He was too old and his refusal to move on impacted her bottom line. I bet you didn't know any of that either," Rex challenged.

Brad rubbed the hint of stubble on his chin. "I didn't," he admitted.

"Of course you're on the team," Viv reassured. "You're

invaluable. You're smart and energetic. The perfect match for the Neighbors in Crime Agency."

Viv's enthusiastic praise for Brad annoyed Rex. *She's deliberately buttering him up.* He started to disagree with Viv and stopped short when he realized that Brad's connection with the police might prove to be useful.

Brad directed his gaze toward Viv. "Mia expected to inherit from Wally. He named her in his will. One hundred grand on the stipulation she return to school and get a four-year degree."

Rex whistled. "I knew there was something going on between those two. The grandfather and the helpless pie maker relationship didn't fool me. They struck a deal. She wanted to go back to school so she made nice. Paid him off with attention and pie. She cozied up to him, gave him what he wanted, all because she knew he had the dough."

Viv looked thoughtful. "Did she deliberately feed him apple pie and Bloody Marys to speed up a health crisis? That's what I'm wondering."

"I wouldn't put it past her," Brad mumbled.

Rex felt a pang of sympathy for Brad. He'd been disappointed by women with ulterior motives in the past, so he knew how the kid might be feeling. *I had to harden my heart over the years. Otherwise I'd be broke. Or worse yet, dead like Wally Walker.*

"Okay, so we've got suspects," Rex said. "But I think it would be best to take this conversation elsewhere. Someone might overhear us."

Viv tapped Brad's arm. "Let me text you the gate code. You won't need to talk to the security guy."

Brad reached for his cell right as an alert pinged. "I got a message from another student at Mojave."

When he finished, he explained. "There's a rally. Here, look for yourself." He held up his phone for Viv to read.

TEXT In one hour meet at the outdoor quad. Bring signs.

Viv handed back the phone. "What rally?"

"Students are planning a rally to protest about what happened in the sixties."

Rex had no idea what Brad was talking about. So much happened in the '60s and early '70s. He was young then but his mother was very active in the civil rights movement. As a grad student in political science, she'd been arrested more than once.

He could hear her voice, her animated tales as if it were yesterday. Her emotions ran high, leaving an impression. He'd not thought about feeling frightened by her intensity for a long time.

A twinge of insight made him think, *Viv's like that. Very passionate about who and what she loves.*

He quickly dismissed the comparison, remembering a specific year. *Martin and Bobby were assassinated in 1968.* Then more memories from his past rolled out one after the other. "Don't eat that," his mother had said, slapping a bunch of green grapes from his hand.

"Cesar Chavez led farm workers on strike in Central California. My mom boycotted." Rex frowned trying to recall the exact dates. All the memories ran together like a patchwork quilt of activism.

"And don't forget the Vietnam protests. Now that was a really big deal in '68." Berkeley led the way. His mother had dragged him up north to help roll bandages for the students on the picket lines. He was one of the only children there.

And then one of his last memories of the turbulent years included Kent State. This time he was left home with a neighbor while his mother, fueled by her anger at the government, returned to Berkeley. He realized then that her activism held priority, even over him.

"I guess," Brad finally said. He had that tone of disinterest that Rex associated with someone not listening but thinking about what they wanted to say next. Sure enough...

"Then you might not know," Brad began, "Palm Springs had their own share of problems around the same time. Things came to a head during the '60s. By 1968 bigwigs finally decided no one deserved compensation. Commerce is God, always has been," he added.

"The idea of reparations was recently considered but it got stuck in the court. That's what we're trying to draw attention to at this protest."

"What kind of problems did Palm Springs have?" Viv prompted.

"They called it Palm Springs Section 14 urban renewal. Where people on the city council, along with the Bureau of Indian Affairs, voted to evict residents with little to no warning. One square mile of dry desert land needed to be cleared so that developers could build retail space and restaurants. That stretch now occupies the most expensive end of main street in Palm Springs."

Rex felt his fingers tingle. The kid finally got his attention.

Brad continued. "Cops arrived one day and pulled people out of their homes. Machines bulldozed the bungalows with all of their belongings. Some cops burned the houses to the ground to scare families from returning to grab their valuables."

"That's just horrible." Viv sounded shocked. "I had no idea."

Brad's face flushed. "The majority of the people on the

council didn't even own the land. They convinced the Agua Caliente Band of the Cahuilla Indians to do the dirty work because they held the land rights."

"So why have the students suddenly taken an interest?" Viv asked.

Rex answered, "The kids just wanted something to complain about. You know students. Anything to get out of papers and exams. They think this is a noble cause and they'll get lots of attention."

"That's not true!" Brad's face turned red. "This is a legitimate social injustice issue. Many of those students had grandparents who were dislocated. So they're demanding reparations from the city of Palm Springs.

"Businesspeople got nothing but rich after the redevelopment. While many of the students' families never recovered. That's a big deal. How can my generation get ahead without some inherited money to buy a house or go to college?"

Rex had not expected Brad, the laid-back kid from Lily Rock, to care so much about the plight of the less fortunate. "Your grandparents or great grandparents...were they evicted?" Rex asked.

"No. But that's not the point. When one of us is chained, none of us are free."

Rex recognized the phrase from a song. Coming from Brad's lips, it seemed a bit incongruous. But obviously the kid believed what he was saying, he'd become so passionate.

"Why don't you come with me?" Brad said. "You're students of a sort. Maybe it's time to open your eyes to what's going on."

"I suppose..." Rex's voice dragged with reluctance.

"It's been years since I've been at a protest," Viv said.

"I'll add you to the Project 14 text chain. You can find

all the details. One hour. I'd better get moving. We can meet at your place later."

Brad stepped from the curb to hurry across the street.

Rex tugged at Viv's elbow. He needed to get something off of his chest. "All of this is very interesting, the protest stuff. But I think it's a big distraction from our case.

"Plus there's the pocket watch. I might get arrested again. I don't want to tell the kid."

She appeared thoughtful "I agree. Let's keep the whole pocket watch theft between us two. Brad won't understand about your inner images. Plus the psychometry piece might seem airy-fairy. Brad's been working with Jets for too long. He's strictly a by-the-books kind of cop-to-be."

Rex exhaled with relief. "Thanks. Brad doesn't seem to be the kind of guy who would appreciate my peculiarities. It's taken me this long to appreciate myself."

"But don't worry about Brad," she insisted. "He's a lot like you in other ways. Arrogant. Smart. Privileged and a lady magnet." She smirked.

He felt indignant. *What does she mean, I'm like Brad? I'm nothing like him. If I didn't know better, I'd think she really meant that. Ridiculous.* Shoving his hands into his pockets, he hurried across the boulevard.

"Coming?" he called over his shoulder.

When she didn't answer, he looked back.

"I want to stop and say hi to Jason." She nodded toward her favorite boutique.

45

VIVIENNE ROSE

Viv wondered what to wear to a protest rally. She'd promised Rex she'd only be twenty minutes so it was time to decide.

A pair of skinny jeans and a black tee would work. She'd pull on a sweater and black sneakers. No use trying to look other than she was; a woman of a certain age dropping in on the younger generation's party.

Her phone buzzed with a text from Mojave Mesa Community College. It was an incoming text.

> Introduction to Private Investigation 101
> will resume next Monday at eight o'clock.
> Type STOP if you will not be attending.

It had only taken the community college a week and they already found a replacement professor. The ease of the transition felt off, especially in light of the fact that the previous professor was found dead at his desk.

I wonder if Dr. Morales had someone in line waiting for an opening. She stood to benefit from the old instructor's death. Had she anticipated his leave taking, getting someone else lined up? If that's the case, she's very organized. And calculating.

The principal's name rose to the top of Viv's suspect list. Right underneath Jackson Walker.

She'd only met Seraphina the one time. Even then she'd not liked her haughty manner. All those photos with the Palm Desert mayor and the California governor didn't help. *Out for her own self-interest,* Viv concluded. *Like everyone else in this case.*

Half an hour later Rex and Viv hurried toward the center of the community college campus. Voices raised in protest reached her ears. "What do we want!" came the call.

"Justice for all," the crowd responded.

"What do we want," the voice repeated.

"Reparations!" The crowd cheered.

Rex gripped her hand as they made their way through the group of students. Tents had been erected behind the quad stage. The path to the stage was filled with men and women from their late teens to early twenties huddled in small clusters.

Bold statements on signs were attached to poles in front of the stage. Photos of the victims of Project 14 looked decades old. They served as reminders of the faces and lives that had been impacted by the dislocation. A few signs held black and white images of burned-down homes. Underneath in bold letters she read, Honor the Past.

More people congregated in front of the banners. Drums beat in the background, maintaining a steady rhythm. People chanted, many sang out in Native dialect. Viv did not understand the words but the intensity of the voices communicated anger.

"Take this." A flyer was thrust into her hand by a young girl. Print on both sides explained the history of Section 14 and a call to action. *Shut down the campus. Force funding for reparations. It's time to show up.*

To one side of a tent encampment, a lineup of observers kept a close eye on the students. *Faculty members*, Viv surmised. Maybe a few community bigwigs. She spotted Seraphina Morales next to the mayor.

"Figures," Viv mumbled.

"Check out the security guards." Rex nodded toward men and women dressed in matching dark blue uniforms. A Mojave Mesa patch on the shoulder of their jackets. Black boots shone with polish. Each one inscrutable behind dark sunglasses.

Viv felt their collective energy. Each one balanced to instantly respond if necessary. "Do they have weapons?" she asked.

"Maybe not a gun but a taser for sure. Pepper spray and a baton. You can see one dangling off his belt." Rex pointed.

Hisses and boos erupted from the crowd, right as Seraphina Morales made her way to the microphone. "Students," she began with her voice of authority. "Classes have been canceled."

A wild cheer rose from the crowd, soon followed by a chant. "We won't go. We won't go."

"You will get one day to express yourselves in a peaceful demonstration," she added. "But let me be clear. No one stays the weekend on this campus."

The crowd hissed and booed her to silence. Once they calmed down, she added, "Classes begin on Monday morning just as scheduled."

Seraphina smiled. Oblivious to the jeers of the crowd, she adroitly ducked an orange that had been lobbed her way. More fruit pelted the back of her tan blazer as she turned to leave. She hurried off the stage as the crowd continued to protest.

Viv leaned closer to Rex's ear. "I think I've had enough," she told him. "We're obviously going to arouse suspicion due to our age."

"I agree." He took her hand to weave his way back through the crowd. The loud protests followed them to the parking lot. Finally Rex stopped, observing another group of concerned citizens who'd been sectioned off on the other side of the lot. He noticed a familiar face in the crowd.

Viv blinked. "Do you know that man?" She pointed toward a guy waving his arms in the air coming right at them.

"That's Jax Walker," Rex realized aloud. "Looks like he's watching the commotion from the sidelines."

"Not anymore. He's coming straight for you." Viv's eyes were wide.

"You're going to pay, Redondo," Jax screamed. "I know you have my watch. Hand it over now or I'll have you arrested." The realtor's chin jutted forward, inches from Rex's face.

"My grandfather's watch." Jax poked Rex in the chest. "You know you stole it out of the evidence bag. It had to be you."

Rex placed one hand on each shoulder of his accuser to give Jax a shove backward. "Come on, buddy. Why don't you calm down."

46

REX REDONDO

Rex knew the shove could be considered assault. Making his arrest even more certain. But he also knew that the only reason he wasn't already arrested was because his crime had to be low on the lieutenant's priority list.

Jax lowered his fists. "Okay, tough guy," Jax fumed. Then he glanced to Viv. His jaw visibly softened. Rex knew that was her superpower. *She has a way of making people see reason, without even saying a word.*

"I've been keeping close tabs on you because I really want my pocket watch," Jax continued in a calmer voice. "If you hand it over right now, I might let bygones be bygones. What would I have to do to convince you?"

Rex knew desperation when he heard it. Jax needed to get his hands on the watch. For whatever reason. But that only made Rex realize his power in the situation. Jax's neediness gave Rex more leverage.

"I'm open to negotiate," he said. "But I want to have the piece appraised. Then I'll know if it's valuable. Get your checkbook ready. I'll expect to close a deal or offer it to another buyer."

"That's coercion," Jax cried. Then he shrugged. "Plus it's not worth much. My grandfather's watch isn't a priceless heirloom or anything."

"How do you know that?" Rex asked.

"He kept it for sentimental reasons. Kind of dangled it in front of me a few years back to get me to reconsider joining the police force. It didn't work."

Rex sensed family drama in that statement.

"So you didn't join the force. Why was that an issue? You're a very successful real estate man."

"You don't understand," Jax insisted. "My dad was also a cop. He died on duty. My grandfather was so proud. He'd given the watch to my dad when he joined the police.

"When Dad died the undertaker laced the watch chain in his fingers for the viewing so that he could be buried with it. But my grandfather took it back. At the funeral he lifted the watch out of Dad's dead fingers when he bent to say goodbye. Then later, when he couldn't convince me to join the academy, he refused to give me the pocket watch."

Rex felt Jackson's disappointment. An important clue. The heaviness over his chest told him that the watch represented a rite of passage. Without having it in his possession, Jax felt betrayed. That he'd been denied what was rightfully his. No wonder Jackson had such strong feelings.

This emotional connection only made Rex more certain. "Nice story. But I'm still getting the watch appraised. I'll let you know what the professional says and then we can come to an agreement."

Jackson's shoulders slumped. He no longer looked like the irate guy hurtling across the grass screaming at the top of his lungs. He'd been deflated, as if someone popped him with a pin.

Rex knew he had no leg to stand on. Jax had every

reason to prop himself up on the higher moral ground, since he'd stolen the watch for a second time, right in front of the police lieutenant no less. So when Jax was so willing to compromise, this only made him more suspicious. He took advantage of the unexpected reprieve. "We'll be going now," Rex stated calmly. "I'll be in touch."

A fifteen-minute drive through the neighborhood and Rex and Viv stood in his driveway. He ran his hand through his hair, searching for words to explain what he'd felt with Jax earlier.

"I can feel the importance of the pocket watch right here." He tapped his chest. "There's an emotional tie-in. Something to do with Wally's death. Apparently he and Jax weren't on good terms. Do you think he got left out of the will? I think he's the main suspect."

"Not according to Gloria," she said. "Jax took over the selling of Wally's condo immediately. He had full access and signed all the legal paperwork. She had no doubt he was the executor."

"That doesn't necessarily mean he inherited the estate," Rex reasoned. "Maybe Grandpa stuck him with the work but not the payout. If the old guy was feeling vindictive enough, that would hurt."

"It would," Viv agreed. "We still don't know for sure that Wally didn't end his own life."

"That's true." Then his stomach growled. "Any chance you want to make us dinner so that we can talk and figure things out?"

"I don't want to go out. I'm still unnerved by the student protest, if you must know. A lot of noise and potential violence."

"We can talk over a good meal at your place," Rex coaxed. "I'll bring something over to your house to grill." He nearly choked on his own words, realizing he'd made the offer impulsively and that he'd have to step out of his comfort zone.

"Pick up some vegetables for a salad while you're at it. Oh, and a good blue cheese for the dressing," Viv added instantly. She did that wave thing with her fingers over her head as she walked away.

Caught up in the moment of admiring her toned legs, he nearly forgot.

I have to do grocery shopping. Wait a minute. Was that a bait and switch...

Rex had no idea where Sutton did their marketing. He narrowed his options to the top five grocers in Palm Desert. His mouth watered remembering their meals together.

In the past Sutton grilled the steaks, laced with just enough fat to make them sizzle. Each bite made him feel grateful to be alive. But that was before...

Rex sniffed. He'd given up on her returning his calls. Though he felt truly sorry, he also felt profoundly rejected. In the past Sutton always accepted his bad behavior once he apologized. What had changed?

He closed his computer once he picked the closest grocery. The Community Corner Market was only five miles away. He'd seen people come and go from the parking lot when he'd passed. *I'll be home in time for a shower before dinner.*

.   .   .

Rex approached the entrance to the market, admiring the bright banners waving in the breeze, advertising weekly specials. A small row of shopping carts were parked in a rack by the entrance. He yanked the closest one by the handle.

He couldn't remember the last time he'd gone food shopping. Probably when he was a child with his mother, it had been that long ago. One step inside, he stopped to admire the aisles evenly spaced with shelves stocked from floor to ceiling. Bulk items like family-sized cereal and instant mashed potatoes caught his attention.

An image flashed in his brain. How his mother would let him read the back of the cereal box to keep him busy. He'd save box tops to earn prizes. It wasn't often that Rex thought about his mom. She'd passed away in his early twenties. But this time he felt oddly comforted.

This must be a family market, he concluded. Right then, a mother issued orders to her two older children. "Fernando. You get the bread. Alisha, the vegetables. Don't bring me anything mushy." The youngest sat in the cart holding a cracker in his hand. The mother pushed the cart down the aisle as the older children scrambled to complete their assignments.

Rex read a sign advertising today's specials. There was a black and white square box in the corner. He stepped closer to watch a woman who held up her cell phone to take a photo.

He gathered his courage to ask, "Did you just take a picture of that?" He pointed to the box.

"Coupons," she stated flatly. "It's called a QR code. Now I have the list on my phone for all the bargains." She showed him her screen. Then looking him up and down, she added,

"Are you lost? There's a fancy market down the street. More to your taste." She hurried away before he could reply.

Is it that obvious that I don't shop here? he wondered. *What gave me away? The question or my appearance?* Rex rarely felt self-conscious. Most of the time he traveled in circles where people recognized him right away. If they didn't, they often made the connection because of the casino advertising. "Oh, you're that mentalist," they'd say. He liked being known.

He stared at another brochure covered with brightly colored photos. Taking his phone, he clicked on the QR code. "Move over, buddy," an older man told him. "I don't have all day."

Rex scrolled the coupons, discovering a few deals at the butcher counter. Inspired by conquering the QR code, he suddenly felt like a man on a mission. A hunter ready to gather. He pushed his cart down the aisle toward the butcher.

A robust middle-aged man named Hank Alvarez stood behind the counter. He waited on a woman with a toddler balanced on her hip. "I'll cut up that chicken for you, Sylvia. Just give me a minute." He disappeared into the back.

Rex was next in line. "I'm looking for two top sirloin steaks to grill." He felt like a man who'd figured things out. *What was I worried about? This is easy.*

The butcher nodded. "What grade of sirloin? I've got USDA Choice top sirloin steak. USDA Prime top sirloin steak. Grass-fed top sirloin steak and the top of the line, organic top sirloin steak."

"I don't know," Rex admitted.

"The wife send you on a search and seize today?" the butcher chuckled. "So let's break it down to how much you want to spend. The cheapest is eight bucks a pound. The top of the line organic is $25 a pound."

Rex whistled. "That's a lot of dough."

"Inflation. Where you been, buddy? It ain't cheap to feed yourself nowadays. Look around. How do you think these families do it? Not by eating top sirloin, I can tell you. Why not bring your lady home something else to grill. I can cut up some chicken that would be delicious and a lot healthier."

To his surprise, Rex didn't mind the butcher's interest in his finances. In fact, he felt oddly seen. As if someone cared about him. It was obvious to him that the butcher was more than an employee. He was an expert in meat.

"I told her beef, so I'd better bring home two steaks," he admitted. "The USDA Prime top sirloin—how much would that cost?"

"I get it. You wanna splurge." The butcher nodded. "USDA Prime top sirloin is on sale today. Check your phone, you'll find the coupon. Have the cashier scan it when you check out. Twelve bucks a pound. I'll be right back."

He disappeared to the back room, giving Rex time to ponder. *I've driven past markets for years. I let other people make my food. But now I'm thinking I missed something important. A kind of a connection...*

The butcher returned with two slabs of meat. Once wrapped, he wrote the price on top and handed the package to Rex. "You can pay on your way out. Pick up a nice bottle of red while you're at it. The missus will think it's a special occasion."

"Hey, Ms. Gomez, how are you today?" The butcher greeted the next customer before Rex could even say thank you.

Not until later, when he replaced his shopping cart, preoccupied with the spirit of his shopping adventure, did Rex look up. He'd nearly missed seeing Gloria Ramirez, who held a stack of pamphlets.

She pinned one to the bulletin board. Finished, she turned and started handing them out to shoppers. He could hear her tell each one, "Weekend vigil at Mojave Mesa."

Some people shook their heads, refusing the flier. Others absentmindedly dropped the paper into their carts. No one stopped to chat.

47

VIVIENNE ROSE

Viv held a cup of tea. She was doing her best to make sense of things. The Mojave Mesa visit had upset her. All those young people worked up for an issue that didn't seem relevant to their lives. At least in her opinion.

Practically speaking, because Viv always considered her logical self first, she couldn't image how the students had time to protest for social justice, what with their classes. Plus most of them had full-time jobs. Some, the older ones, had families and childcare challenges. She knew that from her own experience, working with her doula team in similar circumstances.

Yet the students stood in front of their professors and hired security, demanding that an injustice that happened before they were born be acknowledged. Not just that, but repaired.

Viv knew better than to dismiss her confusion as unimportant. That had gotten her into trouble recently. Just ask Desert Doulas, her once thriving small business. A smile came to her lips. She remembered her son, when he was small. Whenever he got puzzled, he'd get a look over his face. He'd say, "What's up with that!"

What is up with that, she wondered.

Half an hour later she knew a lot more about Palm Springs and the Section 14 relocation project. The description made her shudder. There were photos. One that made her heart ache. A family sorting through the rubble of their home, looking for lost valuables. Smoke rose from the ashes.

Now she felt guilty. She was alive in 1968 and had never heard about the incident. It turned out that the most unsettling aspect of the student protest included her ignorance of the history of Palm Springs. The famous city filled with Hollywood vibes and homes of the rich and famous aside, it came with a price.

Another example of the wealthy leaning on the poor to enhance their lifestyles. Somehow the community college students resonated with the plight of the past, maybe because they were also scraping to make ends meet.

"Meow." Miss Kitty took one leap from the floor to her lap.

"Hello there." She stretched her fingers to scratch the cat's neck.

Viv wondered. How many families still live in this area who were personally affected in the Section 14 uprooting of low-income families... Maybe they are the ones who expect reparations.

Who wouldn't want something for their loss. Look at Palm Springs today. The land that they were evicted from now holds high-end boutiques and very expensive restaurants. If there were grandchildren who've heard the story from their parents and grandparents, maybe they are the ones making demands.

Energized by the injustice and her own lack of awareness, Viv wanted to take a stand. A small part of her wanted to carry a placard, join the students.

She bent to kiss Miss Kitty's head. Her enthusiasm faded away, as it did when she was confronted by the past and realized anything she might do would be too small to make a difference.

Scooting Miss Kitty off her lap, she sighed. It turned out that ignoring the uncomfortable had only gotten harder as she aged. This reminded her of her grandmother. She sat in a corner for most family gatherings. Now Viv had wondered what Grandma was thinking. But she'd never asked. Left alone, her grandmother would eventually nod off.

Viv had assumed this was the way the older generation stepped back. No longer able to help, they stayed out of the way.

Maybe I can be different, she thought. *I can pay attention. Look at my blind spots. Keep listening. Refuse to tune out and think I know better.*

Viv put her cup into the dishwasher. *If I want to be a private investigator, I'll need to take a deep look into my own assumptions.* She felt daunted at the prospect. *I'm not sure I have what it takes to confront my own blind spots after all of these years.*

But then a common phrase came to mind. *No time like the present.*

Rex arrived right at six o'clock, a grocery bag from the Community Corner Market dangling from one hand. "I've got two steaks and a salad bag." He deposited the bag on the counter.

"So what am I supposed to do?" Viv asked in a teasing

tone. "Now that you've accomplished the hunting and gathering you expect me to...

He looked perplexed. "Aren't you supposed to do the preparation? Isn't that how it works?"

She knew this was hard for him. When he'd offered to bring food, she'd leapt at the chance before he changed his mind. It would take some getting used to. Rex had no idea how dependent he'd become. Picking up the pieces Sutton left behind would take time.

Knowing all of that, she was in no mood to soothe his ego with compliments. At least not yet. She raised her eyebrows and waited.

"I thought you'd be pleased," he insisted. "I had to go out of my way. Took me an hour to walk through the market and get the lay of the land. The butcher helped."

She kept her look of pleasant surprise but didn't say a word. *I refuse to make a big deal out of something so small as going grocery shopping.*

He was obviously at a loss. So he continued to talk. "But then I ran into our favorite stager Gloria Ramirez. A one-woman do-gooder with fliers." He held his hand to his forehead. "Getting your own groceries takes so much time," he moaned.

"What were the fliers about?"

"Not a property advertisement like you might think," he said. "She posted information about a weekend vigil at Mojave Mesa."

"Does that mean the students aren't clearing out?"

"Stubborn bunch of kids." Rex nodded. "That must make Dr. Morales pretty mad."

"They want reparations." Viv remembered what she'd just researched.

Rex pointed at the shopping bag. "Aren't you getting

hungry? Time to put on your Betty Crocker and make me some dinner." He rubbed his belly with a huge grin.

"I have a better idea. I'm more of a Julia Child. I give directions. Why don't you take that meat and rinse it in the sink. Pat it dry with a paper towel. Set it on a platter. Use salt and pepper from that drawer over there to season. Both sides need a sprinkling. You can even add a dash of garlic powder but not too much.

"Cover the meat with another paper towel and place it on the top shelf in the refrigerator. While you're there you can retrieve the bottle of wine I've been chilling. Open the bottle to let it air while you use that salad bowl." She pointed to the counter. "Toss the salad. With the tongs. Place it back in the refrigerator next to the meat.

"And don't forget to leave the dressing for last," she called over her shoulder. "I'll be sitting by the pool when you're done."

Viv felt quite pleased. *This man is clueless*, she concluded. *I want to blame Sutton. But his behavior is more about him. How did he go so long not having any idea how to make himself useful in the kitchen?*

She slid the door closed, pretending not to hear his complaints.

Viv left Rex by the pool to clear the dishes. When she returned, he had a thoughtful expression on his face. "So how did you like the steak?"

"It was delicious. More tender than I'm used to. You must have made a good impression on the butcher. He gave you prime beef."

"Until today I had no idea there were specific grades of meat," he grumbled.

"Live and learn." She used her I-don't-care cheerful voice.

Rex changed the subject. "So I've been thinking..."

"Go on."

"I'd like to do some on-foot information gathering about the pocket watch. Like I said earlier, I got a hit. Jackson Walker seemed really upset, irrationally so. An overreaction, considering it's probably not that valuable."

"Not compared to selling his grandfather's mid-century bungalow kind of valuable," Viv admitted.

"Come with me tomorrow," Rex said. "Let's start by getting an appraisal from a swanky jeweler. I'd like to know the genuine value."

"I have another idea. Let's check out that pawn shop in Palm Springs. The proprietor is in his seventies and would have been around to see pocket watches come and go. The shop is one of the only original buildings left downtown."

Rex looked toward the pool. "Good idea."

"About the dinner," Viv began. "You did a great job. But are you ready for the next step?"

He sent her a puzzled glare.

"You need to add a snack before the main meal. I'm thinking cheese and crackers to begin with. I'll show you how to assemble them on a plate. Presentation matters.

"I left a tray of cheese in the refrigerator and crackers on the counter. Did you ever think about arranging them yourself?"

"No." He sounded clipped. "I was waiting for you to take care of that."

"To tell you what to do," she calmly added. "But I won't do it for you."

"Why not?" He sounded exasperated.

"This isn't rocket science, Redondo. Take a risk. Dump

some crackers on a plate. Pour the wine. I left the glasses next to the bottle. Then bring everything outside. Surprise me."

"But you're so much better at that type of thing," he reasoned.

"That's not true," Viv said. "I make food available for you because I want you to feel comfortable in my home. But now that you're spending the night and practically living here, it's time to take initiative."

"At least you did the cleanup," he groaned.

"That's the trade-off. I cook, you tidy up. You cook..."

"You tidy up. I suppose that's fair." His voice dropped. "Is this how relationships are supposed to go? I've never been in one before," he admitted.

Despite his age and experience he was clueless in many ways. *Like I was clueless about the history of Palm Springs,* Viv thought. *We all have our blind spots.* Her heart softened.

"You've been pampered for a long time by Sutton," she told him in a soft voice.

"I did pay her," he reminded.

"No excuses. You deliberately overlooked the obvious. Sutton was more than an employee. She was a former colleague and a friend."

"I suppose," he mumbled. He ran his hand through his hair in exasperation. "I don't want to talk about this anymore. I'm going to get more wine."

48

REX REDONDO

Rex pulled his SUV into a parking space right behind Sunset Treasures. "Interesting name for a pawn shop." He glanced down at the cup holders, feeling slightly nervous about the pocket watch he'd placed there earlier. Viv released her seat belt.

He cleared his throat. "Would you mind picking up that watch for me? Tell me what you feel."

She gave him a curious look and then reached for the chain. Lifting it slowly, the watch dangled in the air. First spinning clockwise, then reversing to the opposite direction. They both watched with fascination as it began to spin in place, slowly at first, then faster, gathering momentum.

"Touch the case with your finger. I'm curious if it feels hot to you." He kept his eyes on the case.

Viv snatched the watch mid-spin. She closed her fingers around the metal. Rex waited. When she kept smiling, he felt relieved. "Not hot..." he asked.

"Not even warm. Rather cool actually. It's metal, right?"

He eyed the watch in her hand with increased distrust. "Every time I pick it up it burns my skin. Even if I hold it in my pocket my thigh gets scorched. That's one reason I stole it the second time, to figure out what was going on."

"And..."

"I got a confirmation when I saw the melted plastic evidence bag. It did it occur to me. Maybe it burned to get my attention." He smiled ruefully.

Viv released the watch, watching it slip back into the cup holder. "Since you're the psychometrist and you read objects, you must be intrigued."

He shrugged. "I remember realizing the importance. That time I held that Fortune Globe in my hands on the cruise. I'd read the globes that felt cool to the touch were most likely authentic. That's why I paid attention.

"But I've never experienced the temperature shift with other objects. That watch has more intensity." He stared at his palm and then added, "Though no scorch marks on my skin.

"Would you mind taking the watch in your purse for me? I don't want the pawnbroker to know its power...at least over me."

She picked the watch out of the holder for the second time and dropped it into her bag. "Got it. Now let's find out how much this beauty is worth."

The air inside Sunset Treasures smelled of musk, leather, and metal. And to Rex, a bit like his grandma's house before she moved. A man stood behind a glass display case with vintage watches and antique jewelry displayed inside. Behind the counter, three levels of shelving held vinyl records and old cameras. The top shelf tilted forward, as if ready to dump and run if one more thing were added.

The proprietor greeted Viv. "How can I help you, young lady?"

She lifted the pocket watch from her purse. "We were wondering if you could tell us how much this old watch is worth."

He took it from her hand, lowering a magnifying glass over his eye. Rex watched for a reaction to the temperature of the metal. *Must not be hot for him*, he concluded.

The man turned the case over and then flipped open the top. Under the cover was an ivory face with bold black Arabic numerals. The hands were blue steel. All of the inner workings stood at a standstill, giving Rex pause for thought.

Questions flooded his mind. *I wonder when this watch stopped working. Who held it in the past? Was it shoved into a drawer, replaced by a wristwatch, considered obsolete?* He felt a quickening sense of compassion hover over his chest. *I can relate to that*, Rex thought. *An old watch and an aging guy.*

The pawnbroker closed the top. He lifted the magnifying glass to relay his findings. "What we have here is a vintage Waltham Vanguard circa 1930s. They're known for this classic white background with the bold black Arabic numbers. See how the hands are blue steel...

"This is a railroad-grade timepiece, by the looks of it. It may have a 23-jewel movement which would make it worth more. In their day the Walthams were real popular because of their reliability, especially with railway workers. The gold case is unusual, which would also add to its value."

He continued, "This timepiece can be brought to working order in the hands of an expert watch repair person who works with antiques. It could be worth eight hundred. More if I can establish the provenance and research the engraving." He lowered the magnifying eyepiece to have one more look.

Rex felt a jolt of surprise. *Only eight hundred. I thought it would be worth more.*

The man looked up. This time his voice held an undercurrent of emotion. "As it so happens, I can help with the provenance on this watch." He faltered, then continued, "Because I know this particular timepiece. Look at the unique engraving."

He flipped open the top to point inside the cover. Intricate swirls had been engraved along with two initials. "See here. The letters ERV. Very distinctive. It's been nearly seventy years now, give or take, but I never forget a watch."

Rex felt his pulse quicken. He glanced out of the side of his eye toward Viv. She stared at the watch in the pawnbroker's hand. *Now we're getting somewhere,* he thought.

The man closed the top and then handed the watch back to Viv. "You might want to have it appraised after it's up and running. Check with the jeweler across the street. A watch guy comes in every week to do repairs. I heard he takes on antique pieces occasionally. He may be interested, you know, as a challenge."

Viv slipped the watch back into her purse.

"How did you come by this timepiece, if you don't mind me asking." The broker's forehead wrinkled.

Viv glanced at Rex. He knew what she wanted without her having to ask. He had to come up with a backstory. Something he was better at inventing than she could ever be.

"We found it in an antique store." He launched into an impromptu tale, his voice resonant, relishing each word. He'd polished this technique so well in his act that no one could tell he made it up on the spot.

He glanced behind the counter. "I found the watch hidden behind cameras on a shelf at an antique store."

Viv smirked. He knew she remembered where he got that detail.

"I've always liked pocket watches," Rex continued. "I'm a mentalist. You might have heard about me. Rex Redondo. I work at the Pair-a-Dice. Anyway, I had a bit of luck with scrying recently and I thought, why not use a pocket watch in my act. You know—to hypnotize or at least mesmerize the audience."

Viv raised an eyebrow.

Rex loved entertaining her, but now he wondered, *Is she appreciating my storytelling expertise, or is she thinking I'm a hopeless liar?*

The broker scratched behind his ear. "I haven't heard of you. No offense. We get all kinds in here. But I don't mind telling you, being a psychic and all, that this watch has a difficult past."

Rex flinched at the word psychic. But he didn't have time to explain how that didn't apply to him. Mostly because he felt as if the guy wanted to get something off his chest, and Rex didn't want to distract. Sure enough, the broker launched into his own story.

"The watch belonged to a Latino guy. It was the mid '60s when he started coming into my shop regularly. He'd get a few bucks to make ends meet. He told me he had a wife and a couple of kids to feed.

"I'd hand over the cash and he'd come back the next week to buy the watch back. I could tell how nervous he was leaving it behind. But then he'd be so happy when no one else bought it. He never seemed to mind paying more."

"Do you remember how much you charged him?" Rex asked.

A look of embarrassment came over his face. "I'd hand over fifteen bucks and price it at thirty. When he came back, he'd pay the thirty plus some interest and sales tax."

"So you gouged him," Rex commented dryly.

"Did he ever say what he needed the money for?" Viv interjected.

"He had to pay his bills. He worked in Palm Springs at one of the big hotels but only got a paycheck twice a month. He'd run out of cash before the next pay period. People lived hand-to-mouth in those days."

Viv's lips tightened. "You mean certain people. The ones who worked as staff for the others who came to Palm Springs for vacation. Those kinds of people. Who, by the way, are still living hand-to-mouth."

The pawnbroker's face flushed. His hands on the counter curled into fists. "Latinos and Blacks were lucky to get the money from me then," he said. "I provided a necessary short loan opportunity. I'm not apologizing. I'm not running a charity here."

"So this was his watch?" Viv pointed to her handbag. "You know that for certain?"

"Yeah, it was. He told me his whole backstory. I guess the guy moved from New Mexico and had gotten the watch as a gift. He worked the Santa Fe Railroad. He came to California for a better life, and the Fred Harvey Corporation gave him the watch as a parting gift.

"He was a brakeman. Those were the days." The broker nodded at Viv. "Folks certainly knew the value of good workmanship then. You can just tell by the gold plating, steel hands, and the engraving."

Rex worded the next question carefully. "Do you happen to know the name of the man who pawned this watch in the '60s?"

The man's brow wrinkled. "Some Mexican name," the broker said. "Let me think. I don't recollect his name but I now remember the date. The last time he pawned this piece was to pay a hospital bill. His wife had a baby. He returned one more time to buy the watch back, but I never heard from him again after that."

"So what was the date exactly?" Rex prompted.

"The middle of March. That's when they started burning down the houses of people in the Section 14 project. Everyone was laying low at the time hoping not to get involved."

Viv's voice sounded clipped. "I think we have the information we need."

"Thanks for your help," Rex said. "We'll take it to a jeweler to be appraised."

49

———————

VIVIENNE ROSE

A quick walk across the busy street brought them to the Mirage Jeweler entrance. The brief distance delivered them into what seemed like an entirely different country. The high-end store, the expensive allure, the opposite of Sunset Treasures.

The well-known boutique exuded an aura of elegance that looked similar in design to all the other shops on the main street. The boutique had a minimalist facade, constructed in cool alabaster stone with warm bronze accents that glistened under the sun's bright rays. This is where celebrities and influencers wanted to be seen. Glass doors slid open, welcoming them into unimagined luxury.

Soft ambient music filled the store. She was reminded of the spa on the cruise. *This must be a track they pipe in to give customers a false sense of security.* Plus a scent, floral with hints of citrus, lightly blended in the atmosphere. She looked for a candle but was unable to find the source of the aroma.

Viv shivered. The contrast from one shop to the other felt alarmingly unsettling. Rex followed right behind. She watched him closely as he adapted his posture to suit the situation.

He had an unconscious way of mirroring who he needed to be in any given circumstance. Just like a chameleon. He stood taller, his shoulders pushed back, looking as if he'd added two inches to his height.

He shoved one hand in his pocket, a nonchalant nod to Cary Grant. He looked as if he belonged in the upscale establishment, his glance taking in the glass counters and ambient lighting with a look of slight disdain.

"Come along, dear." He took her elbow in a proprietorial way, ushering her toward the biggest display case in the front of the shop. The glass on top held no evidence of a fingerprint or a speck of dust.

A woman glided from the back, impeccably dressed in a black suit. Underneath the jacket was a pink cashmere sweater. Diamonds sparkled in her strikingly understated necklace. Each earlobe held a karat-sized diamond stud to match.

She stood smartly at attention behind the counter. "May I interest you in our Desert Light Collection," she purred. "You seem like a very discerning couple." She unfolded a velvet-covered display board.

Viv reached for her purse and pulled out the watch. She set it on the cushioned board without comment.

The woman frowned.

Viv held back a chuckle. *Not exactly from Tiffany.*

"We would like to have this watch appraised," she stated, biting her cheek. The woman's disappointment was so apparent, she almost laughed out loud.

"I see," the woman commented dryly. "Our watch expert is here on Wednesdays. I can have you fill out the paperwork, including your insurance information. I suspect you'll be put on the waiting list. He's very busy." She pushed the watch back with a thinned-lipped look of distaste.

"We also want to have a look at engagement rings," Rex volunteered.

The woman's face lit up. "Of course I can help you with an engagement set. We have several exquisite examples in the case right here. Just last week a very famous celebrity"— she leaned over the counter as if to conspire—"bought the exact same set to pop the question to his intended."

"Who was that?" Rex shot her his biggest grin. "Maybe he's a buddy of mine."

"Oh, I can't divulge," she replied haughtily. "But it will be all over social media very soon."

Viv sighed loudly. *One more female succumbs to the silver fox charm.*

In a hasty voice the woman added, "Once you've selected the rings, I can ask our watch expert if he'll move you to the top of his list and even reduce his price for that other appraisal." She waved her red nail-polished fingers over the pocket watch with an air of dismissal.

"People stop by frequently to have an old piece of jewelry appraised. They find antique items at the bottom of an old drawer or at an estate sale. Everyone thinks because it's old it has to be worth something.

"We hate to disappoint our customers, but in most cases the appraisal costs more than the item is worth. I just want to warn you."

She poked at the watch with one finger, as if it were a poisonous snake. "I'll mark this at two thousand for insurance purposes. But the cost for the official appraisal will be double that. Just so you know."

Once the watch had been disposed of, slipped into a paper envelope and marked, she placed the envelope to the side with a bright smile. "Let's have a look at the Desert Light collection. I'm very certain you'll find exactly what you're looking for." Selecting a key from a large ring, she bent to open the glass case. "I know what would look best. A fabulous choice. We can start with this set..."

She unfolded a fresh velvet display board to place a man's and a woman's ring set in the middle. Pink diamonds glittered from the oversized engagement ring. Viv blinked. Then she reached over to take the envelope. She dropped it inside her worn bag.

"Honey," she addressed Rex. "Let's have lunch before we start spending your money. I know just the place." She made her way toward the door without a backward glance.

The Just Desserts outdoor patio hummed with activity. The host found them a table for two in the corner. "We've got brunch or lunch," he said, handing over two menus.

They both ordered. As the server walked away, Viv spoke first. "I found that pawn shop and jewelry store experience quite unsettling. How is it that the pawn shop, maybe the oldest establishment on Frank Sinatra Drive, is located right across the street from the most fancy upscale jewelry shop in Palm Springs?"

"They're catering to two very different clientele," Rex said. "It's surprising the pawn shop stayed in business. Surrounding retail shops and restaurants are all very different. Upscale. Fancy.

"Thanks, by the way, for getting me out of the jewelry lady's clutches. I only mentioned we were looking for rings to get her to take us seriously."

"So we're not getting engaged..." Viv blinked her eyelashes seductively.

"Is that what you want? I mean, I could consider marriage if you think..."

She grinned. "Marriage isn't important to me. But thanks for asking."

His look of relief made her chuckle.

"You've never struck me as a woman who wants to get married again." He glanced toward the pie bar and shrugged. "Something about this case has me off balance. Maybe I wasn't ready to go back to work."

She detected a new hesitancy in his normally confident demeanor. He'd had a lot of changes recently. From the personal residency retreat to Sutton's disappearance.

He's softening a bit. Not a bad thing.

Viv leaned closer. "Did you get any, you know, vibes at the pawn shop? That guy had so much information."

"His recollections felt genuine. It takes a storyteller to know a storyteller," Rex mused. "Pawn shop guy didn't strike me as someone who deliberately exaggerated."

"Like you," Viv teased.

"Like me," he admitted. "But now I'm wondering about that pocket watch's story. What do you call it—provenance. Lately I've been reminded of an old film by Alfred Hitchcock. I thought it was just one of my things, you know, a detective thriller. But it keeps popping into my mind. I'm not sure how the film and the watch are related. But I sense there's a connection."

"What film is that?"

"*North by Northwest.* A classic Hitchcock. Have you seen it?"

"Years ago," Viv said. "Cary Grant was the star and I remember the plot. Something about government secrets. Grant played the character of a guy named Roger Thornhill."

Her cheeks flushed. "I must admit I paid more attention to Cary Grant than the female lead. What was her name..."

"Eva Marie Saint," Rex replied. "She actually reminds me of you. Elegant and aloof."

Viv felt her neck grow warm. "Is that a compliment?"

"Absolutely." He stared into her eyes. "We can look for *North by Northwest* on cable and watch it together some evening," he added, before turning away.

"I may have an insight. Ready for a bit of mansplaining?" Rex grinned.

"Of course. Bring it on."

Viv ignored the server who stood with their two plates. She pointed to the table, her eyes on Rex. "Mansplain away. I'm all ears."

50

REX REDONDO

"The pocket watch—I'm thinking it's a MacGuffin," Rex explained.

Viv looked puzzled. "I'm not sure what that means."

"In *North by Northwest*, Hitchcock made the MacGuffin famous. The secret documents drove the plot. All the characters were after those documents but when it came to the end, no one knew why. Hitch never revealed their particular importance, other than they were 'secret.'" Rex used air quotes to make his point.

"I have to think about that." Viv didn't dismiss him out of hand. One of things he liked best about her was how she considered his opinions first, no matter how outlandish.

But he could tell she wasn't convinced, so he kept explaining.

"The point I'm making is that the specific details of the secret documents held no bearing to the plot. Hitchcock did a remarkable thing in *North by Northwest*. He used the documents to move the story, confuse the characters, provide drama with resulting action. Now it's part of screen-writing folklore."

A dreamy look came over her face. "The only scene I remember from that film is when Cary Grant stands on a runway. An airplane comes right at him. He ducks to avoid being struck down."

"That was exciting," he agreed impatiently.

"I heard Hitchcock filmed that scene at LAX," Viv added.

"That's what I also heard," Rex mumbled. He could see that she'd considered his opinion and dismissed it as a possibility already.

Viv reached for her glass of water. "Enough about Hitch. What I want to know is what's the MacGuffin in our case?"

Maybe I underestimated her...

"From my perspective," Rex began, "my images, the ones that spin, they're important. I've learned not to ignore them. I also don't dismiss repeating tunes that stick, you know, the ones you can't get out of your head. I feel the same about ideas that pop in from nowhere, that don't give up. Especially ones that remind me of old films or books. But mostly old films."

Viv smirked.

"Come on. You have to admit. My mentalist work saved our first three cases. Do I have to remind you..."

"Your superpower," Viv said. "Candles going out for no reason. Your steely gaze into the eyes of a mark, causing them to confess. Especially women. Now that I think of it, the last person was a female. So two superpowers."

She looked quizzical. "But the sounds and images... Harder to understand," Viv said. "But you're the first to tell people you aren't psychic," she reminded. "Instead of focusing on images and movies that play in your head, why don't we pay closer attention to the facts. What we're learning from Wally's closest friends and relatives and the forensic evidence."

Rex sighed. Viv was technically correct. But what she failed to realize...

All the facts remained separate pieces of a jigsaw puzzle until he gave them meaning with his images and intuition. And now that pocket watch... It held the key to solving this crime.

51

VIVIENNE ROSE

On the drive home Viv ignored Rex. He'd gotten quiet when she refused to give him credit for his MacGuffin theory. Now she felt impatient. Ever since they took on the case, he'd made nearly everything about rationalizing his theft of the pocket watch. Literally stealing it twice. And how it burned hot in his hand.

Viv wasn't a woman who appreciated excuses. Mostly because they didn't lead to taking responsibility.

When he'd raised his palm for proof, she couldn't see a burn. Nor a red mark. *I think he was making that part up,* she concluded. *A MacGuffin... Blah blah blah. I want some facts.*

He broke the silence. "Want to talk more at my place?"

"I suppose," she sighed.

"Mad at me?"

She turned to face him. "Did you grab the pocket watch or did I forget to give it back? Check your thigh for burns, why don't you." Sarcasm dripped.

"I have it right here." He patted his pocket.

I don't think he even heard me. Probably lost in his MacGuffin theory.

Kevin barked a greeting from inside the house. Viv couldn't wait to head home.

"Come inside," he said, reaching for her arm.

She sighed. "I suppose."

They sat at his dining room table. "Here you go." He slid a legal-sized pad of paper toward her.

She felt less annoyed, what with Kevin's effusive greeting. How could anyone stay out of sorts with that kind of enthusiasm? The dog had helped her gain perspective.

"I know I dismissed your Hitchcock theory, but let's be reasonable," she began. "I think old-fashioned detective work is necessary. We need a list of our suspects. Then we need to figure out the three most important questions. Did they have motive? Did they have means? Did they have opportunity?"

"Hence the legal pad," he groaned. "But I'm already bored." He glanced at his palm.

"I don't see any burn," Viv said. "So let that go."

A look of surprise came over his face. He lowered his hand and hid it under the table.

"Let me add a few facts," Viv insisted. "We have a dead man. He had a number of health problems. He took drugs and supplements to bring down his A_1C, which resulted in erratic blood sugar levels. I think Mia and Gloria are the most likely suspects. They both wanted the old guy's money."

"Sounds like a CSI show to me," Rex grumbled. "I think his grandson wanted him dead," he added reluctantly. "That's a motive."

"How did he go about making that happen?" Viv asked.

"He knew Gloria and Mia. Maybe he encouraged them to fiddle with Wally's pill boxes. We saw more than one at the scene of the crime and at his house," Rex said.

"I think he's conniving enough to do that," Viv admitted. "Jax worked behind the scenes to undermine his grandfather's health. I'll write that down. Anything else?"

"How about Seraphina Morales? She wanted Wally out of the way. He blocked her path to hire a better employee and to attract younger students."

"She's very ambitious, I'll give you that. So I'll write her down."

Rex looked at the pad of paper. "Four suspects who wanted or participated in Wally's demise."

"This list isn't terrible," Viv said. "We've spent the last several days getting to know the people close to Wally, and it's paid off. But what about means? We need to clarify who gave him what drug that led to the coma."

"I hope we don't have to interview his doctor," Rex groaned. "I hate being told the information is confidential without a warrant from the cops. Talk about a no-win rabbit hole."

"We have the information," Viv calmly replied. "Brad gave us the report."

"The kid could be a suspect." Rex's eyes lit up. "He was at the scene. He had opportunity."

"If that's the case, we are also suspects. Have you thought of that?" Viv said. "We were on the scene, remember?"

"I suppose." Rex's chin dipped. He'd apparently not considered either of them looking suspicious. "Okay, back to means. Brad showed us the paperwork from forensics. It was pretty clear Wally was overdosing on semaglutides."

"GLP1s," Viv agreed. "Who supplied the GLP1s? His physician, or did Wally access compounds online?" She tapped her pencil on the pad of paper. "I know from my OA group that once people lose weight, their A1C levels drop. Lowered weight pushes them out of the obese category. Often insurance companies refuse to keep paying for the semaglutides after that. Plus he lost weight. He may have dropped on the body mass index scale. If he wanted to continue to lose, he had to pay out of pocket. That can run up to a couple grand a month.

"That's why people turn to compounds," Viv added. "They're cheaper. Maybe one of our suspects helped him get the drug online."

Rex leaned back in his chair. "I suppose. Any one of them could have encouraged him."

"So we need to talk to Jax, Gloria, and Mia," Viv concluded.

"Don't forget Seraphina. I could see her advising Wally about his health," Rex added thoughtfully.

"You see? Detective work is mostly about facts. Checking the boxes. We do not require a flimflam MacGuffin to solve this case."

"So where does that leave us?" Rex asked. "What's the next step?"

"We need to circle back to Wally's closest friends and find out who steered him toward the GLP1 prescriptions or compounds that killed him. That would give us means at least."

Rex's eyes got that faraway look again. *He's seeing images*, Viv realized. She knew it was useless pulling him back to their conversation, so she waited.

"He was the only one in the classroom." Rex blinked. "Even the paramedics were locked out."

A loud pounding came from his front door. She rolled her eyes. "What happened to the safety of the gated community? There's another stranger at your door. Unless you got a call first..."

Rex pushed back his chair. "I'll take care of this."

He glanced through the peephole and groaned. "It's Jackson Walker. I need to have a word with the security guard. He's letting in every Tom, Dick, and Harry." Rex opened the door and planted himself squarely in front of the irate Jackson.

"Where's the watch, Redondo? No more stalling," Jax demanded.

Rex's face went blank. He rubbed his temple. *More images, or is he deliberately acting as if he didn't remember?*

Oh, oh. More images. Then Kevin brushed past, nearly knocking her over to get to the visitor.

"Bork." Kevin leapt at Jax. He growled and circled, inserting his nose to the back of Jax's knee.

Jax stumbled forward. Kevin barked a series of warnings, his teeth bared.

"Get away from me," Jax cried.

Kevin lunged forward. He nipped at the tassel on the realtor's Italian leather loafer. Grasping it in his teeth, he tugged. Jax stumbled. Arms flailed. He landed on his butt.

Kevin placed both paws on his chest and sniffed his shirt. The dog's tail wagged as a victory salute.

"Kevin's not a biter," Rex informed him.

"I'm filing a police report!" Walker roared.

"Come on, Kevin." He grabbed at the dog's collar. "Give the trespasser a chance to stand up."

Jax stood. He brushed his slacks, glaring at the dog. "I thought those doodle breeds weren't violent; figures you'd have an odd one."

"Why don't you come inside," Rex offered. "My partner Viv and I have some information about the pocket watch to share. Maybe we can come to a solution."

"I'm not here to compromise," Jax said, resuming his angry tone.

Kevin growled.

"The watch is a family heirloom. It belongs to me," he insisted.

"Ah come on, Jax. Let's have a beer and make nice." Having lost patience, Rex pulled Jax by his shirt. He dropped his hand to his side. "But only if you want to get the watch back."

"I just want what's mine." Walker's voice sounded less insistent. He finally added, "I guess a beer wouldn't hurt."

Once inside, he sat down at the farthest end of the kitchen table.

"Be right with you. I have to feed my dog. Then I'll meet you both outside at the firepit. Viv will show you the way."

Rex's voice could be heard from the kitchen. "Thanks for protecting me. You're a good boy." Followed by the sound of Kevin's jaws crushing a treat.

"Now go hang out," came Rex's voice. "Consider yourself disciplined."

Viv smirked.

With three beer bottles in one hand, Rex met them at the firepit. He bent to kiss her on the cheek and hand her a beer. "We've got a number one suspect ready for an interrogation right in our backyard," he whispered.

Viv's mind reeled. *Jax had the means. He's just the type to con Mia into feeding the old man more and more pie. Don't forget the morning Bloody Marys. You'd think Mia would know better than to give a diabetic such a breakfast.*

Opportunity, the exact time of death, may not be that

important. Jax didn't even need to be there when his grandfather died. He knew a coma was around the corner. All he had to do was pretend to be at work. The cops wouldn't even look in his direction.

Rex handed a bottle to Jax, then sat down and took a long sip. He rubbed his temple with his forefinger.

Not again. Viv inhaled sharply.

52

REX REDONDO

Images rolled. Wally Walker in a cop uniform. Circa 1960. The size of the hat was a giveaway. The second also of Wally Walker, slumped over his desk at Mojave Mesa. The pill container lay open near his hand.

The third image kept spinning. Rex's heart skipped a beat as it slowed. This time it was an image of Viv and him outside the glass classroom door. Brad May and Eddie stood nearby. All stared from the hallway.

I have no idea what to do with that, Rex thought. *No insight for now.*

"So how did you get past the security guard to my front door?" Rex asked Jax.

Rex deliberately used the calm tone of voice that he often adopted for a mentalist performance. This inspired confidence to soften the effects of his often impertinent and unwelcome questions. "I am curious," he added, when Jax didn't answer right away. "This is a gated community."

Rex turned to Viv. "Honey, it looks like our gated community is less than secure. First Brad and now Jax. I wonder who's coming next."

"We can take that up at the next HOA," she replied in a tart tone.

"I got in the usual way," Jax finally relented. "Real estate professionals know how to bribe their way inside any community. I slipped him a twenty." He took a long sip of beer. "You need to give the booth guy a Christmas present next year," he added sarcastically. "Maybe he'll turn people like me away."

Rex changed the subject. "So you're here to make an exchange for the pocket watch."

"The pocket watch is rightfully mine. Any court of law would agree. Plus now I can add assault and battery to my list. The dog for one and you trying to yank me indoors."

"Okay, okay," Rex grumbled. "I get it. The pocket watch is yours. But don't forget, possession is nine-tenths of the law."

"You're not going to get anywhere by threatening him, you know," Viv chimed in. "He's a mentalist. We met when he swiped a key from my house. I can't take him anywhere." She tried to make light of Rex's odd propensity, hoping to disarm Jax.

"Hand over the pocket watch," Jax demanded.

"Keep your shirt on, buddy. I'll get it as soon as we're finished with my peace offering. A good IPA, don't you think?" Rex waved his bottle in the air.

Jax sniffed. "Have it your way," he muttered.

"So," Rex approached his next question, "why don't you tell me more about the watch. Why it's so important. There must be a story. It's a family heirloom, you say?"

"The watch belonged to my grandfather. He gave it to my father when he joined the police force. Once Dad was killed on the job, the watch was supposed to come to me."

"I'm so sorry for your loss," Viv said sincerely. "How old were you when your dad died?"

"I was still a teen," he answered. "It was tough on me. I really wanted to hold on to something of his, to keep his memory alive. I remember how he took it with him to work every day. He told me it was his good luck piece." Jax's voice dropped. "Lot of good it did him."

Rex heard the young-boy tone in his voice. He felt his heart twist. *Maybe that's a genuine emotion. I can't blame him for that.* In that moment he identified with Jax.

I've felt abandonment too. Rex waited for something else that lingered on the outskirts of his impression. Another place of commonality. Betrayal. *Jax feels keenly that he's been betrayed.*

"When did your grandfather join the police?" Viv asked.

"He was young. In the late '60s."

"Palm Desert?"

"No, Palm Springs. He transferred to the Palm Desert precinct after a few years."

Viv nodded. "Mia, the waitress at the pie bar, told me that your grandfather came by every morning before work. Sometimes he talked about his early years on the force."

"I know her." Jax nodded. "She knew my grandfather pretty well. In fact, better than I did toward the end."

"Was there a problem between you and Walker senior?" Viv asked.

"We had a falling out."

The lobe on Rex's right ear burned, alerting him to pay attention.

"Over what, if you don't mind me asking," Viv said.

"Such a stubborn old coot. I felt betrayed when he refused to let me keep the pocket watch."

"That had to hurt," Rex said.

"He refused to give it to me because I didn't take his advice and apply to the police academy. He pitched a fit and when I didn't relent, he took back his heirloom.

"I stood by my decision. I even consulted Dr. Morales at Mojave Mesa. She steered me into real estate. She said it was a better fit for my talent with finances and sales. So I took classes and then went to Cal State Fullerton for a business degree. I've made a good life for myself, watch or no watch."

"You and Gloria make good partners," Viv said softly.

"Gloria is my stager," he snapped. "She has a real estate license but she works for me. I'm mad at her. I don't know what gave her the idea that she was going to list my grandfather's bungalow."

"You can't blame her. Gloria saw a clear path to getting the listing. You'd have done the same," Viv said.

"Gloria cozied up to him; I knew what she was up to. All about profit. As soon as he passed, I swooped right in to set her straight. Darn right I blame her. I stay out of her family business. She should stay out of mine."

Rex considered what he learned. Betrayal or not, he had more questions. "Viv and I saw the bungalow the day before it was staged. I remember looking at your grandfather's weekly pill container and the injection needles. Did he ever get confused what to take when?"

"Gloria helped him out," Jackson said. "Once his insurance company refused to cover the semaglutides, she showed him how to get a compound equivalent online. They called it SlimVance.

"She'd take him to the compound pharmacy to pick up the injections. He got what he could from her, the old con. Grandfather baited her but he never signed the paper. Crafty old codger."

"So I'm curious," Viv said. "If you and your grandfather weren't speaking, why didn't he pick someone else to be the executor of his estate? He could have taken you out of the will with one phone call to his attorney."

"I had something over him," Jackson admitted. "Something he wasn't proud of. My grandfather cared a lot about his reputation. Legacy was important to him. I hated to use what I had..."

Jax's statement had the undertone of a lie, which Rex instantly picked up. *Jax didn't hate blackmailing his grandfather at all. Something's relevant here.*

Jax continued. "He didn't speak to me but he didn't disinherit me either."

Rex felt his fingertips tingle. *Okay, I get it. He has to convince us that his grandfather had no intention of changing the will. Otherwise he might look guilty. A coverup for another lie or because he's guilty.*

"I'm done here. Where's the watch?" Jax stood abruptly.

Rex reached into his pocket. "Got it right here, sonny boy." He dangled it by the chain. Jax snatched it midair.

"You don't need to press charges now," Rex insisted. "You got the watch. No money exchanged. Just a misunderstanding."

Jax slipped the watch into his pocket. "Wait a minute. You said you got an appraisal. How much is it worth? I'm curious."

"A couple thousand at most," Viv said. "We were advised that the appraisal would cost more than the actual value. So we didn't get any official paperwork. It's an heirloom so the value is in the story. The provenance is the key."

. . .

Rex closed the door behind Jax, convinced they'd uncovered important information. He turned to Viv. "We got more motive and connections. He's gotta be the guy. Mia and Gloria were pawns."

"Maybe..." She didn't sound convinced. He pulled her into an embrace for more convincing. She buried her nose in his shirt. "Jax is a mixed bag, that's for sure. I wonder what he meant by having something over Wally. Sounded ominous."

Rex rested his cheek next to hers. "Do you want to stay up to talk, or should we call it a night?"

"I'm beat," she admitted. "I need to get home and check on Miss Kitty."

"Any chance you want to spend the night at my place? I have fancy sheets and fluffy towels," he teased. "You go check on the feline and come right back. I'll have a warm drink waiting for you. If you're interested, that is..." He held his breath. Coaxing didn't always work with her.

Viv tapped his chest. "What are your motives, Redondo? Companionship or someone to fix breakfast in the morning?"

He chuckled. "I love a good breakfast," he admitted. "But I really want to go to sleep and then wake up with you by my side. I can make coffee. Afterward we can go out."

She wrapped her arms around his middle. "Let's compromise. I'll bring eggs and a fresh loaf of bread for toast. We can fix breakfast together. Sound good?"

His lips met hers.

53

VIVIENNE ROSE

Rex held up a mixing bowl. "I cracked them like you showed me but I still see a few shells." He gulped. The yolks reminded him of eyeballs.

Viv took the bowl. "Take that piece of cracked shell on the counter. If you dip it close to the tiny shell in the bowl it will naturally attach. Lift slowly and you're in business."

"Okay. I've got this." He held his breath as he dipped. "I thought, since we're having scrambled eggs, the bits might not matter. Just extra crunch," he grumbled, still fishing for the last piece.

"If the crunch is a fresh vegetable maybe. But no one likes shells in their scrambled eggs," she told him. "You have a lot to learn about cooking."

He sighed. "I guess. Sure used to be easier when Sutton was here."

"None of that. No bemoaning Sutton." She didn't want to start her day with another complaint.

"I miss her," he insisted.

Viv ignored him, knowing full well catering to his feelings would only lead to another discussion about Sutton's behavior. *Which will get neither of us anywhere.*

She busied herself with the eggs. "You butter while I scramble," she instructed. "Then we'll sit down and get back to our investigation."

Later they sat at the kitchen table. He dabbed at his mouth with a napkin. "Good eggs." He seemed surprised.

"They're better when you scramble them at home," she said. "I hate cold eggs. That's what you often get when you go out."

"I need to hire a cook," he told her. "Not that I couldn't be a good one if I set my mind to it."

"Maybe..."

"A cook who can also clean," he insisted. "I know I don't want to do that."

"Possibly..." She made an effort to sound agreeable.

"And who can take care of my bills and do research for Neighbors in Crime." It was as if he were detailing an offer of employment for her.

She gave him a hard stare. When she didn't offer, he continued.

"I'll need at least four people to replace Sutton. I haven't even started with someone to gather intel when I return to the stage."

"Which reminds me, Wally Walker relied on the women in his life too. Look where that got him."

"I suppose." He frowned.

"Wally relied on Mia to organize his medications every morning. She'd pack his favorite food for takeaway. The pie and the Bloody Mary," Viv explained.

"Probably died because of Mia," Rex grumbled.

"According to Brad, Mia got a payoff. Money to go back to school. That's a great inheritance."

"And a decent motive," Rex agreed. "More than Gloria got." He reached for the last slice of toast.

"Wally didn't take responsibility for his own health or his daily life," Viv said, returning to her point. "Gloria never got him to sign a contract. Would her resentment be enough of a motive for murder?"

"I have a hunch about that," Rex said. "I think Wally might have eventually signed the contract. Gloria was certainly persistent. But the bigger issue was Jax. If he got wind of Gloria benefitting from his estate, he might have retaliated."

Viv nodded. "So you think Gloria wanted to keep Wally alive longer, just to get him to sign."

"But Jax, if he knew about Gloria's motive, would want his grandfather to die sooner, to avoid him changing his mind." Rex looked thoughtful. "Jax admitted that his grandfather cared a great deal about his legacy. I have a gut feeling that is important." He swallowed the last bite of egg.

To her surprise, this time he changed the subject.

"I wanted to ask you something about last night. It's the first time you stayed over." He winked. "Did you adjust to the mattress? It's firm. Supposed to be good for your back."

Oh no. Here he goes...

"Yes," she said.

"I'm not asking for feedback about my lovemaking prowess," he insisted. "I just want to know that I made you comfortable." When he looked into her eyes, she glared back.

He made an obvious effort to shift gears. "And I remembered that I forgot to tell you... I saw more images last night.

I was afraid to mention them to you since they're not facts."
He used his fingers to air quote "facts."

Viv nodded toward the kitchen. "Time to do dishes."

"Oh no. You just reminded me." He sounded miffed. "I have to hire a cook and a dishwasher. Will this ever end?"

She shot him a withering glance. "There's another option."

"Sutton refuses to return my calls," he complained.

"You could stop trying to replace her and do the work yourself." Viv wanted him to come up with the solution, but apparently she needed to hit him over the head.

"I got a call." He nodded at his cell. "Hello," he said, putting the phone on speaker.

"Mr. Redondo. This is Lieutenant Darius James. How soon can you drop everything and head on over to Mojave Mesa Community College?"

Rex's eyebrows raised. "Good to hear from you, Lieutenant. I hope this isn't about my arrest. I gave the pocket watch back to Jackson Walker last night. Maybe you didn't realize..."

"Not about that," James snapped. "An entirely different matter. We have a hostage situation on the Mojave Mesa campus. The students trapped Dr. Seraphina Morales in her office and refuse to let her go without having their demands met."

"Is that so." Rex's eyes brightened.

"For some reason Dr. Morales thinks you can negotiate her release."

"I'll bring my associate and meet you on campus. You're in good hands now. Redondo and Rose are on the case."

54

REX REDONDO

Police vehicles sped throughout the Mojave Mesa faculty parking lot. Rex pulled the SUV forward and leaned out the window. "I'm Rex Redondo. Lieutenant James called me in for a consultation."

"We know. Go ahead. Park over there. Follow the noise. You'll find the protesters in front of the administration building." The officer lifted the yellow tape for Rex to drive past.

Viv and Rex made their way across the sprawling campus. The tension in the air brought him to a standstill. He inhaled deeply. Viv echoed his thoughts.

"It's usually so quiet here," Viv murmured. "I'm feeling anxious."

Rex nodded in the direction of students who'd gathered in clusters on the lawn. Viv pointed to signs held in the air. "Justice for Section 14. Reparations Now!"

A makeshift barricade, constructed around the administration building, was made up of bicycles, trash cans, and a few benches. Rex did a quick visual surveillance. "I don't see any weapons. Guns would be very dangerous."

278

"Look up." Viv pointed to brightly painted banners hanging from the building's windows. The bold colors and slogans created a stark contrast to the institutional beige of the campus buildings.

Rex squinted, taking in the assembled crowd. Nearly everyone held a cell phone, some in outstretched arms. He assumed they were recording the scene. A lineup of uniformed officers stood behind them. *Not cops*, Rex realized. *Campus security.* They'd formed a perimeter, looking grim.

"I hope things don't escalate." Viv sounded nervous.

"Isn't that Brad and Mia?" Rex asked. "I thought they broke up."

"Let's go chat them up," Viv said.

Brad nodded a greeting as they approached. "Hey, Rex. Hey, Viv. Glad you could join us." Mia gripped Brad's elbow with both hands. She stared up at Brad with adoring eyes.

"I've been called in as a consultant. Dr. Morales wants me to negotiate her release," Rex explained. "But we're not at liberty to discuss any more details because this is an ongoing investigation." He felt good saying that. Even if it weren't true. He hoped to put Brad in his place as an outsider.

"I see." Brad's jaw tightened.

"I need to tell Lieutenant James that we're here." Rex reached for his phone. He texted.

We're here.

You can approach the building.

Came an immediate response.

We have to go." Rex nodded his head at Viv.

Hair rose on his neck the closer they came to the entrance of the administration building. "I see Dr. Morales," Viv said, looking up to the top floor. "She's standing just inside a window."

The principal looked out over the campus. Her customary smile gone, her shoulders drooped toward her chest. *She doesn't like not being in control,* he concluded.

"I suppose she's taken a training class in student protesting 101," Viv suggested. "Oh look. There's the custodian. Eddie Vargas." Eddie manned the entrance, his arms folded in front of his chest. He looked serious.

He's the one with all the access codes, Rex reasoned.

Eddie acknowledged their approach with a nod. "You can go right in. They're expecting you." He punched in a code and the doors slid open.

"Over here," Lieutenant James called. A young female stood next to him. Dressed in jeans and a tee that read Reparations Now, printed in bold black letters.

"This is intense," Viv whispered. "Look at her body language."

"I'm feeling it," Rex admitted. "I've been in situations like this before, in the military. These students are the same age as the soldiers in Afghanistan. At least they're waving placards, not M16s."

The weight of the moment hit Rex's gut. He tried not to stare as the woman marched closer to a group of police officers. Arms gesturing, her voice raised, she made her case. The officers stood impassively, arms at their sides. They looked over her head without comment.

"She's ready for a fight," Rex observed.

Lieutenant James stood across the room and lifted his phone. He walked as he talked, making his way closer to

Rex and Viv. "I'm going to let the college administrators and the police officers know you're here," he told them.

"What's her name?" Rex nodded toward the agitated female.

"Marisol Alvarez. She's the lead protestor. Got quite a mouth on her."

The elevator door swished open, revealing two police officers. They exited as Rex turned to Viv. "Wish me luck."

Marisol followed him into the elevator. She pushed the button to close the door, creating a sense of privacy. Turning toward Rex, she began to explain. "Since 1968 Latino, Native, and Black families have expected some kind of acknowledgment about this injustice. You just stand there with your arms folded as if none of those people matter."

Rex held up his hands. "I understand where you're coming from," he said with a calm and steady tone. "Your concerns are real and valid."

She stopped talking and registered surprise. Rex took the opportunity to explain more.

"But holding Dr. Morales as a hostage isn't the answer."

"What do you know!" Eyes narrowed, she glared at Rex.

"I know what it's like to live in a world that ignores your suffering. I was in the military. No matter how loud you scream to be heard, you're shoved aside and marginalized. I've spent my life in rooms with higher-ups who refused to listen."

He noted a softening in her expression, her bottom lip trembled. He lowered his voice to match her emotions.

"Section 14 wasn't fair. But Dr. Morales—she's on your

side. She must have approved your protest request. She's actually listening."

The corner of Marisol's mouth hardened. She didn't look convinced. "Morales talks a good game. But nothing's changed," she said matter-of-factly.

"Dr. Morales has made changes, just not obvious ones," Rex explained. "She's offered scholarships for students with no access to inherited wealth. She's pushed grants for aid and made certain to track students from Mojave Mesa to four-year colleges.

"Come on, Marisol." He deliberately used her first name. "You have the right to demand justice, but not at the expense of the woman who's trying to help."

Rex took a step back. He watched Marisol's fist clench and unclench as she considered his words.

"Give me a minute," she said. "I need to think." She turned away. He watched as she pulled out her cell. Speaking under her breath in Spanish, he couldn't distinguish her meaning. She listened to the response and then clicked off. Rex needed no other invitation. He kept talking.

"Let's show that we can stand together, support each other. We can honor the memory of Section 14 instead of creating more harm. What do you say... Will you let Dr. Morales go?" Rex didn't plead, he knew better than to appear weak. But he didn't insist. He kept his voice neutral.

Marisol held up her phone. "I talked to my adviser. He says we can let Morales go with a few provisions. Tomorrow we want to meet with administrators. We want to be represented."

Rex knew this was an important opening. *Plus she reminds me of Mom*, he admitted to himself.

Up until going back to college, he'd not even thought about her or his childhood. But now that he had...

He dove right in to help. "I can recommend an attorney. I think I can convince him to do the work pro bono."

"Not legal representation. At least not a lawyer." Her chin tightened.

Rex blinked. *Where is she going with this?*

Marisol glared. "We want to be represented by you."

He shook his head. *What is she talking about? I'm not a negotiator. Let alone an advocate for reform.*

Marisol pushed the button for the door to open. She shouted to all who could hear, "We'll negotiate. We have our representative. This guy over here." She nodded at Rex. "What's your name again?"

Viv moved close. "Good choice," she told Marisol. "His name is Rex Redondo. He can talk the hind leg off a dog and he'll get you what you need."

Marisol's forehead wrinkled. "I've never heard that expression before."

"He'll represent you—as soon as he gets over the shock of being asked."

"That's funny." Marisol smiled.

"What about Dr. Morales? Will you tell the students we've come to an understanding, that she'd being released..." Rex asked.

"If you insist." Marisol turned back to the crowd.

55

VIVIENNE ROSE

Viv watched a gaggle of reporters rush to the elevator. Dr. Morales emerged, her shoulders held back, her face all smiles. "Part of doing business," she explained. "Students are genuinely concerned about justice. They want a fair share. I uphold their right to free speech and will arrange for a series of meetings to discuss our next step.

"Now I need to consult with our negotiator." She made her way toward Rex and Viv. "Do you have time to chat?" she asked. "We can meet back upstairs in ten minutes. I have another issue I'd like to discuss."

"Do you want me there?" Viv asked.

"I do," Morales said. "You two are a team, right?"

"We'll get a cup of coffee first," Rex explained. "Then meet you upstairs."

Rex tugged on Viv's arm. "I want to ask you something."

As they walked away, she didn't hesitate to tell him, "You were masterful, by the way. I felt the empathy and your connection."

"Thanks." He ducked his head, obviously embarrassed. "I've used my empathy to con people for so long, I had no idea it could actually be useful. I didn't expect to be pulled in by the students. How will I get out of that?"

"The reward for one good deed is the challenge of another," Viv replied tartly. "My mother's old saying."

"Never heard that one before," he admitted. "But there's something else. Check out Eddie the custodian over there. He's still protecting the entrance."

"That's his job. Unless..."

"The way he used the code to get us in the locked building," Rex said. "It got me thinking..."

"Again, that's his job. He's head custodian."

"It reminded me of when we found Wally." Rex's eyes darkened. "I just get a feeling about him. That he's been overlooked somehow."

Viv thought back. How she'd felt so helpless watching Wally slumped over his desk behind the glass doors. In the moment she'd feared the worst. He wouldn't be helped in time.

Did I miss something that day?

Oh my goodness. Her eyes grew round. *I never stopped to think. With all of the confusion and the breaking in, we investigated everyone close to Wally. Then we got all of his medical information. But we missed something crucial. Rex is right. The head custodian knows the door codes. Eddie Vargas stood outside the locked room...*

"We have to contact Lieutenant James!" Viv insisted. "I think I saw him leave as soon as Marisol agreed to let Dr. Morales go."

"But what about our meeting in the principal's office?" Rex seemed confused.

"She can wait. We have new evidence."

. . .

They sat in interview room number one at the Palm Desert Police Headquarters. Lieutenant James propped his elbows on the desk. "All right, you two. I've got five minutes. Rotten kids. They took up my entire morning with their reparations nonsense."

"We know who killed Wally Walker," Viv said. "We know means and opportunity. The motive is a bit iffy, but now that I see clearly, there's only one person who could have done it."

Darius James rolled his eyes.

"You can doubt all you want," she said tartly. "I feel certain."

Lieutenant James glanced toward Rex. "She's got this," he scoffed. He returned his gaze to Viv.

"But I don't need you two. I know who killed Wally. It's just a matter of arresting him. Jackson Walker. He's got the strongest motive. Money grabber," James grumbled.

Viv disagreed. "I don't think so. Jackson was mad at Wally over a family squabble that erupted over a keepsake. Not a strong motive to kill him, in my opinion."

Rex let out a long sigh. "Like I said. The power of the MacGuffin."

"A what?" asked James.

"Not this again," Viv fumed.

Before Rex could launch into an explanation, Viv cut him off. "It's not the MacGuffin. I have facts."

"It all started that day I stole the watch," Rex began, his voice launching into a storyteller's drawl.

James tapped his wristwatch. "You've got three more minutes. Then I'm arresting the grandson."

56

REX REDONDO

"Not so fast," Viv interrupted. "Let me explain. The solution to the murder was right in front of us the first day. We stood outside the locked room with the killer."

"So what. I knew that!" James fumed. "If not Jackson, then maybe that other kid. He was there the first day. Brad May. We took his testimony. He probably lied."

"Come on, not the kid. He's a pain but he wouldn't kill an old man." Rex surprised himself, defending Brad aloud.

"If it's not Brad May, then who else? The only person left is Eddie Vargas, the custodian."

"That's right." Rex took over the conversation. "Vargas."

James scowled. "Can't be Eddie. I've known him for years. He's an institution at Mojave Mesa. Beloved by everyone, students and faculty alike."

James adjusted his tie, his face flushed.

"Eddie Vargas killed Wally Walker," Viv stated flatly. "It's obvious."

Rex spoke. "Vargas told me that Walker locked the door to the classroom. He said he warned Walker and he went ahead anyway. Vargas lied. I don't know why I didn't pick up on it at the time. But he distracted me from even considering him a suspect. Who does that? Right at the Roadkill over a beer. We were just two guys shooting the breeze. He has no shame."

Lieutenant James looked thoughtful. "I've got background on Vargas right here. We filed it away because we didn't think he was a suspect. Everyone said he was good friends with Walker. Even Dr. Morales made mention when we interviewed her." He turned away from his computer to prompt Viv. "I'm listening..."

"He was the only person who could override the electronic door opener. That was his job," Viv said.

"What else?" asked James.

"He'd called the paramedics the first two times that Wally slumped into a coma. By the third emergency he made himself scarce. Probably locked the door from the main panel. Then he took his time returning to the scene to stand outside with us and pretend to be surprised," she explained.

"That makes sense." James held up his hand. "Don't move, you two. I'm going to have a couple of my guys pick up Vargas and bring him in for questioning."

As soon as the door closed, Rex turned to Viv. "Do you suppose they are listening in on our conversation?" He nodded to the speaker on the wall underneath the mirror.

"Maybe."

"I don't care," he said. "You're right about Vargas. Plus I love how you confront people, especially James, with your facts."

"You love how I confront people." Viv smiled. "Really..."

"Everyone but me," he admitted.

. . .

An hour later they sat across the table from Eddie Vargas. He wiped perspiration from his forehead with the back of his hand. "So it's the Latino, right. You're going to blame me for the old white guy's death. Figures..."

"This isn't about race," Lieutenant James stated sternly.

"Easy for you to say," Vargas added. "Everything's about race for me. I'm brown, remember?"

"How's that?" Rex asked. He'd heard the anger in the voice of the student protester. Eddy's tone sounded similar.

Vargas's eyes flashed. "I just recently realized that Walker was on the Palm Springs force. Back in the '6os. Early in his career; let's just say it made me furious."

"It wasn't a secret. Wally Walker's transfer back in the day was public knowledge. At least two, maybe three people told me the story," Viv said.

"I didn't put it together. All of these years we were amigos. His son told me a month ago. By accident, an aside. You know Jackson Walker, the real estate mogul. I heard him arguing with Wally about some pocket watch. I listened outside while he confronted the old man, called him out.

"How Wally switched precincts, took a cut in pay, started over, because he led the dislocation of families in Section 14.

"Walker didn't even try to deny his involvement. He said he felt remorse afterward and that's why he quit. Started over in Palm Desert. Easy for him. Starting over. But it wasn't easy for my grandparents."

James cleared his throat. "Granted, the police stepped over a line. But it happened a long time ago. Are you still carrying a grudge?"

"My grandparents lost everything because of people like Walker," Vargas shouted. "They lived in that neighborhood with pride, year after year. Then some council decides they want the land for development. And the cops show up and pull them from their homes. Burned down their houses. The day after, looters picked through the rubble.

"My grandfather didn't get to transfer to another department like Wally. He'd lost his dignity and his roots when their home burned to the ground. Walker got to have his career. His famous son and a grandson who's wealthy and a big deal in real estate. Not a custodian picking up other people's trash like me. Walker got to teach at Mojave Mesa as if he were some kind of hero, students flocking to hear his stories.

"So yeah, I'm angry. I have no bungalow to cash in for inherited wealth. No reputation to coast on for community pride. Not even a keepsake from my abuela or abuelo."

Rex folded his hands in front of his stomach. He had no words. Tears welled in Viv's eyes. Lieutenant James stood, his face masked in professionalism. "I assume you're not sorry about Walker's death. I also assume that you fiddled with the electronics to lock down his classroom."

"I made sure he wasn't going to get a third rescue, if that's what you mean. You'll have a hard time proving that I locked the electronic door. I know that much."

"That might be," James said. "But the exact proof isn't my problem. That's for someone else, including a judge and jury to decide." He walked around the desk. "I have enough evidence to arrest you.

"Eduardo Vargas, you're under arrest for the murder of Wallace Walker. You took justice into your own hands, which is punishable by law." He tightened the cuffs. "Anything you say now can and will be used against you. So I'd suggest you save the rest of your story for your attorney. We can appoint someone if you'd like." He took Vargas by the elbow to guide him toward two officers who stood in the doorway.

The following Monday, Rex and Viv sat in the front row of their Mojave Mesa Introduction to Private Investigation 101 class. Rex looked anxiously toward the door. No sign of their new instructor.

This time twenty students sat at the desks behind them. Brad May sat close by. "I think the murder and arrest increased enrollment," he whispered in Rex's ear. "Do you know who our new professor is?"

The door to the classroom swished open. In walked a professional woman, dressed in a black tight pencil skirt and a snug matching blazer. Her red hair had been twisted into a bun at the nape of her neck. Her oversized glasses gave off an intelligent vibe.

"Hey, wait a minute..." Rex blinked.

Laptop on the desk, she walked around to address her class. "Welcome to Private Investigation 101. This is a serious academic class, an opportunity for you to qualify for the PI exam. I'll keep track of attendance. Only one excused absence allowed. You'll be given weekly snap quizzes and assigned two research papers.

"None of the AI nonsense either. I have an ear for plagiarism. I've been taught by the best to suss out liars." She glanced down her nose at Rex, the corner of her mouth twitching.

"I'm not here to answer any questions about the previous instructor. That's police business. Don't even bother. My name is Sutton Drew. You can call me Ms. Drew. And no, you don't get any other questions. It's my turn to talk and yours to listen."

Rex raised his hand.

"Not now," she stated firmly. "Unless you want to stay after class. I'll be available then." She walked toward the whiteboard without a backward glance.

Rex inhaled quickly. He felt his lips burn. The four words that he'd been holding back begging to be spoken.

I told you so. He wanted to shout from the rooftops. He knew Sutton was right for this job. Hadn't he pointed it out right away? Arranged for her to be noticed and hired?

He coughed into his fist. Plus she looked amazing in that tight skirt. And the heels. Those toned calves.

Pay attention, Rex old boy. Time to mind your p's and q's.

"Class dismissed," Sutton said. "If you do have questions you can stay. Otherwise I posted my in-person office hours online."

Viv leaned closer. "Should I wait outside? So you two can talk alone."

Rex felt slightly off balance. He wondered the same question. He didn't want to be chewed out again, after all the things he'd been through. Plus he felt certain that if he worded his apology just right, maybe Sutton would reconsider and come back.

He patted Viv's hand. "Good idea. I'll see you in the corridor."

He watched as Viv stopped to chat with Brad in the hallway. *That kid,* he sighed. *I suspect we won't be seeing the last of him any time soon.*

Sutton studied her laptop. He rose from the chair. "I tried to call. Texted a bunch of apologies. What else can I do?"

"I got the messages," Sutton said. "But I wasn't ready to answer them. We needed a break, you and I."

She didn't sound that mad. "Does that mean you're coming back?"

Sutton finally gave him her full attention. "We can't go back to what we were. I need to move forward and you do too." She nodded to the hallway where Viv and Brad laughed. "She's your focus right now. An excellent choice, by the way."

"I can have two women in my life," he objected.

"Not for long," Sutton said. "Viv's her own woman. She'll eventually get tired of the threesome. No woman in her right mind wants the trouble. Especially with us living in such close proximity.

"Not because of you, she accepts who you are. But because she wouldn't respect me doing your bidding, enabling your little-boy lifestyle. Viv would hate that, no matter what you paid."

"I suppose," he mumbled. "So you took the job after all. The one you punched me for."

"You want me to say thank you?" Sutton teased.

"That would be kinda nice. How about an I'm sorry. Don't forget you sucker punched me. I could file assault charges, you know, even if you are female."

"You stepped over the line," Sutton reminded him. "But I will admit I got the job. In fact I got along so well with Dr. Morales, she offered me a full-time position, despite having my own PI license. She told me that she'd made an exception just for me, being so qualified and a veteran.

"Before you say I told you so, just know that I returned the favor. When Morales called me for advice about the student protest, I suggested you'd be a good negotiator. You can thank me for that recommendation."

Rex shoved his hands in his pockets. The *I told you so* no longer felt right. Especially since she'd returned the favor.

Sutton rose to her feet.

He pretended to flinch, turning his head away, holding up his hands. "Don't hit me!" he cried.

She smirked. "Let it go, Redondo. I want a hug."

He didn't need another invitation. He walked around the desk and pulled her into his arms. "I hate fighting with you," he admitted.

A voice came from the door. "Have you two made up? I'm ready for brunch." Viv smiled. "Want to come along, Sutton? Brad May is saving a table at Just Desserts."

Rex released his former employee. "That would be fraternizing," he warned. "Having brunch with three of your students."

"We're not in the military anymore. I can have meals with whomever I please. I can even date students. It's not recommended, but it's not a rule breaker," Sutton corrected.

"I draw the line at having lunch with the kid," Rex grumbled. "Not the kid!"

"He's a good-looking guy." Sutton smirked. "Plus he may have a future in law enforcement. I've looked over his background."

She turned to Viv. "I'd love to have lunch with you."

Rex stood back to watch the two women share a brief hug. "You won't believe this," Viv said just loud enough for him to hear. "He's learning to cook."

"You are a miracle worker, Vivienne. I knew it the first time we met." Sutton nodded.

You see, Rex thought. *I can have two women. Just give it time. Maybe not like it used to be, but this isn't over.* He felt warmth and hope fill his chest.

They love me, he concluded. *I haven't lost my touch.*

Dear Readers; I hope you enjoyed the fourth installment in the Redondo and Rose Neighbors in Crime series!

I've been thinking about this story for some time, as it explores something dear to my heart. I was born and raised in California and visited my God Parents in Palm Springs from an early age.

Weaving the deeply complex Project 14 narrative into a present-day mystery felt challenging. Fortunately Rex and Viv, my mid-life sleuthing duo, and their evolving relationship, paved the way.

Class Dismissed is not just about unraveling a murder mystery but also about the legacy of history—how events long ago resurface to the present. The 1968 Section 14 redevelopment in Palm Springs, a real-life tragedy where homes were burned, families were displaced, and lives were upended, casts a long shadow over this story.

Wally Walker's role as a young police officer during that time reveals the painful complexities of guilt, shame, and redemption. With recent discussions in the news of reparations reigniting awareness of such injustices, it felt timely and essential to incorporate this piece of history into the narrative.

My hope is that this book encourages reflection on how the echoes of the past shape our communities and ourselves.

We also witness the joys and challenges of midlife reinvention in the lives of Rex and Viv. One of my favorite reviews echoed in my mind as I wrote. "Not your average granny trope."

By the end of Class Dismissed, even Rex recognizes that life need not stop when one retires. He's found the love of his life and a a surprising new ability to use his skills. Viv and Rex's refreshing portrayal of love, friendship, and partnership, sprinkled with humor, exasperation, and undeniable affection, makes them a joy to write—and, I hope, a joy to read.

As always, thank you for joining me on this journey. Cozy mysteries are about more than solving puzzles; they're about creating a world where justice prevails, communities thrive, and characters you care about grow and evolve.

I'm so grateful to share this world with you.

Happy sleuthing,

Bonnie Hardy

BOOK CUB DISCUSSION QUESTIONS

Class Dismissed

Book Club Discussion Questions **Characters & Relationships**

1. Rex and Vivienne's Dynamic: How does the partnership between Rex and Viv evolve in this story? Do you think their differences make them stronger as a team, or do they create unnecessary complications?

2. Wally Walker's Legacy: Wally is portrayed as both a mentor and a man with a troubled past. How do his choices shape the perceptions others have of him after his death? Did your opinion of him change throughout the book?

3. Supporting Cast: Which secondary character stood out to you the most and why? How did their role in the mystery contribute to the story's development?

Themes & Motives

4. Section 14 Incident: How does the historical context of the Section 14 incident add depth to the story? Did it influence how you viewed the motives of certain characters?

5. Family Secrets: Jax Walker's strained relationship

with his grandfather is central to the story. How do family secrets and generational guilt play into the larger mystery?

6. Moral Ambiguity: Several characters, including Rex, make questionable choices (e.g., pawning the pocket watch). Do you think their actions were justified given the circumstances?

Plot & Mystery

7. Red Herrings and Clues: Did you guess the killer before the reveal? What clues or red herrings led you astray or kept you on track?

8. Setting the Stage: How did the Mojave Mesa Community College setting enhance the story?

9. Twists and Turns: Were there any plot twists that surprised you? How did they affect your enjoyment of the book?

Broader Context

10. Rex and Viv's Future: Rex and Viv are considering opening a private detective agency. Based on their performance in this case, do you think they'll succeed? What challenges might they face in future investigations?

11. Social Issues: The book addresses themes like historical injustices and modern struggles (e.g., financial insecurity, drug use). Did these themes feel relevant, and how did they shape the story?

12. Cozy Mystery Appeal: What aspects of *Class Dismissed* make it a cozy mystery? Are there elements of the story that challenge traditional cozy tropes?

Personal Reflections

13. Relatable Characters: Were there any characters or situations that resonated with you personally? Why?

14. Your Role as a Detective: If you were investigating this case, what would you have done differently from Rex and Viv?

15. Favorite Moment: What was your favorite moment or line from the book, and why?

Bonnie Hardy, a retired professional turned author, is celebrated for her two enthralling cozy mystery series. The first, set in the picturesque mountain town of Lily Rock, features amateur sleuth Olivia Greer, known for her uncanny ability to draw out confessions from the most unlikely people.

The second series, set in Palm Desert, features the midlife duo mentalist Rex Redondo and his down to earth next door neighbor doula Vivienne Rose.

Inspired by Agatha Christie, Bonnie's captivating tales

of mystery and community masterfully blend fast-paced whodunits with clever sleuthing.

You can find all of her books at her website https://bonniehardywrites.com/

facebook.com/bonniehardywrites.com

instagram.com/bonniehardywrites

bookbub.com/authors/bonnie-hardy

goodreads.com/bonniehardy

www.ingramcontent.com/pod-product-compliance
Lightning Source LLC
Chambersburg PA
CBHW061641190726
48289CB00006B/1691